I0743395

Sad Lisa

Anne Louise Bannon

Healcroft House, Publishers

Altadena, California

Healcroft House, Publishers, a subsidiary of Robin Goodfellow Enterprises,
Altadena, California
United States of America

ISBN: 978-1-948616-11-9

Library of Congress Control Number: 2020906777

Dedication

To Jane Neff Rollins, a good friend when I've needed one

She hangs her head and cries on my shirt
She must be hurt very badly
Tell me what's making you sad, Li?
Lisa, Lisa, sad Lisa, Lisa

— Cat Stevens

June 15-16, 1984

I hummed along with the haunting tune that I loved so much as I put the finishing touches on the two place settings in the stately Baroque dining room. Cat Stevens' Sad Lisa was my favorite song, bar none, even though it was probably because of my name as much as the early junior high loneliness I was going through when it came out in 1970.

Later, it would seem like an omen that it was playing on the radio at that precise moment. But that night, my mood was in complete opposition to the tune. My boyfriend, George, was coming over for dinner and Sid was out for the night.

I couldn't wait. I hadn't been on a date with George in almost two weeks. We'd been dating off and on for over a year at that point, and the past three months, we'd been going out pretty steadily at least three nights a week. But just after Memorial Day, my work had put a stop to that. George had been getting a little sulky about it, and I could hardly blame him.

But, finally, we were having dinner at the house where Sid and I live. It's Sid's place, and living there had been a condition of working for him because he was really recruiting me for an ultra-top secret organization called Operation Quickline in addition to being his secretary. So, technically, I am his secretary and he is, technically, my wealthy freelance writer boss. But we'd been acting more like teammates both in the Quickline and the writing business. And Sid and both of our businesses were the last things I wanted to be thinking about at that moment. I took a deep breath, lit the two candles, dimmed the lights, then changed the radio station on the wall intercom to a classical one.

The doorbell rang. Motley, my springer spaniel, barked from my bedroom, where he'd been sequestered for the night. Sighing happily, I went to answer the front door and found George Hernandez on the doorstep, tall and broad-shouldered, with black hair, and dark brown sensitive eyes.

"Hi," I said.

"Do you look gorgeous," George said, grinning.

I was wearing a nice little flowered chiffon dress that bared my shoulders. George had on a nice sports jacket over an open Oxford shirt with dress jeans. He also had one hand behind his back. His grin changed to a shy smile. He brought his hand around to his front and presented me with a bouquet of red, long-stemmed roses.

"For you," he said. "Even though they are not nearly as beautiful as you are."

I blushed. "George! Thank you. You're so sweet."

I reached up and kissed him. We stood there, just necking, for several minutes.

I finally untangled myself. "I'd better get these in some water. Come on."

"Great. When's dinner?" He followed me down the hall, past the dining room to the kitchen.

"Right away. It's all ready. I just have to bring it in. Oh, and I sent Conchetta home a bit early."

Conchetta is the housekeeper. She works from ten a.m. to six p.m. weekdays and that is it. She would have been heading home at right about that time, but since Sid had left early, I really wanted to make up the previous two weeks to George and have the house to ourselves.

Motley let out another bark, this time, his pathetic one.

"Where's Motley?" George asked as I got a vase from the cupboard.

"In my room." I filled the vase with water and put the roses into it. "He's such a nuisance when he's begging at the table."

[I notice that you did not point out that the only time Motley begged was when George came to dinner, and that only happened because George kept feeding him at the table even though you kept telling George not to over and over again. - SEH]

After getting the roses in the vase and handing the vase to George, I pulled the main course from the oven. Conchetta had made a gorgeous braised brisket for us, along with roasted potatoes. A pan with creamed spinach was waiting on the stove with the serving dish next to it. A salad waited in the fridge.

I sent George ahead of me to the dining room so that I could get everything onto the wooden service cart. When I wheeled the loaded cart in, George was still standing next to the table with the vase in his hands.

"Where do you want these?" he asked.

"Why not at that end of the table?" I said, pointing at the empty chairs on the side away from where I'd set our plates.

George did as I asked, then looked around. "Your boss isn't around, is he?"

"Sid left around four-thirty," I replied, the relief heavy in my voice. "The doctor officially pronounced him cured and clean and he's out celebrating."

"The poor girl"

I chuckled. "Angelique didn't seem to think so. I talked to her this morning and she seemed to be looking forward to it."

George made a point of seating me and I couldn't help sighing as I sat down.

"Tired?" he asked after we said grace.

"Yeah. I've been running around all day."

"Doing what?"

"Research. What else?"

I wasn't going to tell him what I'd really been doing. George didn't know about Operation Quickline. Actually, no one does except the people who are in it and a few select liaisons. What we mostly do is get documents from one point to another, documents that are so sensitive and valuable that they need to be hand-carried rather than risk postal services losing them. But every now and then, the FBI gets a hold of something a little too hot to handle, so we get to deal with it.

What had been keeping me busy those previous two weeks was just that. The winter before, it had been discovered that there was a leak somewhere in one of the West Coast FBI offices. It's a little hard to send in undercover agents when your target can track who those agents are. However, we'd caught a break in May. Someone, I don't know who, had discovered that a certain attache to the Rumanian consulate in Los Angeles was working as somebody's handler or contact. There were phone taps on the consulate phones and possibly in the man's home, but he was far too cagey to use those phones for anything other than consulate business or personal stuff.

So, since Quickline doesn't supposedly exist, we had been asked to keep a tail on him in the hopes that he'd lead us to his contact. But there were two problems. The main one was that he was a diplomat and if we got caught tailing him, it would get really sticky diplomatically. So, we couldn't stick that closely to him. The other was that even a civilian can spot that kind of surveillance unless you have a whole crew of people changing things up randomly. While we had the crew, the diplomat was really good at what he did and kept ditching us. We were pretty sure he hadn't spotted too many of us because he wasn't doing anything unusual when he ditched us. If anything, he was using the same tactics most of us used when we wanted to be sure no one was following us.

That day had been my turn to tail the diplomat, along with two other people, each from a different line. It had been exhausting, physically grueling work. And while we didn't get ditched that day, we didn't catch the diplomat doing anything questionable. He didn't even go near a payphone, let alone use one. All of his meetings were with people we knew to be innocent because we'd already checked them out. In short, it all felt like a big, fat waste of time, even though we knew it wasn't.

"So, why are you doing so much research?" George asked.

"We've been selling a lot of stories," I said with a shrug. "As Sid says, we have to grab the work when we get it."

"But he doesn't need to work," said George, reasonably enough.

Sid had inherited the larger part of his money. Freelance writing does not pay that well, trust me.

"I know. But he needs something to keep him busy." I grimaced. "You know what he's been like these past three weeks."

I could see George biting his tongue, and it was justified. About three weeks before, Sid had been exposed to a little social disease. He was really careful, and it has only happened one other time since I'd come to him. But you can't fool around as much as he does and not pick up something. [Christ, the things we did before AIDS - SEH] He'd had to wait to fool around for a week and a half to not spread it. But just as that week and a half was up, he'd developed symptoms, which meant another week and a half of antibiotics and no sex. Which meant an incredibly grumpy Sid. Fortunately, he had kept me up to date on what was going on and tried to keep to himself. But it did mean that the tailing job and the research for the freelance business were Godsends of the highest order. The only thing worse was the day before and that morning. With light at the end of the tunnel and a date for that night, Sid began teasing me. It wasn't mean, but it was really the pits and almost worse than the grumpiness.

"Look," I continued. "I really do not want to be talking about Sid or work right now."

George smiled.

We finished dinner, then moved to the rumpus room to talk and watch a movie on the TV. Only we ended up necking. I got out a bottle of wine from the wet bar and we cuddled up in the bean bag chairs, sipping our wine and chatting comfortably, and then kissing.

Maybe it was the wine. I don't drink a lot, never have and especially not as a member of Quickline. Maybe it was because I was so tired. I also think it was because I was so fed up with Sid. Anyway, when George asked me to marry him, I didn't even think about it. I said yes.

Needless to say, the necking got a lot more intense and just barely on the side of decent.

"Well, well, well," cut in a familiar voice.

I jumped, bumped my head into George's nose, then scrambled back.

"Sid!" I glared at him.

He was standing in the doorway, grinning. He's a very handsome man, with dark, wavy hair, a cleft chin, and piercing blue eyes that, at that moment, were twinkling with mischief. He's not a big man - just under average height. He may be slender, but it's all perfectly proportioned. That night, he had on an off-white linen jacket, a pink broadcloth shirt and tie, and khaki dress slacks.

"Hello, George." Sid stepped behind the bar. "Nice to see you again."

"Hello, Sid," George replied in a tone that was unusually genial for his interactions with Sid. "I hear you're feeling better."

I winced as Sid chuckled lecherously.

"Much better." He sighed and bent down behind the bar to open the little refrigerator there. He popped back up. "Lisa, did you take my Chablis?"

"There wasn't a note," I said, taking a sip. Since the rumpus room was considered open space in the house, anything in that fridge was fair game unless there was a note on it. Only we often forgot to write the notes. "Which is what you said last month when you ripped off my amaretto."

"I told you I'd buy you a new bottle."

"Do you see it there?"

"Alright, alright. Put it on my list. I'll have to make do with the riesling." He set the bottle on the edge of the bar, then reached up to get two glasses off the overhead rack. He picked up the bottle, swung around to the door of the room, then turned back to George and me, a not-so-innocent smile on his face. "You two behave yourselves now. Remember, necking is like playing with fire."

"Sid, shut up," I growled.

George laughed. "Sid, I have every right to neck with my fiancee."

Sid, who had already turned to leave, stopped and slowly turned back. He looked at me, utterly bewildered.

"Your fiancee?" he asked.

"Yep." George squeezed my shoulders protectively. "Lisa and I are getting married."

"Hm." Sid looked at me. "Wedding bells on the brain."

He had tried to warn me this was coming and I had refused to believe him.

"Sid," I said softly.

"This is quite a surprise."

"It is to me, too," I said softly.

"Well, that's some consolation." Sid forced a smile. "Congratulations."

He left. I glared at George.

"George, why did you have to tell him?"

"He's got to know. You were planning another way?"

"I hadn't even thought that far. I guess I wanted to break it to him gently."

George shrugged. "It's not like you two are going together."

"But he is a very close friend."

"I think it's better this way. Everything up front, no sweat."

"I guess maybe you're right." I snuggled up next to him, laying my head on his broad shoulder.

This man was going to be my husband. I was going to spend the rest of my life with him. We would be having sex together. A major spasm of doubt took hold in me. I looked up into George's brown eyes and pushed the doubt aside.

Later that night, after George had gone home, I thought about it some more. There was no doubt that I loved the man. I kept thinking about it, and the more I did, the more I convinced myself that marrying him was the thing to do.

The next morning, Sid didn't show up for our morning run. We run six days a week. I loathe it, but it is important to stay fit when you're in the spy business. It was pretty unusual for Sid to skip it, although I didn't question it. I just went back to bed for some extra sleep. When I finally got up, Angelique Carter was at the breakfast table, looking very sleepy and wearing Sid's bathrobe.

In addition to being one of Sid's more frequent girlfriends, Angelique and I are good friends, too. She works at the FBI, not as an agent, but as the civilian secretary to Henry James, who is an agent and public information officer. He's also Sid's and my immediate supervisor for Operation Quickline. Angelique knows nothing about that, however.

"Morning," I mumbled.

"Morning." She yawned. She's tall, with very full brown hair.

I blinked and went into the kitchen to get some cereal and milk. I brought my bowl into the breakfast room and plopped down next to Angelique, who was eating fruit salad.

"Where's Sid?" I asked after a couple minutes.

"Still conked out," Angelique said. "I tried to wake him for breakfast."

"He doesn't wake up."

"I know."

Moodily, we both continued eating.

"By the way," Angelique said. "Congratulations."

"Thanks." I looked at her, a little surprised. "Sid told you?"

"Mm-hmm." Angelique yawned again. "We spent a lot of time just talking last night."

"You're kidding."

Communication is not Sid's thing. We communicate really well because we have to, but I have never known him to spend much time talking with his girlfriends.

"Not about you and George," Angelique continued. "Anything but that. Still, he's bugged."

"Huh." I thought that one over. "Well, George was awfully abrupt about telling him. It's kind of too bad."

"Not for me, it isn't." Angelique smiled at her fruit salad. "I'm behind this one-hundred percent."

"You haven't even met George."

"I don't care as long as he's marrying you and Sid isn't."

"Sid would never get married, let alone to me."

Angelique just looked at me. "Come off it, Lisa. I know where my competition is. You just marry your friend and stay out of Sid's bedroom. With any luck at all, Sid will be so broken up, I'll be able to move in permanently.

"With any luck," I said, grumpily. "You'll probably last the usual two weeks, then Sid will get bored, you'll get hurt, and you'll move out."

It was the usual way it happened when Angelique moved in, which she did every now and then. Actually, it was the usual way it happened when any of Sid's girlfriends moved in.

"I don't know," Angelique said. "We did do a lot of talking last night. I think that's the key."

"That's it alright," I said, trying to figure out how I felt about Sid talking to someone else. Not that it made any difference. "You can have him and good luck."

"Thanks." Angelique stretched and got up. "I'm going back to bed. As soon as you set a date, let me know. I want to come dance at your wedding."

I watched her go. Poor Angelique has been in love with Sid since I've known her. Sid likes her as a friend and took her to bed with him more often than any other woman that I knew of, but that was it. Angelique decided she'd take what she could get. Somewhere along the line, she had gotten into her head that if I ever moved into Sid's bedroom, Sid would pretty much stick with me. I was skeptical. Granted, Sid and I are very close friends. But Sid is about the last person in the world who could handle a permanent relationship, even without strict fidelity. He is just not the settled in, married type. And the only way I'd ever move into his bedroom would be if he married me first.

That definitely wasn't going to happen, I reminded myself. I was going to marry George, sweet, innocent, bear-like George. I smiled and went to call my sister with the good news.

If Angelique was enthused by my engagement, Mae was less so.

"That's that boy you've been dating a lot lately," she said.

"He's hardly a boy, Mae. He's six feet tall and two years older than me.

"I suppose. How's Sid taking it?"

"George told him last night when Sid surprised us. Sid seemed pretty shocked."

"I can imagine. You've been screaming you didn't want to get married for so long."

"Well, I changed my mind. I love George. He's very sweet and cuddly and he loves me very much."

"I'm sure he does. Bring him with you tomorrow for dinner. I want to meet him. Is Sid coming?"

"I don't know, Mae." I fidgeted with the phone's cord. "He's got a girlfriend with him and I think she's staying the weekend."

"Have him bring her."

"Okay. Listen. I've got to call Mama and Daddy. I'll talk to you tomorrow."

Mae said good-bye and hung up. I just held down, then released, the switchhook and punched in the numbers for my parents' place in South Lake Tahoe. Mama was ecstatic when I told her the news.

"That is the best news that I've heard in years!" she squealed, her South Florida accent getting even stronger. "Bill! Come talk to Lisle! She just got engaged!"

Daddy got on the line and asked if I was happy.

"Of course, I'm happy, Daddy," I said

"Well, Lisle," he said, quietly. "I've always said it's your life. I just wish I could have met him first. But if you like him, then I'm sure he's a fine man."

"Thanks, Daddy," I said, sighing with relief.

For Daddy, that was wholehearted approval. Mae said later that Daddy was just glad it wasn't Sid. Sid and Daddy were getting along better than they used to, but they are not friends by any stretch. I heard the click as my mother picked up an extension.

"Now, Lisle, when's the date?"

"Mama, we just got engaged last night," I said, laughing.

"Well, you just hurry up and set one. Maybe I'd better fly down so we can get the plans started right."

"Fly down?" My heart stopped and I checked my watch. Sid's son, Nick, was due in at the airport in just about an hour. "Mama, I just remembered something, and I've gotta run. Don't fly down just yet. We'll talk about it when the date is set. I've got to go. Now."

"Alright, honey. Talk to you later."

I hung up and rushed out of my room, almost bumping into Sid in the hallway. He was fully dressed in a tan linen blazer, dress slacks, plaid shirt, and tie.

"Oh, there you are," I said. "I was just going to go find you. One of us has to get Nick from the airport."

"I'm going," Sid said blandly. "If Angelique wakes up, tell her where I am and that I'll be right back."

"Alright."

Sid left. I sighed. He was acting completely

indifferent, which meant he was very bugged. Nick was going to be spending the week with us, as he was out of school for summer vacation. I hoped Nick's presence would distract Sid a little.

Sid and Nick had met very belatedly when Rachel, Nick's mother, decided that Nick was old enough to know his father. Sid hadn't seen Rachel since Nick's conception twelve years before. Rachel didn't tell Sid she was pregnant, so when they showed up on Sid's doorstep this past spring, Sid was perturbed, to say the least. He hadn't wanted to acknowledge Nick, and Nick, surprisingly, hadn't necessarily wanted a father. However, the two eventually resigned themselves to each other and were getting very close. They occasionally needle the other that there isn't any real proof that the two are related, which is a little ridiculous. They look just like each other.

About twenty minutes after Sid had gone, a buzzing on my hip startled the heck out of me. It took me a moment to realize what it was. About a month before, all the Quickline agents had been assigned pagers. I know. It had taken so long because there was a problem with getting a secure radio channel. It's why we don't use radios to communicate. Anyone with the right receiver can pick up the signal. However, they finally got some super-secure way to scramble codes and the like on the pagers, and so we had them. I had to admit, they were convenient. No more calling a contact twenty times before I could schedule a drop. If a pick up had to be changed at the last minute, all I had to do was send the number of a nearby payphone as my call back number, and I could get things changed. The problem was, I was having a tough time getting used to having the darned thing on me all the time.

I hurried to Sid's office, checking for Angelique as I went. I didn't see her, but I slid the door to Sid's office closed and locked it just in case. I pulled the pager from my shorts' waistband and then dialed the number on the read-out from the Quickline extension.

Sid has multi-line phones in just about every room in the house, but only the phone in the office has the line for our hidden business.

A woman picked up on the other end. I gave the caller code and she returned the receiver.

"I've got a priority two, code one pick up for you," she told me.

I held back my groan. All Quickline business is given a priority and a code, with levels between one and five. Priority is obvious, but the code level indicates how much contact you can have with the person dropping the item. Code one means no contact at all, and you sometimes have to pull off some real sleight of hand to keep an enemy from finding the item. Code five, you can take the item directly and hang around and chat. Priority ones were absolute emergencies and relatively rare.

"Where do you want to do this?" I asked.

She named a drugstore that was actually pretty close to me. I agreed even though the timing would be tight.

"Okay. Got it. In twenty," I said.

"Good. I think I'm being watched."

I hung up and this time really did groan. But there was nothing I could do. I left a note for Angelique on the breakfast room table to let her know where Sid and I were, then grabbed my monster purse and headed out.

I spotted my contact browsing the greeting cards but couldn't see anyone else in the drugstore. I made a show of checking my list, then headed for the aspirin. I checked a few of the bottles. The green plastic wallet was next to the extra-large bottle of the store brand. I did what anyone would do upon finding a wallet. I opened it up to look for some I.D. and in doing so, managed to slip a register receipt out and into my purse. I still didn't see anybody, but that didn't mean someone didn't see me.

I took the wallet to the register, letting them know that I'd found it, paid for my aspirin and left. My contact had already gone, but as I passed the greeting card aisle, a man with dark hair was rifling through the cards my contact had been looking at.

When I got back to the house, Sid and Nick had just arrived. Nick slammed into me with a big hug, then ran off to put away his suitcase.

"Where did you go?" Sid asked.

"Priority two," I said. "I was just going to the office to read it."

Sid followed me there, and I got out the microdot reader. It looks just like one of those single slide viewers that you can pick up at a camera store, only the magnification is a lot stronger.

"The worst of it is, she thought she was being followed, and I think I made the guy," I said.

Sid sighed. "Just what we need. Another line down."

The previous spring, we'd lost one of our distribution lines thanks to that leak in the FBI offices.

"We don't know that it is," I pointed out. "People pick up tails all the time."

Sid nodded and we turned our attention to the magnifier. The drop was a description of the man they suspected of being the leak.

"Well, there's a help," Sid grumbled.

I couldn't blame him. The target was supposedly average-sized, with brown hair, brown eyes, and no distinguishing marks, apart from a scar on his left hand.

"I suppose it's something." I thought back to the man rifling through the cards back at the pharmacy. "And it wasn't the guy I saw this morning. He had black hair."

Sid shrugged and went off to find Angelique so that we could all go to lunch. When we got back, Nick followed me into my outer room. I have a little suite, including bathroom, near the kitchen. The outer room I use as my sewing room. It was originally supposed to be a sitting room with a mini-office. I did leave the couch, but that's jammed up against the far wall. I have two sewing desks under the one window, one with my regular machine and one with the new serger. Sid had actually talked me into buying a top-of-the-line model that used five threads and sewed the seam, as well as finished it.

"What's that?" Nick asked, pointing to it.

"My new serger," I told him. "It helps me sew faster."

I shook out some dark brown heavy twill that would eventually become a pair of shorts and laid it on the cutting board that took up half the floor space in the room.

"You already sew an awful lot," Nick complained.

"It's good therapy," I said. "Lord knows, I need it around here."

Nick laughed, pushing his glasses up on his nose. He was just as near-sighted as Sid, but Sid wore contact lenses.

"What's with Dad?" he asked suddenly.

I frowned and continued folding the fabric, then smoothing it out as I evened up the edges.

"What do you mean?" I asked slowly, hoping Nick didn't mean what was going on with Angelique. I had assumed she and Sid were up to something again, but didn't know and didn't want to know.

"He's acting funny. I thought the doctor said his V.D. was all gone."

"He's, um, had a mild shock. You remember George, right?"

"Your boyfriend." Nick rolled his eyes with the disdain only an eleven-year-old can muster.

"Yes. He proposed to me last night."

"Like, marry him?"

"Yes." I made sure my edges were even, trying not to watch Nick.

"No kidding. Dad always said he was going to. I bet you set him straight."

I took a deep breath. "It depends on what you

mean by that, but I accepted."

"That big old goop?"

"Nick! I love him!" I put my hands on my hips.

Nick shrugged. "You're copping out.

"Marriage is not a cop-out." I went back to laying my pattern pieces on my fabric, looking for the best fit.

"Whatever. Dad must be really jealous. He's got the hots for you."

"Your dad has the hots for every female he's ever met."

"True, but you're not just any female."

"Whatever," I grumbled. I adjusted a piece or two, then looked around for my measuring tape. "If he's jealous, that's his problem. I'm marrying George and I'm very happy about it.

"You don't sound very happy."

"Well, I am."

I found my tape measure where it belonged, hanging next to my machine, and went back to laying out my shorts. Nick watched without comment. I glanced at him and wondered who I was trying to convince.

The next day, Sunday, was incredibly weird on the family side of things. Since Nick is Catholic, like me, I took him with me and George to mass that next morning. I couldn't help being excited. George kept telling me how beautiful I was. We prayed together, which is something I will never share with Sid. I mean, Sid respects my faith, but he was raised as an atheist and doesn't believe. My faith is important to me and being able to share it with George was amazing.

After mass, we went to my sister's place in Fullerton. Sid and Angelique were there, too, in fact, they beat us there. I don't know why Mae thought it would be a good idea to have Sid around when my niece Janey checked George out, but there he was.

Janey is the second oldest of Mae's five. Darby, her older brother, was Nick's age at that time and he and Nick get along famously. Then there's Ellen, who was six and thrilled to death that she was done with kindergarten. Then there are the youngest two, Mitch and Marty, who were three, almost four, and giving the terrible two's a run for their money.

Janey's eighth birthday was in another month or so, and for a kid her age, she had (and still has) a way of seeing into people's hearts and knowing them for who they are. She's got brown hair and big green eyes. I was not worried about her liking George. He was a total sweetie. She still managed to surprise us.

"How do you do, Janey?" George asked when he was presented to her in the family room.

She looked at him, her head cocked to one side. Then she looked at me for almost a minute, it seemed, then looked back at George.

"Very well," she said. "It's a pleasure to meet you."

She looked at me, then ran off to play upstairs.

"Nice kid," said George, looking after her fondly.

He didn't seem to notice that the rest of us had our jaws on the floor. Janey's indifference was unheard of. Even Angelique, who had only just met Janey for the first time, knew something was up. I found out later that Janey had given her a nice, warm hug when they met.

When dinner time came, I went upstairs to the bedroom she shares with Ellen to get her. The door was half-closed and I could hear voices. I paused about halfway down the hall.

"Well, I can't say he's bad when he's not," Janey was telling someone. "He's a very good man."

"But you don't seem to like him very much," said Sid.

"Oh, I like him okay. I just don't want to hurt his feelings."

"How would you hurt his feelings?" Sid couldn't help laughing.

Janey let out her breath as if it was obvious. "He thinks he's going to marry Aunt Lisa and he's not."

"Your aunt seems pretty sure."

"No way, Uncle Sid. It's just not right. Don't worry. She'll wake up in plenty of time."

"Who said I was worried?"

"Uncle Sid."

I could almost see Janey's big green eyes focused on Sid and him squirming.

"Alright. I am concerned. For her welfare and all."

"Of course, you are. She's your best friend. Just be nice to her. She'll come around. But you gotta be patient and don't be too nice to her around Angelique. I don't know if you know it, but..."

"I do know how Angelique feels about me."

"Then why do you keep letting her hang around you?"

"Why do you keep asking the same questions your aunt does?"

"Uncle Sid, what am I going to do with you?"

"Face it, Janey, I'm hopelessly corrupt."

"No, you're not. You've just got to get it out of your system."

Sid laughed loudly, which was a good thing because I had to laugh, too.

"Janey, dinner's ready," I called, then hurried to the stairs before I could see Sid leaving the room.

I have to admit, I was rattled, and it pretty much ruined the rest of the day for me. George noticed something was up and asked me about it as we drove home. Well, he did the driving, as he always did.

"Oh, it's nothing," I said. "I'm fine."

George laughed. "I had a great time, you know. Your nieces are such beautiful little girls. I hope we have two just like them."

"I hope not!" I blurted out, my insides turning into a massive knot at the thought.

"What? They're gorgeous and wonderful."

"And very bright and inquisitive," I said. "Ellen has almost torn that house down with her experiments, and let's not start in with Janey. I mean, I adore them. You know that. But Mae has her hands full and it ain't just the twins."

George chuckled. "Sid told me about Janey."

"He did?" I immediately became suspicious. "What did he tell you?"

"She seems to think we're not getting married." George laughed, then saw the look on my face. "You knew that?"

"Uh-huh." I swallowed. "She's pretty perceptive."

"That's what I'm told," George said. He glanced at me, then frowned. "If you're that worried about it, we can take some time with this. Maybe she'll come around."

"Maybe," I said.

It had never happened before, but it was always possible that was because we'd never given Janey the chance to. The more I thought about it, the more that made sense.

George frowned at the traffic ahead of us. "Oh. Sid asked me not to tell you about what Janey said. He thinks you don't know."

"I wasn't supposed to, but I found out anyway." I bit my lip. I did not want to say how I knew. "It's okay. I won't say anything."

"Oh, Lisa, I love you so much. We are going to be so happy together."

I smiled at him, my insides loosening up and warming. He reached over and picked up my hand. My eyes filled as he gently kissed my fingers. He was so very, very sweet. And while Janey was extraordinarily perceptive, that didn't mean her opinions would never evolve. They were evolving all the time. She certainly liked George. I decided that was enough. George had been very sweet about slowing things down, too. [At least, he got that right - SEH].

The next day, Monday, Sid's turn to tail the Romanian official came up. He left even before breakfast. Angelique had gone back to her place the night before. So that left Nick to follow me around all morning, which he did relentlessly.

"I'm bored," he announced around eleven. "Where's Dad?"

"Out doing research," I told him. "Why don't you go play with Motley? He needs some exercise."

"Okay." He slumped out.

I bit my lip. There really wasn't a lot for Nick to do around the house, and neither Sid nor I liked to encourage watching TV. Nick liked to read well enough but was generally too hyper to spend a lot of time doing it. Nor was Sid's neighborhood the kind of place where kids could play outside. Sid doesn't even have much of a front yard, just a slope covered with ice plant. The yard out back is fairly good-sized, but at the time, there wasn't anything there for an eleven-year-old boy to play with.

As I watched him go, my pager went off. Just what

I needed. I went into Sid's office, locked the door, and picked up the phone, pressing the line for our business.

A man picked up on the other end. I gave the caller code, he gave the receiver.

"I've got a priority two, code one pick up for you," he said. "It's at Union Station, locker four-twelve. They want it to go upline through the Blue group."

"Got it." I opened Sid's desk to get the skeleton key we had for the Union Station lockers. "And the next stop?"

"Uhhh... Here it is. Blue five."

"Okay. Thanks."

The stop number would have been on the package, but it was only courtesy to let my next contact know where she was heading. I hung up and immediately dialed again. There was no answer. I tried the page number only to get a message that the pager was offline or out of the area. I groaned. The only other Blue group contact I had was in Orange County and I did not want to go that far. But there was no help for it.

I dialed again. At least, this time, the contact picked up right away. We did the caller code, receiver dialog.

"I've got a pick up for you, priority two, code one," I told her. "Going upline to Blue five."

She groaned. "It never fails." She yawned and I got the feeling she'd just come back from somewhere else. "When and where?"

"I'll shoot for the Disneyland Hotel drug store. Anything you need?"

"Tampons."

I tried not to snigger. Many of us women in Quickline had developed the habit of hiding things behind feminine products. Most men would not go near them.

"I'll call you right before I drop them," I told my contact. "Should be in the next couple hours."

She yawned again. "Okay."

As I hung up, I looked at my watch. I did not have

much time if I wanted to avoid the worst of the traffic. I found Conchetta, the housekeeper, dusting the living room.

"Conchetta, I've gotta take off," I said apologetically.

She just shook her head but smiled nonetheless. I mean, I figure she knows something's up. She does have a security clearance.

"I'll watch Nick," she said. "But I'm going home at six, as always."

"I know. One of us should be back before then. I'm going to tell Nick, okay?"

Except Nick was not in the house, nor was he in the backyard. I finally found him in Sid's hot tub, which is in the side yard next to Sid's bedroom. Nick was fully clothed and he had Motley in the tub with him.

"I'm giving Motley a bath," he announced cheerfully.

"Don't you dare put any soap in that hot tub."

Nick rolled his eyes. "Are you kidding? After what happened the last time?

"Alright. You and Motley stay outside until you're both dry. You can eat lunch on the back patio, if necessary. Absolutely no tracking water through the house. Is that clear?"

It was pretty warm that day, so I figured both Nick and the dog would be dry in short order.

"Yes, ma'am," Nick said.

"I've got to run an errand. I'll be back after lunch."

"Okay."

"And stay out of trouble."

"I'll try."

Nick did try. That didn't mean he'd stay out of trouble. As an afterthought, I locked Sid's office before I went out to the garage and my blue Datsun pickup. It has the larger cab and jump seats and a shell on it.

Fortunately, the drive to Union Station was relatively straightforward. I went straight for the lockers, keeping a solid eye out as I went. I got the package, a small taped-up manila envelope, then wandered the station a bit, checking time tables for the few Amtrak trains that left out of there.

Sure enough, there was a tail, which wasn't surprising. My contact was supposed to have told me that he had one. But that didn't mean he'd either spotted the tail (this fellow was rather notorious for missing such things), or that he'd thought to mention it. Sid and I often wondered how the man had stayed alive as long as he had.

The tail was a dark-haired man with a mustache and bristly chin. He was hanging fairly close to me, which did not bode well. He was probably looking for an excuse to attack me and take the package. It could also have meant that he didn't have a team in place.

I hoped it was that he had no team. Still, just in case, I sauntered toward Olvera Street, which is across the street from the station and was crowded with tourists that time of year. People make great cover against getting attacked. I am perfectly capable of defending myself in a fight. On the other hand, I abhor violence and always have, which may seem a little weird given my business. However, most good undercover spies try to avoid violence like the plague because violence attracts attention. Unfortunately, violence still manages to find us all too often.

Sure enough, as I crossed the street and walked up the hill to the plaza, my tail bumped me, then grabbed my arm to tug me behind the nearby arbor.

"Hey!" I yelled, just like they teach you in civilian self-defense classes.

That startled him enough to give me a slight edge, even though he didn't let me go. I kept struggling, yelling for all I was worth because sometimes attracting attention is exactly what you need to do. What I wanted to do at that moment was convince my tail that he'd somehow gotten a hold of a civilian. It's surprising how well that works. [It certainly surprises me - SEH]

The tail got his mouth next to my ear and I felt a gun in my ribs.

"I want what you got out of that locker."

"It's my brother's locker," I whimpered. "He gave me the key, I swear it."

My tail shoved me forward, then ran from the arbor. I looked around and didn't see any onlookers. I ran back to the station and dodged cars in the parking lot until I found my truck. My heart still pounding, I got out of the lot as fast as I could and drove around the downtown area for several minutes to be sure that I didn't still have a tail. Satisfied that I was in the clear, I got onto the freeway and headed for Anaheim.

I parked in the lot for the Disneyland Hotel, thanking God and St. Anthony that I'd managed to find a space during the height of the tourist season. The hotel lobby was crowded, which was also a blessing. I passed a coffee shop and saw my contact eating her lunch or breakfast. She blinked at me and nodded. I took my time going to the drug store. Once there, I looked at the box of tampons, shook my head. As I put it back, I slid the envelope with the pick-up in it behind the other boxes. I wandered the store until I saw the contact in the feminine products aisle. I hung back just long enough to be sure that she had the envelope, then left the store and hurried back to my truck. It was well after one by that point, so, I picked up a burger and fries at a drive-through on the way back to the freeway.

Traffic was a mess, too. The Olympic games were a little over a month away, and there were construction projects all over the place, with workers frantically trying to complete them before the games began. I got home a little before three.

I heard music coming from the rumpus room, but the song ended as I got into the doorway. Records littered the floor and Nick stood, studying the back of an all-too-familiar album cover.

"Nicholas!" I groaned.

"Hey, Lisa, listen to this song. It's neat." He put the needle down on the record.

I gritted my teeth as he scraped the needle across

the disc trying to find the track.

"Nick, be careful," I told him as sternly as I could. "You'll mess up the needle and the record. They're both very fragile."

"The needle on my mom's record player isn't."

"I'll bet you anything Sid's is a lot more delicate and expensive. He's finicky about stuff like that, you know."

"I know. Listen to this." He got the needle placed correctly. "Neat, huh?"

It was Sad Lisa.

I smiled in spite of my irritation. "Yes, it is. I know the song very well."

"You do?"

"That's my album."

"Wow."

"Why don't you clean up all these albums you've left lying?"

"Oh. Sure." Nick scrambled after the records, stopping only to put Sad Lisa on again.

He was entranced by the song and kept playing it over and over. I finally had to tell him to stop as I was getting sick of it.

Sid did not get home by dinnertime. George came by to get me for the teen bible study at church, so I took Nick with us. I probably should have stayed home with him. Nick was completely bored to the point that I had to take him out of the church classroom where we met right before break time.

"Why do we have to be here?" he whined.

"I have to be here and there's no one else at home to keep an eye on you," I said.

"I'm not a baby."

"No. But you're a little too young to be left alone."

"So, why are you here? This is for high school kids."

"I help with the leadership. I work on retreats and I'm going to be one of the counselors for their camp at the end of July."

Nick harrumphed. "So, why aren't you and George

talking about being engaged?"

I sighed. "Because we agreed that we'd tell our prayer group first. We don't want to distract the teens just yet."

Nick harrumphed again, but let it go.

The next morning, Tuesday, as we came in from our morning run, Sid suggested that we take the day off.

"I want to spend some time with Nick," he told me softly as Nick ran to his room to get dressed for the day.

"I'm glad, but we've got deadlines," I said. "I need your edits on the bond market piece. I've got a rough draft to finish on mail-order fabrics, and we've got to put together our final outline for signs of child abuse."

"Don't we have a couple weeks on that last one?" Sid asked.

"Yes, but we've had a lot of extra running around to do lately, and it doesn't look like that's easing up any."

Sid winced. "It could be. One of the crew picked up a suspect yesterday. I got word they were going to be in the alley last night."

The alley, which was located in downtown Los Angeles, was a favorite spot for meetings and prisoner transfers. It had gotten to be that way because it had a weird spot, where one of the buildings wasn't as deep as the two on either side, which made hiding there really easy. Also, it was in an area where the buildings were older and had been mostly emptied in anticipation of some urban rejuvenation plan, except for a few offices here and there. In fact, the alley was so popular, we were sometimes warned when someone wanted to use it.

"That doesn't mean we're done," I said. "Even if it does, we've got a whole bunch of holiday queries to get out, as well."

He winced. "I'm not going to insist that you work when I'm taking off, but if you want to, feel free. I want to spend some time with Nick and today's a good day to do it."

He had a point. The problem was I also got the feeling he was avoiding me. Sid and I work pretty closely together and not just with Quickline. It may be our cover, but Sid and I do really work as freelance writers, and business that way was going gangbusters. I was a little worried about Sid trying to dance around the work thing. After all, he's usually pretty strict about being at our desks from eight a.m. to five p.m. At the same time, he will occasionally blow off work in favor of weekday skiing or something else fun, and he's been known to let me do the same. So, I decided not to confront him about it. At least, I was able to work in shorts and a t-shirt, as opposed to our usual office wear, something else Sid insists on.

They spent the morning on Nick's continuing obsession with Sad Lisa. I guess Nick had played the song for Sid, because while I worked, I could hear them in the library, going through Sid's sheet music collection. I was a little surprised that Sid already had a copy of it. Sid's been playing piano since he was six and is a very accomplished pianist. He tends to prefer classical music but is open to playing just about anything. The music went on for a bit and I tried to ignore it. I sighed in relief when Sid suggested that the two of them hang out in the hot tub.

Right before lunch, George dropped by just to say hi. He could do things like that because he was independently wealthy. It was old family money. His ancestry went back to the Californios who owned vast swathes of land in the area before the Americans took over. How his family had managed to hold onto their lands and money when most of the other old Mexican families didn't, I do not know.

George spent his time doing art photography and was very good at it, and had even done a few shows. So, it wasn't surprising that he had his camera bag with him. Nor was the vase of red roses he had.

"George, how sweet," I said, feeling warm and

happy.

I let him in and he followed me into the office.

"I'll put them on my desk," I said.

"That's exactly what I had in mind."

I set the vase on the corner of the desk, then shook my head as he opened his camera case.

"George, I've got a lot of work to do today and you know how much I hate having my picture taken."

"These are not going into a show," he said.

We'd had words before about that when he'd tried to get me to sign a model release the previous spring.

"George, please."

"Oh, come on, Lisa. I have pictures of everyone I care about except my beautiful girl. Please?"

I sat down. "Just a couple, okay?"

I went back to work on my article while George got out his light meter, then opened the drapes to the side yard.

"Oh, wow!" he yelped as he saw what was outside.

"That's why I have those drapes closed," I said.

I'd shut them when Nick had noisily accepted Sid's suggestion about the hot tub. I was pretty sure they weren't wearing bathing suits. Sid is a nudist at heart and genuinely can't understand why people get so weird about being, and seeing someone, naked.

"I think I can work with the light in here," George said.

Shaking my head, I went back to work on my draft, trying to ignore the whirring of his camera. Sid came in a couple minutes later, wearing a towel around his waist, and pair of leather thongs on his feet, and I'm pretty sure, nothing else. The towel was only as a courtesy to me.

"Oh, hello, George," Sid said. He was smiling, but there was something entirely bland in his tone that didn't feel right. "How's it going?"

"Very good, Sid. How's it going with you?"

"Good enough." He tried opening his office door. "Lisa, why is this locked?"

"I had to run an errand yesterday and couldn't take Nick," I said. "I thought it might be wise."

"I see. Good thinking."

I handed him my keys. "Here."

"Thanks." Sid unlocked the door and went in.

George set his camera down on the desk and came around and crouched next to my chair.

"How much more have you got to do?" he asked.

"Just two more lines, I think." I looked over my notes on the desk as George slid his hands around my waist. "But I've got other things to do besides this."

"Busy girl."

"Well, I don't have a rich family."

"Soon you will. I'm going to sweep you away to a beautiful mansion and all you'll have to do is order servants around." He kissed me.

He was a very good kisser, and caught up in the kiss, I decided that the mansion and servants were him being silly and not any real plan. But something else occurred to me.

"Aren't we going to live in your condo?" I asked when I could. "And what about Jesse?"

Jesse was George's best friend and roommate.

"No. We'll get our own place. I'm going to sign the condo over to Jesse."

"He's not going to accept it."

"We'll see. There's plenty of time to worry about that."

He moved in for another kiss, but I caught the office door opening out of the corner of my eye and pushed away.

"Excuse me, lovebirds," said Sid, stepping outside.

"Sorry about that, Sid," I said, turning back to my keyboard.

"About what?" Sid asked. "Anyway, it's lunchtime. Why don't you and George go out? Unless, George, you want to eat with Nick and me."

"No thanks, Sid," George said with a laugh. "I'll take Lisa out."

I really did not want to go out to lunch, and briefly wondered if Sid needed me out of the house for some reason. That didn't entirely make sense, but then I remembered what Janey had told him the day before, the part about being extra nice to me. I quickly decided that it wasn't worth getting into any arguments over and agreed to go as soon as I'd finished my draft.

That night, at the adult's bible study, George and I announced our upcoming nuptials. Everyone was pretty enthusiastic.

Well, almost everyone. Our youth minister, Dan Williams, looked at me a little strangely. We'd dated briefly when he first arrived in the parish and I'd told him that I didn't want to get married to anyone and he'd stopped dating me. On the other hand, he'd just gotten married earlier that spring to Sarah.

Jesse White already knew about the engagement and had told his girlfriend, Kathy Deiner. Kathy is also one of my closest friends. She's a tall, very elegant Black woman, with her hair cut short. She's a junior partner in an accounting firm and Jesse's a photographer, like George, only at the time, Jesse was still building his business by doing weddings and portrait settings and whatever else he could scrape up.

Jesse and Kathy had been the odds-on favorites to announce their engagement next, instead of George and I. Nobody could figure out what the hold-up was, but Kathy had confided in me that Jesse did not want Kathy supporting him. As Kathy explained, it had a lot to do with negative stereotypes about Black men, which was kind of hard to argue with.

"It seems like everybody is getting married except me," she complained quietly to me during the break.

"Hang in there," I whispered back. "George told me today that he's going to sign the condo over to Jesse when we get married. We'll find a way to get him to take it."

Kathy shuddered and shook her head. "Wish me luck, because that's what it's going to take. As my granny says, that man is more stubborn than an ornery mule."

My other girlfriend, Esther Nguyen, was too wrapped in her own problem, namely that her father had moved into her apartment. Esther, who's an engineer, doesn't tend to be too interested in what she calls "girlie" stuff. I was sort of surprised by our other friend, Frank Lonnergan. He's a musician and he and Sid have become good friends, as well. Frank clearly disapproved.

"Jealous, Frank?" George nudged him playfully.

"I'm not," Frank said as if he knew someone who was.

That bothered me. I couldn't say why, but it really bothered me.

June 21–22, 1984

Wednesday, it was my turn to tail the official. Nothing happened. Sid had the night shift and didn't come back until time to run, Thursday morning. He ran with us, then at breakfast, gave Nick permission to watch the pile of movies they'd rented the day before. After that, Sid went to take a nap and I went back to the office.

He woke up in time for lunch. I took mine back to the office while he and Nick chatted. When Sid finally came in, he stopped and looked at me.

"That's a very nice blouse you have on," he said smiling gently.

The blouse in question came from a McCall's pattern with a square neck, front buttons offset to the right side and full, three-quarter length sleeves. I'd made it out of a linen with a flower print in apricot and light green.

"Thanks, Sid." I was still a little suspicious. Sid complimented my clothes all the time, but there was just something off about his comment.

"Did you buy it?"

"No, I made it."

"You did a nice job. That's a good color for you."

"Thank you," I replied.

Sid went into his office. I bit my lip. Things were just too awkward and it was beginning to get to me. On the other hand, I really didn't want to have a fight, and that seemed all too likely. Sid and I fought all the time, so it wasn't that so much as me being afraid that he would use my engagement as an excuse to avoid the confrontation, which would eventually mean a really nasty dragged-out fight, which meant that if we were going to be fighting anyway, I might as well get it over with. I groaned inwardly, then followed Sid into his office and plopped down into the chair in front of his desk.

"Yes?" He glanced up at me, then returned his attention to the article draft that he was marking up with the fountain pen he reserved for red ink.

"Don't you think it's about time we talked?"

"About what?" He made a mark on the printout.

"About George and me."

He looked up and shrugged. "What's to talk about? You obviously love the man. I've taken great pains to avoid any of those sorts of ties between us. I have no right to stand in the way and I'm not going to."

I somehow managed not to roll my eyes. "Sid, there's more to it than that."

"Of course, there is." His grumble was sarcastic as all get out, but he capped his pen and sat back in his seat. "Alright. I'm not terribly thrilled about it. But what can I do? I'm not about to offer you the same thing."

"I'm not asking for that, and I'm not even sure I want it." I looked down at my hands. "I am worried about our friendship."

"How does George feel about it?"

"I don't know." I began picking at a hangnail on my thumb. "I haven't really talked to him about it."

"Well, you'd better."

He was right, but I glared at him, anyway.

"What difference does it make?"

He held his hands up. "I don't want to be an obstacle between you and your husband."

"I'm not going to let that happen. And I refuse to let George determine who my friends are going to be. Sid, you're my closest friend. I don't want to lose that."

Sid looked away, then back at me. "Are you planning on working for me after the wedding?"

"Well, duh." I stopped and frowned. "I guess it isn't that obvious. I mean, I want to. I've just got a feeling that George isn't going to want a working wife. His mother doesn't." I put on a smile. "We'll just have to talk that one through."

"That's not the only job problem you've got." Sid's eyebrow lifted.

Wincing, I got up from the chair and shut and locked the office door.

"I don't want to be reassigned," I said, sitting down again.

"That's not what I'm worried about. Have you told George anything?"

"Of course not. But I'll probably have to tell him something sooner or later."

"Probably." Sid shook his head. "Will you promise me one thing? Don't tell him until after the wedding? I realize there's always the possibility of divorce, but I'd feel a lot better if you waited until then."

"Yeah. That makes sense. Alright. I promise." I looked away and shut my eyes.

"Don't feel you can't break that promise if you have to tell him to keep him. But that's the only condition."

"I know, Sid."

He still seemed a little uncomfortable about something. "Who knows? We may end up recruiting him."

"I'd rather not," I said, my heart skipping a beat. "At least, not immediately."

Sid grinned. "I wouldn't until closer to the wedding. Speaking of which, do you know when yet?"

"That." I grimaced. "Probably not until next year or later, with any luck. We're supposed to have the meeting with Father John..." I looked at my watch. "Shoot. In just about half an hour."

"Oh." Sid's face fell.

I realized we still hadn't discussed what I really wanted to.

"Sid, could you do one favor for me?"

"What?" He uncapped his pen.

"Could you not avoid me?" I know it's a little awkward, but we can adjust. I don't like having things between us."

"I'll try, Lisa." He looked at me a little sadly.

"Thanks, Sid." I got up and left.

There wasn't much more I could ask for and I did believe he would try. At least, there hadn't been a fight and Sid hadn't completely avoided the topic.

My only other problem was the coming meeting with Father John, our pastor at our parish. George had talked me into it that Tuesday after Bible study. I pointed out that he had agreed to take things slowly, but he came back saying that the best reception sites were usually booked over a year in advance, so it made sense to have the date set sooner rather than later. Then my mother called after I'd gotten back and told me the same thing. Worse yet, she had a reception site that she really liked for the following April and needed to put a deposit in as soon as possible. So, when George called me the next day with the meeting time, I agreed to go. I also made the mistake of telling him what my mother had said.

Father John Reynolds is the only person I've ever told about Quickline. He's a tall, gentle man with a special talent for helping me get and keep perspective on a lot of the questionable things I find myself doing. He'd been doing ministry over at UCLA, then was assigned to my parish as pastor right before I got there. Kathy, Esther, and Frank had known him from UCLA and followed him to the parish. George and Jesse knew each other and Father John from some other ministry John had been involved in and followed him to the parish. Which gives you an idea of just how special Father John is. The Church tries to encourage people to stay with the parish they live in to avoid anyone getting too dependent on one person. But Esther pointed out that as young adults, none of them had any ties anywhere and they might as well develop said ties with people that they like. It's thanks to John that I'm up to my hips in the high school group and other activities.

As John ushered George and me into his office, the

priest seemed unusually uncomfortable.

"Is everything okay?" I asked as we settled into chairs.

John shifted in the beat-up office chair behind his cluttered desk. "Yes and no. I just don't know about this."

"But why?" asked George, completely baffled.

"A lot of things, George," John said. "It's not that I don't think you'll have a good marriage. It will probably be nice and solid. You two love each other and you have a strong sense of commitment. You have a decent idea of what you're getting into. So, for those reasons, I can't refuse to marry you."

"But," I said.

Father John took a deep breath, then looked at me and George.

"But," he repeated, "I don't think it's the best of all possible choices. It's not a bad one. It's just not the best."

"John, I don't understand," George complained. "What could possibly be wrong with it? I love Lisa. I want to make her happy."

"I know, George." John looked him up and down. "But there are problems on both sides. For instance, I have to wonder about your motives, George. I've known you for a long time and you've been wife hunting almost since you got out of high school. It could be that you're more in love with the idea of being married than you are with Lisa, herself."

"But I love Lisa," George's voice took on a whiny edge.

"I know you do," John said, more patient than I would have been. "And I said that." Then he turned to me. "As for you, Lisa, I know you love George, too, but I also know you love your career. Are you sure you're not running away from something by marrying George?"

"You mean Sid?" I asked, then sighed. "I don't think so. Maybe, at first, there was a little of that. But we did get to talking about it this afternoon, and I'm confident in our friendship and I plan on maintaining it."

"I see," John said, still looking less than convinced.

"John, this is not a rush job," George said. "I waited, just like you told me to."

"Uh-huh."

George rolled his eyes. "Okay. We both know I've been wanting to get married. And maybe I jumped the gun once or twice."

"Four or five times, George," John said.

"But I really took my time with Lisa," George said. "I've never loved anyone more than I love her. I've thought long and hard about this and prayed about it."

John looked like he wanted to say more.

"I know," he said, finally. "That's why I don't really have grounds to refuse you marriage. I am going to ask you one favor, though. Wait. Don't set a date for another few months."

I was about to say okay, but George groaned loudly.

"We can't," he said. "All the good reception sites are already booked until next year. And my mom has been bugging me as it is."

"So has my mom," I said with a sigh. "But if you want us to wait, we will. Mama's important, but not that important."

"Hmmm. When did you have in mind?"

"Next April," George said quickly before I could suggest the following July. "Lisa's mom found a really nice hotel for the reception and she wants to put a deposit down as soon as possible."

John looked at me.

I shrugged. "She's pretty excited."

John looked at us both for a very long minute.

"April," he said finally, then reached over the desk to where the wedding book sat waiting. "I suppose I can work with that. Let's see what's available."

George grinned and I smiled. We were able to get April 20, 1985, at ten a.m. Mama had told me to get the time a little later in the afternoon, but we didn't have the option. All of the other Saturdays that month were booked and May was mostly full, too.

John wrote us in and told us about the preliminary paperwork and other requirements. George was so excited I don't know how much he heard. As we started to leave, John held me back.

"I want to talk to Lisa privately for a minute," he said.

"Sure." George all but floated out of the office.

I sank back into my chair as John closed the office door.

"I think I know what this is about," I said as he got back into his chair.

"I don't know what you've told George about your little side business, but I thought I'd better not take any chances," John said.

"That's good because he doesn't know a thing."

"You're going to have to tell him eventually."

"I know." I looked away, feeling guilty. "But I promised Sid that I wouldn't until after the wedding unless I couldn't keep him any other way."

"That makes sense," said John. "But it's not all that fair to George."

"The problem is, once he knows, he's pretty much caught," I said. "There really is no way to be fair to him that way. Heck, Sid couldn't even tell me about it until I was already recruited."

"I suppose not." John looked at me again. "Are you sure you're not running away from Sid?"

I looked at him, puzzled. "Sid and I are friends and that's not going to change. So, there's really nothing to run away from."

"What about children?"

"What do you mean?"

John snorted. "What's going to happen if and when you get pregnant?"

"I don't know. I suppose I'll have to go into some type of retirement."

"You'd better find out before too long. That could put you into quite a bind."

I shrugged, not wanting to admit he was right. "It'll work out. I know of a whole family that's involved. Sid was even talking about recruiting George."

John's eyebrows rose. "How do you feel about that?"

"Fine." I stopped. "I don't know, I guess. I don't like involving George in the danger, but it would be nice to work with him."

"You haven't thought this out very completely."

I squirmed. "We've only been engaged for less than a week."

"Lisa, you should have thought of these things before you gave George your answer."

"Maybe." I was annoyed because he had me. Unfortunately, that only got my dander up. "But I'm committed to this now, so I'll just have to work it out. I love George and I do feel good about this."

"Alright. I'll talk to you Sunday, then."

John got up and opened the door for me.

"What was that all about?" George asked as we left the rectory.

"Oh, nothing. Just some minor issue." I looked over the parking lot. "I don't know, George. Maybe he's right."

"Of course he is, Lisa." George pulling me close to him. "We have lots to think and pray about. But this is still right for us. We are going to be so happy. I love so you much, my heart is overflowing and I'm only going to love you more."

George swept me into one of his gorgeous, wonderful kisses, and I let it fill me with his confidence.

June 23-24, 1984

On the fourth Friday of the month, the adult bible study hosts a potluck. Dan Williams, the youth minister and leader of the adult bible study, had wanted to do some more active evangelization. After his attempts to hand out bible tracts at the local shopping center failed utterly, Frank suggested that maybe just being friends with non-Christians would be more effective. That led to a regular party where we could invite our non-Christian friends and hang out.

I'm pretty sure Sid was the main target, especially since the more fundamentalist part of our group doesn't tend to have friends who aren't Christian. Anyway, Sid went to the first one and it did not go well. The fundamentalists made their first mistake by trying to convert Sid with brilliant arguments from the Bible. Sid answered back with a contradicting verse to every verse they threw at him. Then he pointed out, quite reasonably, that the foundation of their argument was that because Scripture is God's word, it is therefore true. He didn't believe in the existence of a Supreme Being at all, so they were going to have to prove their point some other way. Then he really got them by saying that he'd read the Bible a couple of times and had been completely unmoved by it. At least three of the girls burst into tears at that one.

Then there was the time Sid picked up on Mary Phelps' non-Christian co-worker. Mary is still mad at me about that, even though I pointed out to her that I'm not responsible for Sid's behavior, that she knew what Sid was like, and that her co-worker had started it by coming on to Sid. It was also about that time that I realized that Sid was mostly going in order to tease the fundamentalists. [A bunch of self-righteous bullies who deserved every bit of the tweaking - SEH]

Still, I was surprised to find Sid at Sarah William's mother's house in Bel Air when George and I arrived that Friday. Sid had flown up to San Jose with Nick earlier that afternoon. Nick had tried to convince Rachel that he wanted to spend another week, but as we were fast learning, as soon as we suggested something, Rachel was going to insist on doing the opposite. So, when I told Rachel that it was fine by us if Nick stayed, she insisted that he be on the next plane to San Jose. Sid went with him because it had been too late to arrange for Nick to fly by himself with the airline. I figured Sid would just go out wherever while he was up in the Bay Area or when he got home.

There he was, however, playing piano with Frank playing guitar. Mary Phelps had her teeth gritted and was glaring at me, and that's when I realized Sid and Frank were playing Vatican Rag. It's a funny tune, but not exactly respectful, which meant that Sid was in one of his moods, and Frank even more so. Frank only played the song to bug Mary and her cohort, which you'd think they would have figured out.

"I think I want to go home," I hissed at George, setting down my dish of Conchetta's truly wonderful chiles rellenos on the buffet table.

"Just ignore them," George said with a chuckle. "That's what you always tell Dan to do."

I sighed. He had me there.

I went back into the living room where Frank was belting out the final refrain. Sid looked up as his fingers danced like lightning over the keyboard and grinned at me. The applause as the two finished was both tepid at one end of the room and enthused by the group around the piano. The latter group included Jesse, Kathy, Esther and, oddly enough, Sarah's mother.

"Hey, Frank, do you know Sad Lisa?" Sid asked.

"I do believe so," said Frank.

I tried not to groan.

"Turns out it's one of Lisa's favorites," Sid said.

"Then play it, we must," Frank said in his Yoda

voice. He is quite the Star Wars fan.

Frank sang as Sid played. It was beautifully done, but I felt an odd shudder ripple through my body, what my mama would call someone walking on my grave.

I turned away and focused on chatting until the song ended and Dan led us in an overly long grace. Sid, Frank, and Esther were muttering along and chuckling. They were probably making fun of Dan's long-windedness. Part of me wished I could join them and part of me was glad I'd stayed where I was. George slid up and put his arm around my shoulders.

"Honey, don't let him get to you," George whispered.

"He's not," I said.

George laughed and kissed me full on the mouth. As we pulled apart, I noticed Sid looking at us, but he looked away before I could get a good look at his face. After everyone had eaten, Frank and Sid led the sing-along. I found myself finally relaxing. I couldn't help watching Sid as his fingers touched the keys, gently but sure and strong. He glanced up, caught my eye and smiled.

Shortly after that, he finished a song, then turned on the bench.

"What I need is a woman," he announced. "Any takers?"

Half were mortally offended, the other half were laughing hysterically. No one was taking him up on the offer.

"No?" Sid got up. "I didn't think the odds were too good anyway. I'm taking off."

As he left the living room, he was stopped by Sarah Williams, who was just going in.

"Leaving already, Sid?"

"Yes," said Sid, his eyes glittering mischievously. "While the night is still young, I'm going to get me some."

"Some what?" Sarah asked.

Sid goosed her on her backside and sauntered out of the house. Sarah screamed and Dan looked like he was about to commit murder. The rest of the room sat in stunned silence, except Frank and Esther. They laughed like hyenas.

"You walked into that one, Sarah," Esther gasped.

"Did she ever," Frank managed to add.

"Quit laughing, you two," Kathy said, failing to hide her own giggles. "She doesn't know Sid that well."

"She should after Carol and Dean's wedding," said Esther.

Carol and Dean pressed their lips together in disgust. They'd only heard about the incident, which had happened a couple months before. Unable to snag a date for the wedding, Esther had asked Sid on a dare. The thing is, Esther has a rather raucous sense of humor and her mind is almost as filthy as Sid's. She blames it on all the engineers she hangs around.

Anyway, Sid went and, at the reception, the two were seated next to Sarah and Dan, who had only been married a few weeks at that point. Sid and Esther spent the entire party trying to one up each other with dirty double entendres, and Sid made indecent proposals to both mothers and all of the bridesmaids. Esther said it was the most fun she'd ever had at a wedding.

I shuddered and tried to put the memory out of my mind. I was surprised at how easy it was to convince George to take me home early, although I shouldn't have been. When we got home, I was going to send him on his way, but he just kissed me and asked to come in.

"Okay," I said, reeling from another of his kisses. "But just for a little bit. I'm really tired, George."

Which was the actual truth, for a change. I didn't have to follow anybody until sometime the following week.

We sat down on the couch in the living room and George told me to close my eyes.

"Why?" I asked.

"Just close them and hold out your hands," he said.

I did and felt him slip a ring onto my left ring finger.

"Oh, George!" My eyes flew open.

It was a simple diamond cut into a circle, and it was huge.

"Oh, George," I said again. "I'm going to be scared to wear this."

George laughed.

"That's okay." He patted my hand. "You deserve it."

"It fits, too."

"It does?" George looked surprised and elated. "I was just guessing. I'm so glad. I thought I was going to have to bring it back."

"No. It's perfectly beautiful."

"Not as beautiful as you are, Lisa. I love you so much."

We kissed again, then George yawned loudly.

"I guess I'm not the only tired one," I said, giggling.

"It's okay," he said, sliding backward until his head was propped up by the arm of the couch. "I guess I am kind of sleepy. I was up all night in my studio."

George had a darkroom and studio in one of the buildings his family owned, which was in downtown Los Angeles. He mostly kept it for Jesse, so that Jesse could do portrait sittings, and to keep an eye on the building because the area it was in was supposed to be getting redeveloped soon. I had never been there, and at that moment, it struck me as a little odd that I hadn't.

"There's been some weird stuff going on in the alley," George continued. "Jesse says he thought he saw a kidnapping going on a couple months ago. There were a whole bunch of men and a guy in handcuffs. So, we've been taking turns watching."

"Really?" I asked. "What have you seen?"

"Well..." He gave me a funny look, then laughed and pulled me down next to him. "Nothing for you to worry about."

"And maybe not you, either," I said, snuggling next to him. "You two didn't necessarily see what you thought you did."

"I know what I'm doing, Lisa." George squeezed my shoulders.

I didn't say anything but snuggled a little closer. I couldn't tell him that I probably knew better than he did how to handle what he'd seen in that alley.

A few minutes later, George started softly snoring. I slid out from underneath his arms and he slid down all the way onto the seat and rolled over to face the back of the couch. So, I covered him up with an afghan we kept inside one of the end tables, then went off to bed in my own room.

I couldn't help wondering if Sid would jump to the wrong conclusion when he saw George. But Sid never found out that George had stayed the night. George left around seven the next morning, and I know because the silent alarm on the front door went off. I went to check it and saw George heading down the driveway to the street below us. Sid hadn't come in, either. His BMW was gone from the garage and the alarm readout didn't show him coming in.

It wasn't unusual for Sid to stay overnight somewhere, so I really didn't think anything of it. Besides, he was on tailing duty that Saturday, so while I had figured he would, at least, call, it wasn't any big deal that he hadn't. I spent the day getting some sewing done and went out that night with George.

Sunday, Sid still hadn't called, but there wasn't much I could do. I went to mass with George, then out to brunch, then he talked me into spending the rest of the day with his family at his parents' place in Malibu. Well, it was only fair. I'd dragged him out to visit my family the week before. Unfortunately, it was not much fun. George had three older sisters, only one of whom was married at the time, and she and her husband had no interest in children. All three sisters and the one brother-in-law were there, and Mrs. Hernandez spent all afternoon complaining that she didn't have any grandchildren. Most of her remarks were aimed at her daughters, but I was targeted just often enough to get that I would be expected to produce as soon as was decently possible after the wedding.

It did not make for a comfortable ride home. George was bubbling over, talking about how wonderful it would be when we had our own little ones.

"I think we should have six, don't you?" he asked.

"We don't necessarily get to decide," I said, hedging.

Truth be told, I was not planning on using traditional birth control, but I'd heard about some interesting options called natural family planning. Even then, I wasn't entirely sure I'd be able to have children, never mind that my sister wasn't having any problems that way. My mother had had a lot of trouble, not only getting pregnant, but carrying babies to term. After I'd been born two months premature, she'd had a couple other pregnancies which she'd miscarried, and her doctor and her priest finally convinced her that the birth control pill would be a lesser sin than potentially killing herself with another pregnancy.

"Well, I hope we have six," George said.

"Then you get to take care of them," I snapped. It had been a wretched afternoon, and I was trying not to worry about Sid.

"Of course, I'll help." George grinned, obviously very proud of how modern he was.

"If we have six kids, you'll do more than help. That's a lot to handle even if I wasn't going to work. And I fully intend to keep my job."

"You don't need to."

I sighed. "I want to."

"But what if I don't want you to?"

"Well, George, you may just have to get used to it. I want to keep working."

"Lisa, I'm not worried about Sid. I want you to stay friends with him. But I've got enough money to keep us comfortable. You don't need to work. And you and Sid can still be friends."

"Even if Sid weren't around, I'd still want to work."
I glared out the passenger window of George's car. "I
like working. As much as I love Mae's kids, if I had to
do what she does, I'd go nuts. I know. I've had to do it
once or twice. I'm not that maternal."

"It'll be different when it's our own kids."

"Maybe."

He looked at me, a worried frown on his face.
"Don't you want kids?"

"Yes." I paused because it suddenly hit me that I
wasn't all that sure that I did. "But I also want to do
my job. I'm good at it and I love doing it. Asking me to
stop would be like me asking you to quit doing your
photography."

"You wouldn't do that. I have to do something."

"Well, so do I."

"We'll have kids to take care of." He reached over
and held my hand. "Trust me, Lisa. It's going to be
wonderful. We're going to have a beautiful life. You'll
see. I love you so much, Lisa."

"I love you, too, George."

"Hey, we're here." George pulled into the driveway
at Sid's house. "Tell you what? We're both tired. Let's
give this a rest and we'll talk again later, okay?"

I nodded. "Okay. I'm going to head on in and go
right to bed." I got out of the car. "See you tomorrow."

George looked a little forlorn as I went up the
walk to the house and I felt guilty and really mixed up.
On one hand, I hated that it didn't seem as though he
heard a word I said about what I wanted. On the other,
I really hated that he seemed so disappointed in me.
As I went inside, I reminded myself that these sorts
of bumps in the road were normal for relationships
and that I had gotten Sid to communicate with me. I'd
eventually get through to George.

Then I forgot about George when I realized that
Sid still wasn't home and he hadn't left a message on
the answering machine. I shouldn't have, but I checked
the alarm readout and he hadn't been home, either.

It was still the weekend, so he could have been at an extended party. I went to bed thinking that I was telling myself a lot of things I didn't really believe.

June 25, 1984

Monday morning, Sid still wasn't home. It wasn't unheard of for him to take off for the weekend and he did sometimes forget to call and let me know. But he would have been back by Monday or, at the very least, have called to let me know.

On the other hand, with me being engaged to George, things had changed and it was possible that Sid simply hadn't called. So, I forced myself to give him the benefit of the doubt before calling Henry James. I also decided to check his office. There wasn't a phone number on the desk, which probably meant that he hadn't planned on staying over anywhere. In fact, he kept a packed overnight case in his car just in case he wanted to stay over someplace.

I bit my lip, then unlocked his desk. His address book was in the top drawer, near the front. No, it wasn't a little black book. It was about five by seven inches and covered in the same tan leather all his desk accessories are. I flipped through it, hopelessly. I recognized a few of the names, but not many. It felt weird. Sid and I shared so much, but that part of his life was a complete mystery to me.

I sighed and glanced into the open drawer. The glare off a glass pane caught my eye. It was surrounded by a wood frame. I pulled it out. I knew the photograph. Sid had taken a picture of me with my camera while we were on this one trip for Quickline. It had been an awkward day and Sid had found a way to make me laugh and pressed the shutter release at just the right moment. We had gotten so close on that trip. I swallowed thinking about it.

But now there was George. I quickly put the picture back and returned to the address book. It had fallen open to the N section. As I scanned the names, one caught my eye: Andrea Norton.

I had heard Sid mention a woman named Andrea in passing a few times. He'd usually been either very horny or bugged about something or both. He hadn't seemed unusually horny or bugged, for that matter, that Friday night. It didn't mean he wasn't, however. I decided to try.

The voice that answered the other phone was rich and sensual.

"Yes?" she asked.

"Is this Ms. Andrea Norton?" I asked as calmly as I could.

"Yes, it is," she replied.

"This is Lisa Wycherly. I work for Sid Hackbirn. I believe you know him."

She chuckled. "As often as possible."

"He hasn't been home all weekend and hasn't called. Is he there, by any chance?"

"That doesn't sound like him," she said. Her voice was still rich, but not quite so languid. "He was here Friday night but left Saturday morning. I haven't seen him since."

"What time did he leave?"

"He left to go running at six. Came back and then left again. I think it was right around nine but can't be sure."

"He didn't, by any chance, say anything about where he was going?"

She sighed. "Not Sid. You must be really worried."

"Yeah. I guess I am. Thank you for answering my questions, though. So sorry to have disturbed you."

"You haven't." She paused. "Tell Sid to give me a call when you find him."

"Sure."

We said goodbye and I hung up feeling even more worried.

Some days, I know God is working. A moment later, Sid's regular line rang and it was Henry James on the line.

"Morning, Lisa," he said pleasantly. "Is Sid out?"

Normally, Sid answered his own line unless I was home and he wasn't.

"Uh, he's missing, actually," I said. "I mean, it's possible he took off and didn't call, but I'm getting a bad feeling, Henry. He hasn't been home since Friday. I've traced his movements until Saturday morning around nine, but after that, it's a mystery."

I could hear Henry shuffling papers on the other end of the line. "I believe he was on the rotation to tail that official. I picked up some chatter that he was onto something."

Sid and I didn't know why, but Henry was being kept in the dark about the case. Henry had figured that much out, as well, and while he accepted it, you could tell it rankled.

"Oh, no," I said.

"It is possible that it didn't pan out and he went on to his usual pursuits."

"That's what I've been trying to tell myself," I said, shaking my head even though he couldn't see it. "But you know what, Henry? I've got a really bad feeling something's gone wrong. Sid would have at least called and left a message."

"He has been a little shy of you since you got engaged."

"Not that shy," I said. "At least, I hope not."

"Me, too." Henry shuffled some more papers. "Tell you what. I'll make some calls and see what I can do."

"Thanks, Henry."

We hung up and I sighed deeply. There was plenty of work to do. Sid and I had gotten caught up on our freelancing work after all and all I had left to do from the week before was print out the final query letters for the holiday pieces we wanted to do and get them in the mail. But I was so worried about Sid that I put the dot matrix paper in the letter-quality printer, which meant I had to re-print all twenty-three letters. Then, after getting the letters printed, I mixed up the copies of our past clips and had to sort those out. I did get the envelopes printed okay. But then I lost about five of them when I realized I had put some of the wrong queries with the wrong addresses. Fortunately, the others hadn't been sealed, so I was able to get those double-checked and in the right envelopes. But I had to print the five new envelopes three times before I got those aligned, and another two that I realized had typos on them. Then I ran out of postage.

I was about to run to the post office when I realized I wanted to be home just in case Sid called. I was really torn. The queries were late as it was - most magazines plan their Christmas issues six to eight months in advance (one of the reasons we had put together so many that year). Even then, it probably wouldn't have made that much difference, except that I was so very worried about Sid.

I left the queries spread out on my desk and went to get a drink of water and ended up prowling the house. I wished I hadn't waited so long to call Henry. Sid had to be in trouble. He really would have called. I was certain of it. So why hadn't I touched base with Henry? Why hadn't I tried to find out where he was going that Friday night? Why the heck did he have a picture of me inside his desk drawer and how long had it been there?

I had gotten the slides developed, and Sid put together the slide show for Mae and family, which was probably when he'd gotten the print of me made. But why had he chosen to hide it in his desk? I had a couple pictures of him on my office wall. Admittedly, one couldn't necessarily tell the one was of him, as it was a silhouette of a sunrise over the Grand Canyon. The other was one I'd caught while playing with one of George's wide-angle lenses.

So, why had he hidden my picture? Neither of us had photos of my family or friends out, that was true. We didn't want to give an enemy anything to grab onto. But pictures of ourselves, well, if any enemy was in the house, they probably already knew what we looked like. So there was no real reason for Sid not to have the photo on his desk or on his wall.

Unless his feelings for me were a little more than friendship. That was ridiculous. We were best friends and Sid's feelings were probably pretty strong. But he was in no way able to handle the emotional commitment of a permanent relationship. He could barely last two weeks of being faithful to someone. He just wasn't into commitments and love and had told me so on several occasions.

The phone rang. It was Nick.

"I want to come down there," he complained. "It's boring here."

I debated asking him if he was alone. The odds were decent that he was. Rachel was an emergency room doctor, and it was hard enough to find childcare for a kid Nick's age, let alone during the crazy hours that she worked. Nick got left alone far more often than Sid and I were happy with, but there wasn't much we could do, short of taking full custody of the boy. That was assuming Rachel would let us without one big, nasty fight (not likely) and terribly impractical considering Sid's and my little side business.

"I know, Nick," I said with as much sympathy as I could muster. "But Sid had to go out of town on a last-second assignment and I don't know when he's going to be back."

"Aren't you going to be there?"

"I've still got a lot of running around to do," I said. "And, besides, is your mom going to go for that?"

"She's the one who told me to call you guys."

I shuddered. At the beginning of June, Nick had asked to come down for an extended stay, and Sid and I were pretty sure Rachel was hoping we'd take him for the summer. Sid had told Rachel (through Nick because Rachel would only speak to Sid or me directly if she absolutely had to) that Nick would have to go home periodically. Sid had even written Rachel a letter with the dates that we knew we couldn't take him, adding that there might be additional dates when Nick couldn't visit. So, when Rachel had demanded that past Friday that we send Nick home, we were a little surprised. Only now I wasn't. I was as sure as I could be that Rachel still wanted us to take Nick for the entire summer but was going to make demands every so often just to show us she was still in charge. That was going to make things difficult, especially right then, because Sid and I really couldn't keep Nick for the summer or we would have.

"I'm so sorry, Nick, this is not a good week," I said. "Your dad did tell you that it could happen this way."

He sighed and I braced myself. Nick had tried the manipulation thing a few times before but had quickly learned that it did little but make Sid and me angry.

"Okay," he said, understandably sadly.

"You know we'd love to have you if we could," I said. "But we can't."

"I get it," said Nick. "Can I come next week?"

"I'll check with Sid and call you by Friday," I said.

"Okay. Thanks."

As I hung up, I wondered if Rachel would call, but she didn't. Henry did, however.

"They found Sid's car," he told me. "It's been sitting in the parking lot at a new housing tract in Mission Viejo."

My heart stood still. "Could they be keeping Sid there?"

Given that Southern California was going through a major housing boom, certain bad guys had discovered they could hide out in a newly-built house that was waiting to be sold. There were hundreds of housing tracts all over the region, all in varying degrees of development. As long as the neighbors hadn't moved in and the bad guys took care to muffle any noise and black out the windows, there was no one to see or hear anything nasty going on.

"Hard to say," said Henry. "The development

is huge, for one thing, and there's no guarantee that someone didn't move Sid's car to throw us off the track."

"Or, come to think of it, that Sid wasn't moved for some reason," I said. "Shavings. Now what?"

"I'm coming to get you and we'll go out to Mission Viejo," Henry said.

He arrived about fifteen minutes later. He's a tall man, balding with gray hair and a face that is perpetually flushed for some reason. It took a little over an hour to get down to the new housing tract being built in the southern part of Orange County. Sid's BMW sat in the small parking lot in front of the sales office for the tract. An Orange County Sheriff's car was parked next to it. The tan-clad deputy stood next to Sid's car shaking his head at another man in a dark gray three-piece suit with a small metallic bronze nameplate pinned to the lapel.

Henry walked up first, flashing his badge at the deputy. The deputy, who was about average size with dark hair and a square, tanned face, nodded at Henry, then turned back to the small man in the suit.

"I'm telling you, there's no reason he can't park here," the deputy said.

"We put a sign out," yelled the suited man. According to the nameplate, he was James Martens. He pointed to a small white sign at the edge of the lot.

"I'm sorry, sir, but a sign by itself has no legal standing. You need a citation from the state vehicle code to get that."

"Then why do we have a sign out here?"

"I can't tell you, sir," said the deputy. You could tell he was doing everything he could to keep his eyes from rolling.

"That car has been here since Sunday morning, maybe even Saturday," Martens yelled.

Henry smiled at the smaller man. "Why do you think it could have been Saturday?"

Martens glared at him. "I don't have to talk to you."

"You might want to," said Henry, with far more patience than I felt. He flashed his badge again. "Henry James, FBI. This car may be connected to a case I'm working on. So, why do you think this car could have been here as early as Saturday?"

"I dunno." Martens shifted uncomfortably. "I think I saw it when we locked up that evening. Yeah. That's it."

"I see," Henry said.

Martens looked again at Henry. "Did you say FBI? Is this connected to that house you guys borrowed from us?"

"Could be." Henry kept his face blank, but I could tell he'd been caught off guard. "Why don't you show it to us?" He looked over at the deputy. "In the meantime, can you get this towed to the L.A. lab?" Henry got out his wallet, shuffled through it and handed the deputy a card. "Here's the address and phone number. They'll ask you for a case number. Just tell them that it's under review." He glanced at me. "Agent Donaldson's case."

Given that I had an alter-ego as Janet Donaldson, I wondered what Henry was doing and why he didn't want to use his name.

"Yes, sir," the deputy said with a sigh.

Henry turned to Martens. "Can you tell us where the house is?"

"Sure. I can even take you up there."

"How about we follow you in our car," Henry said.

Martens shrugged. "Give me a minute to get the keys." He waved at a black Cadillac in the lot. "That's my car."

He took his time in the office, but that could have been my own impatience. We followed the Cadillac up through the winding streets of the subdivision. It was huge, covering most of a hillside and it looked as though no one lived there yet. Most of the lots were empty, and what few houses there were did not have yards yet.

"I may not have need to know," I said. "But why

put the car under Agent Donaldson's name?"

"I don't want the lab techs looking at it," Henry said. "They won't do anything until the paperwork comes through, so we'll have some time to get it released before the techs start asking for it. Hope you don't mind going in tonight to get it."

"I'll have to," I grumbled.

The house we were directed to was an enormous two-story with tile roof and beige walls. It sat at the end of a long street of mostly finished houses waiting to be sold. It looked as though they'd built that part of the housing tract first.

Martens parked on the street while Henry pulled his car into the driveway. We got to the door and Henry took the keys from him.

"I'll bring these back to the office when we're done," Henry said. "And I'll need to see any paperwork you have on the place."

"Paperwork?" Martens gulped. "There isn't any. We were told it was a top-secret operation. The man's credentials looked legit. Just like yours."

"Really?" Henry asked.

"Yeah. His name was, um, Lou Parsons."

"Did you get his ID number?"

Martens sighed. "Uh, no. It was only going to be for a week or so. I thought it wouldn't be a problem."

"We'll see," said Henry. "Thanks for your help."

Martens went back to his Cadillac and Henry unlocked the door to the house.

It was bare of carpeting and other flooring, those were presumably custom elements that would be added when the house sold. There weren't any kitchen or bathroom cabinets, either. Whoever had been hiding out there had done a very good job of getting most of the traces out of there, but Henry and I found several windows with bits of masking tape and black paper on the frames. I went upstairs right away. There were five bedrooms, and they were all huge. Still, I looked for the smallest.

I found it at the back of the house. There weren't any bloodstains, thank God, but the door had a few fresh gouges in the hole where the knob would eventually go. The windows also had secure locks on the frames and I could see scratches where someone had tried to break the lock. Sid always had something on him that he could use, so I wasn't surprised. I looked around the room more carefully as saw some tiny scratches on the wall next to the closet, just above the baseboard. I looked more closely and laughed.

"What?" asked Henry, coming into the room.

"Sid was here, alright," I said, pointing to the scratches. "He left a message for me. Proverbs twenty-seven, fourteen."

"Sid's quoting the Bible?"

"'He that greets his brother with a loud blessing in the early morning, a curse shall be laid to his charge.' It's one of my favorite verses." I sniffed a little. "I am not a morning person and Sid really is."

Henry looked the room over. "I don't see any signs of scrubbing or fresh paint."

I nodded. "Thank God."

"They must have taken him somewhere else." Henry looked a little grim.

There were reasons why they would have done that, but the big reason is that it's easier to move a living person than a dead one. It didn't look good, especially since there wouldn't be a good reason to keep Sid alive.

"I'd better see what more I can get out of our salesman," Henry said.

We agreed that I should let Henry lead, even though I had my FBI ID for Janet Donaldson on me. The fewer names Martens had, the better, just in case.

Martens didn't have anything to add, though. He shrugged helplessly when Henry asked for a description of the agent.

"He looked pretty normal," Martens said.

I nudged Henry. He glanced at me with a quizzical

frown, then nodded.

"Was Agent Parsons an average-sized man, brown hair, brown eyes, with a scar on his left hand?" I asked.

"Yeah." Martens' eyes lit up. "That was him."

"It was?" Henry asked.

"Yeah. He had that scar right along here," the man answered, running his finger along the outside of the back of his hand from the wrist to the pinkie. "Big old white one. Don't want to think what did that."

"No, you don't," said Henry with a tight smile.

There was something definitely very odd about how Henry was acting, not that Martens noticed. I looked at Henry, who thanked the man and we left.

Henry was silent in the car as we drove back to Los Angeles.

"Did I screw that up?" I finally asked.

"What?" Henry glanced over at me. "Not at all. Where did you hear about that description?"

"It came from Upline last week," I said.

"That's interesting," he muttered.

"We've gotten the impression that they've been keeping you in the dark on this case."

Henry sighed. "They most certainly have, and now I know why."

There was a pause.

"Let me guess," I said. "You're not going to tell me."

"Nope."

I sighed. "So, now what?"

"We get Sid's car released. We'll say they towed the car by accident."

"So, I tell them I left the car to go tail someone with my partner?"

Henry nodded. "That sounds good. I'll have to get the paperwork generated at the office, but I'd rather no one saw you pick it up. In fact, I'd rather you didn't come by the office at all for the time being."

"Just me?"

"Nope. Sid, too." He glanced my way again. "Look,

I know you'll probably jump to a conclusion or two. That can't be helped. Just don't act on anything, okay? Not without orders from Upline."

"Yeah. Sure. But how am I going to get the paperwork?"

Henry suddenly smiled. "Lydia has been after me to invite you and Sid over for dinner. Why don't I call her when I get back to the office and you can bring your fiance over, too."

Lydia as Henry's wife. Sid and I were friends with her, too, so that made things a lot easier. However, Henry must have been really worried about someone connecting us to him for some reason. I tried not to speculate, especially since Sid and I had already made some guesses.

When Henry dropped me off at the house, I was mildly annoyed to find George's car in the driveway. He was waiting on the front porch for me.

"Did you track Sid down yet?" he asked after giving me a big hug and kiss.

"No," I said, unlocking the front door, then disarming the alarm. "I'm getting really worried."

"He'll be alright," George said, following me into the office. "So, when do you want to go to dinner?"

"Dinner?" I dropped my purse onto my desk. "I just made a date to go to Henry and Lydia James for dinner. He invited you, too."

"I was going to take you out tonight."

I smiled at him. "That's sweet, George. Thanks. I hope you don't mind, but I'd really rather eat with the Jameses."

"I suppose," George said. "So, what do you want to do until then?"

I rolled my eyes. "Work. I've got a lot to get done and it's been hard enough to concentrate with worrying about Sid."

I also did not want George around for any phone calls, but he didn't get the hint. I did get him to run to the post office to get the extra postage for the queries.

He came back all too quickly and hovered until it was time to go to Henry and Lydia's. Fortunately, the only call I got was Henry confirming the dinner invite.

George and I got to the James house in Encino at six-thirty. It was a large, sprawling ranch-style house. You could tell the James family had been living there forever. Lydia was a warm, full-figured woman, not quite as tall as her husband, with dark blonde hair.

"I hope it wasn't too much trouble having us over at the last minute," I told her after I'd introduced George and Henry had led George into the living room.

"No trouble at all," she said, with a laugh. "I just threw another potato into the pot."

"Is there anything I can do to help?"

She led me into the kitchen, which was just to the left of the front door. "Why don't you help me bring everything into the dining room?"

She had a salad bowl out, filled with salad, two dishes with vegetables, and another with a pot roast swimming in gravy dotted with bits of potato and carrot.

"Looks like you did more than just add another potato," I said, picking up the salad and a bowl of green beans.

"Well," Lydia chuckled. "When I heard you were coming, I threw in more like four or five."

I laughed and blushed. I have to admit, my appetite is pretty phenomenal. Much to Sid's dismay, I eat like a small horse and never gain an ounce. George thought that was great, but then George thought anything I did was just great. After dinner, I was about to offer to clean up, but Henry nodded at me. So, I nudged George into offering. Henry got me alone long enough to hand me a manila envelope, which I stashed in my purse.

"You know where the lab is, don't you?" he asked.

"I've got the address."

"Good. Make sure you get in there tonight. Like I said, there isn't any other paperwork on Sid's car and I don't want anybody either asking for it or looking at that car.”

Sid and I both had specialized radio and tracking equipment locked in our glove boxes, and the trunk in Sid's car had a false bottom.

“Tonight?” I winced. “How late can I go?”

“The lab is open twenty-four hours, but I'd get there before eleven or so. After that, it slows way down and you might get noticed.”

I looked back at George, who was saying something to Lydia with an earnest expression on his face.

“That might be a little dicey,” I said.

“Do your best.”

We finally got out of there just before nine and got back to the house at a quarter to ten. George wanted to stay and talk for a while.

“I hate to do this to you, George, but I'm really bushed,” I said as we stood on the front porch.

“Lisa, I just want to be with you.”

“I know, but I'm tired.”

“You don't seem very tired.”

I sighed, thinking how very tired I really was. “I've been very worried about Sid and...”

“Then why don't you let me stay and take care of you?”

I threw up my hands. “Because I don't want to be taken care of. I just want to be left alone.”

“Why would you want that?” It figured George would be baffled.

“Because I like being alone.”

George looked at me. “Lisa, that doesn't make sense.”

“Of course it does.”

“You're upset and worried. No one wants to be alone when they're upset and worried. You'll just brood about it.”

“Well, then let me brood,” I snapped.

“Lisa, you're holding out on me.” George frowned at me.

I squirmed a little. “No, I'm not.”

"I'm going to be your husband. We can't have secrets between us. Tell me the truth."

"I am. I want to be alone!"

"Why?"

"I don't know!" I glared at him. "I just want to be alone."

George sniffed. "I think you're trying to get rid of me."

"Yes, George, I am." I crossed my arms and stepped back. "Sid isn't really missing. He's in the back bedroom and I'm trying to get rid of you so that we can continue our clandestine affair."

George's eyes grew wide. "Lisa?"

"Oh, come off it, George. I was being sarcastic."

He sighed. "You're getting angry. Let's calm down and we'll talk about this tomorrow. Come on and kiss me goodnight."

I kissed him quickly and there wasn't quite the rush I usually got. Once again, George was avoiding the issue, and that really bothered me, especially since I was beginning to notice that we never seemed to talk about it later. On the other hand, it was getting George on his way home.

As soon as he left the porch, I hurried inside. Leaving the lights off in the living room, I slid to the front windows. The headlamps from George's car lit up and the car drove off down the hill. I called the limousine service to take me to the lab, which was near the airport. While I waited for the limo to show, I got out my blonde wig and put on a lot of make-up, shading and contouring my make-up so that anybody who saw me would have a hard time recognizing me again. It's not a perfect disguise, but it's good enough.

The limo driver was a bit on the chatty side, so I told him that my car had been towed and I had to go to the impound lot to get it back. I didn't want him remarking on the odd address or anything. The driver went off on an extended monologue on the perfidy of the parking regulations in Beverly Hills and environs.

I just nodded and let him go. I was annoyed enough as it was. It didn't help that it was a little after eleven when I finally got to the lab building, which was in an industrial park just south of LAX. I figured it was just as well that I was cranky. If my car had been towed by mistake, I would be.

The man behind the window in the lobby was skinny and wearing a white short-sleeved shirt with an ugly blue-striped tie and ugly black-rimmed glasses. The name on his ID said Fred Stubens.

"What's this?" he demanded when I handed him the three-part form.

"My car got towed here today," I explained. "It was a mistake and I need to get it released. It's been approved."

Stubens read the form, then looked at me. "What are you doing here at this hour?"

"Trying to get my car back," I said.

"I understand that," he replied, his voice far more testy than necessary. "Why are you doing this now?"

"Because I need it."

"You know what the rules are. Or you should."

"My supervisor told me to get it released tonight." I looked down at the form. "It says emergency release, right there."

"I know what it says." He looked me up and down. "But the rules say we do not release any vehicles of any kind except during business hours."

"Even with an emergency release?" I asked.

"Those are the rules."

I tried not to groan. "But I'm in the middle of a hot case. I need that car."

"Maybe you should have thought of that before you had it towed."

"I didn't have it towed. Some other idiot did. I didn't even know where it was until four hours ago. That's why I was given an emergency release. Do I have to call my supervisor?"

His sigh was deep, profound and made it very

clear just how completely put upon he was.

"I'll go ask my supervisor," he said, picking up the form with his thumb and finger.

He retreated to a room at the far end of the office he was in. The roar that emanated through the open door was quite gratifying. I could hear the whining, but not what Stubens said.

"The rules allow for an emergency release!" yelled a deep voice between an assortment of swear words. "That's why it's an emergency release, you idiot."

There was another whine.

"Go ahead. Write me up. We'll add it to the stack. You know, the one buried under all the complaints about you!"

More whining.

"Never mind!"

A minute later, a stocky man in a tan dress shirt, no tie, and creased polyester slacks came over to the window with my form.

"Sorry about Stubens," he grumbled, scratching behind his ear. His badge said that he was Dominic Fanelli. "They put him here because no one else will work with him."

"No surprise there," I said.

Fanelli grinned. "Yeah. I'm still trying to figure out who I pissed off enough to get him. Now, let's see." He read the form. "You got your ID?"

"Right here." I pulled Janet Donaldson's ID case from my monster purse and flipped it open.

"Great. Donaldson." Fanelli picked up a pen and check a couple boxes on the form. "Oh, crap. It's the Beemer."

"Yes," I said cautiously.

"Mr. Charm School back there, when he heard it belonged to one of ours, wanted to report the owner for corruption."

"Oh, no!" I squeaked, trying to think of a good reason why a lowly Special Agent would be driving a very expensive car. "It's part of my cover. That's why I need it tonight."

Fanelli looked me over critically. "It's okay. No one reads any of that a— Uh, jerk's complaints."

He went back to making notes and stamping paper while I fretted and tried not to show it. After Henry had gone to all that trouble to avoid being connected to Sid's car and the Donaldsons, I was afraid our cover been blown.

The next morning, I was awakened by my phone ringing. As I fumbled for the phone by my bed, I noticed that it was the office line ringing. It was also nine a.m. I suppose I should have let the answering machine get it, but it could have been an editor with a story for us. I cleared my voice and tried to sound alert.

"Is this Lisa Wycherly?" the woman on the other end of the line asked.

"May I ask who's calling?" I replied, blinking my eyes.

"This is Ventura County Hospital. We have you listed as the contact for a Sid Hackbirn."

I sat up, my heart pounding. "This is Lisa. Is Sid okay?"

"He's with the doctors now," the woman said.

"Oh, no," I sniffed.

There was a slight pause. "He's not in any immediate danger, Miss Wycherly."

"Oh, thank God." I swallowed and started breathing. "What happened?"

"He appears to have been the victim of an assault. The ambulance brought him a short while ago. He does have some head trauma, but he is conscious and lucid."

"Thank God," I whispered. "Okay. I suppose I should go there. You're in Ventura, right?"

"Yes, Miss Wycherly."

I got directions to the hospital, then called Henry to let him know that Sid had been found.

"What happened? Where is he?" Henry asked.

"At Ventura County Hospital," I said. "They said he'd been assaulted. I'll be heading up there as soon as I can get out of the shower and dressed."

"For sure. Keep me posted, okay?"

"I will."

I showered as fast as I could, and quickly put on some jeans and an Oxford shirt. Grabbing a couple tote bags, I shoved some clean underwear into one, some shorts and tops and another pair of jeans. Then I went into Sid's bedroom. I seldom went in, but it's not as though there was anything terribly embarrassing in there. It was just his room and I didn't trespass. Nonetheless, I grabbed some fresh underwear from his dresser and some sweats and t-shirts, and put those in the other tote. I wasn't sure what else he'd need.

I was about to head out to the garage when I realized I'd better call George.

Jesse answered the phone.

"Jesse, it's Lisa."

"Hi, Lisa. What's up?"

"Is George there?"

"He's asleep. You want me to wake him?"

George was even more of a night owl than I am.

"No, don't. Just tell him we found Sid."

"Well, thank God for that."

"Anyway, I've got to go out to Ventura to the county hospital there. I'll call George later when I have a better fix on what's going on."

"Okay."

I debated calling Nick, but there wasn't anything I could tell him and he didn't really know there was anything wrong, to begin with. I rushed out to the garage, stopping only to get the toiletries bag out of the overnight case that Sid kept packed in his car. It took over an hour to get through traffic to the hospital.

When I got to the hospital, Sid was still in the emergency room, even though the nurse told me that they were going to admit him.

"What happened?" I asked her.

"We don't really know," the nurse said. "The paramedics on the ambulance said that he'd been assaulted. Apparently, the cops took the report on the scene. He got knocked around pretty badly, but he doesn't have any broken bones. Just assorted bruises and a nasty concussion. The doctor wants to keep him for a couple days for observation."

"Can I see him?" I asked.

"Sure. Right this way."

She led me to a curtained area. Sid was laying on his back, with a hospital gown covering his chest, staring at the ceiling. The dark stubble on his chin and cheeks made his skin look almost ashy.

"Hi," I said quietly.

He gingerly turned his head and squinted at me. "Hi."

"How are you feeling?"

"I ache all over and I have one hell of a headache."

"I can imagine. Can you tell me what happened?"

"Not right now."

I glanced around at the curtained alcove. "No, I suppose not. I hear they want to keep you around for observation."

"Yep." Sid looked miserable.

"If it will make you feel any better, I'll stay here in Ventura while you're here."

"What about your fiance?"

"George will have to do without me or come up here. Unless you don't want him to come."

Sid shifted and winced. "It doesn't make any difference to me."

"And God didn't make little green apples."

Sid blinked and sighed. "I have no right to say no."

I left it at that. I probably shouldn't have, but he was feeling so bad that I didn't have the heart to argue.

"When's the big day?" Sid asked suddenly.

"What?"

"Your wedding, honey. You were supposed to pick a date last Thursday and you never told me what day."

"Oh. It's April twentieth. Mama found where she wants to have the reception and the first opening was in April."

"I see."

"Nick called yesterday. He wants to come down."

Sid winced again. "This is not a good time for that."

"I know, but I think he's at home alone again."

"Damn her." Sid tried shifting again, then squeezed his eyes shut. "I'll take care of calling him."

"I told him I'd let him know about next week by Friday. And I only called Henry and George before coming up here, so Nick doesn't know you've been hurt."

Sid grunted and winced.

"You look pretty uncomfortable. You want me to fluff up your pillow or adjust your bed or something?"

"Nah. I'm just hoping the pain pills start kicking in."

"Mr. Hackbirn." The nurse swiftly pulled the curtain open. A pair of orderlies stood behind her with an open gurney. "We're going to move you to your room now."

"Can you give us a moment?" I asked, then turned to Sid. "I'll go get myself settled while they're moving you and make a couple phone calls. Can I get you anything while I'm gone?"

"How about a woman?" Sid smiled at me.

"You're in no shape for that and besides, that's in direct violation of our original work agreement."

"Can't hurt to ask."

"I'm not going back to L.A., so can I get you anything from the store?"

The nurse glared at me but I ignored her.

"A razor and soap might be nice. My beard is itching like hell and scratching it makes my headache worse."

"Oh!" I held up the tote I'd brought in with me. "I brought you some fresh underwear and sweats. And your toiletries bag is in there."

"Thank you," Sid sighed, grabbing the tote. "Now, if only I have a spare pair of contacts in here."

"Later, Mr. Hackbirn," said the nurse firmly.

"I'll see you in a bit," I told Sid and turned to go.

"Lisa," Sid called. "I know I'm pretty grumpy right

now, but I want you to know that I really appreciate you sticking around."

"Thanks, Sid," I said. "I'm glad to do it.

As I left the hospital, I reflected that I really was.

[I guess now's as good a place as any to lay out what happened to me when I got captured. We were using a three-person team with two switching off sticking close, and a look-out observing with a pair of binoculars from a distance. It's a tough tail to spot, let alone ditch.

That Saturday morning, I was on look-out duty, observing from my car. There wasn't much going on. We were on Santa Monica Boulevard, not far from where the street would cross into Beverly Hills. The subject was going through his usual routine. The two close-in tails had just switched off when the second tail spotted the contact walking past the subject. There was no way to tell if anything had passed between them. It didn't matter. We wanted the contact.

He was pretty average looking, brown hair parted on one side, wearing a tan sport-shirt and jeans. Once the alarm went up, even I could see the white scar running along the top of his left hand. I kept my glasses trained on him while the first tail went after him and the second went for her car. Sure enough, the contact walked down the street, turned a corner and found his car, a Toyota sedan. Since I was on wheels, I had first shot at tailing him. The other two tails radioed in and we took turns switching off as the Toyota slid through traffic to Robertson, and from there to the Santa Monica freeway.

He headed west to the 405, and from there down to Mission Viejo. It was my turn to stick close as he pulled into a brand new housing tract. We all had a pretty good idea what was going on at that point. I went ahead and parked in the lot for the sales office and went on the model tour. The other two tails held back, although while I was on the tour, the contact left the tract and the tails went after him. My job was to check out the houses where the contact had gone.

I wasn't entirely expecting three paid thugs when I got to the house. They jumped me and knocked me on the head. When I came to, I had been locked into a fairly large bedroom. The windows were blacked out and locked. They'd taken my jacket and shoes and somewhere in all that, I'd lost my contacts. I tried the locks with the pick from my hair, but that didn't help. So, I scratched a message on the baseboard, one I knew Lisa would get. At least three times, I was brought hamburgers and water. I couldn't figure out why they wanted me alive, so I decided to play the civilian kidnap victim, offering each thug all kinds of money to let me go.

I had completely lost track of time, so I have no idea when they decided to move me. All three of them showed up this time, one with a gun on me. I held up my hands.

"What's going on?" I yelped. "My family will pay. I promise they will. You just have to let me go!"

I could see the thugs look at each other. They were definitely not trained agents, which was also very telling. The one with the gun gestured at the other two. I'm not sure what happened, but I think they injected me with something. Or maybe there was another hit on the head which joggled my memory. Either way, the next thing I knew, I was in yet another new house. The bedroom was considerably smaller, although just as unfinished as the other one.

The weird thing was that my jacket and shoes were heaped in a pile in the corner. The thug who'd had the gun at the other house sat in the corner with the gun trained on me. My head was a mess and I upchucked all over the floor. The thug yelled and a different fellow came in to clean up the mess.

Once the mess was cleared and the new fellow gone, the thug with the gun got up and stood over me.

"What do you want?" I asked, sounding as panicky

as I could. "I've promised you money."

"Where's your yellow card?" the thug demanded.

"My what?" I swallowed because I really didn't know what he was asking for.

"Your yellow card. You're supposed to have one."

"All I got are my charge cards. You can have them."

The thug raised his hand as if he were going to hit me. "I'm not going to waste my time with phony IDs."

That was even weirder. It was almost as if they knew what to expect, since I did not, in fact, have my real ID on me.

"Huh?" I asked.

"Where's your yellow card?" the thug yelled.

"I don't have one!"

The thug frowned. He knocked me down and left the room. I was a little surprised that he had given up so easily, though hardly complaining about it. I went through my jacket and shoes. Sure enough, the pager was still there, so I triggered it. I kept triggering it every hour or so, and it eventually paid off. It was a pretty small task force, I'm guessing there were a couple Navy Seals. Those guys know extraction like no one else, and this was a quick and relatively painless operation. Well, painless for me and the agents. The thugs were hurting even worse than I was by the end of it. I didn't get to see that part. Me, they hustled into an ambulance, which was fine.

I'm not sure whose idea it was to send me to Ventura. It was a long enough ride that someone from Upline was able to debrief me as we went. She seemed puzzled when I mentioned the yellow card. She clearly knew what it was, but it didn't seem to make sense. Yes, I was tempted to ask, but knew better.

And that's pretty much what happened. - SEH]

I found a motel reasonably close to the hospital, but couldn't check in quite yet, so I stopped for lunch at a nearby cafe. By the time I got back to the motel, it was after one-thirty, and I was able to check in. I called

Sid at the hospital to let him know that I was running behind and he told me he needed his spare pair of glasses because the nurses wouldn't let him wear his contacts. Sid, who is very near-sighted, must have been pretty desperate to see something.

I next called George.

"Lisa, what happened?"

"He got mugged," I said. "He'll be alright, but he's going to be in the hospital for a few days."

"That's good. When are you coming home?"

"When Sid gets out of the hospital."

"Then I'll go up there."

I bit my lip. "I'd rather you didn't, George."

"But I can help you."

"I don't need the help."

"Oh, come on, Lisa." George was almost whining. "Why don't you want me there?"

"Because I don't think it will make Sid feel any better."

"He won't have to see me. Please, Lisa?"

"I suppose," I said. It was a terrible idea, but I was so tired, I didn't feel like arguing.

I gave George the name of the motel and asked him to wait until the evening to come up.

"I'll probably be at the hospital," I told him. "So there won't be anything for you to do."

"Don't worry, Lisa," George said. "I'll take care of it."

I called Henry next.

"I don't have any details on what happened yet," I told him. "The good news is that Sid's going to be alright. The worst of it is a concussion, so they're going to keep him in the hospital for a few days just to be on the safe side."

"They must have wanted something," Henry said, his voice getting grim.

"Well, I'm glad they did," I said. "That's the only reason he's still alive."

"I'm not complaining." Henry sighed. "But I'm

going to send Angelique up to see you this afternoon. Upline sent something addressed to Sid, and it must be pretty urgent if they're sending it through me."

"Must be. Can I talk to Angelique then?"

"Sure."

Henry connected me. Angelique was more than willing to come up to Ventura, not to mention swinging by the house to get Sid's glasses. After talking to her, I made one more call to Conchetta to let her know that Angelique would be by, and that was that.

Calls made, I went back to the hospital. As I came down the hallway, a nurse left Sid's room with a tray in her hands and shaking her head. She was Black, a little on the short side and well-padded, and laughing to herself.

"Don't tell me," I said as I walked up. "He made a pass at you."

"Did he ever." She laughed. "It's a good thing I'm married."

"That doesn't make any difference to him."

She laughed again, even harder. "That's what he said. He's a charmer, alright."

"I know. You might want to warn your co-workers. He won't violate mutual consent by any stretch, but he'll be getting desperate soon, and he can make himself really, really tempting."

"I'll warn them," she said, her eyes glittering. "Or maybe not. You never know when a little bit of temptation might be just what the doctor ordered, so to speak."

I had to laugh. "It may just be."

"You're not going in there, are you?"

I grinned. "He knows better than to try it with me."

"Well, I just hope he doesn't get any of my girls pregnant."

"Don't worry about that. He's fixed."

She laughed and I went into the room.

It was a private one. I did not want to ask how

much Sid would be paying for it. [You did not, but it was worth it. - SEH] Fortunately, Sid is independently wealthy. Believe me, espionage does not pay that well, and freelance writing even less.

"Well, well, well," I said, going over to his bed. "Up to your old tricks again, huh?"

He shrugged as well as he could. "What can I say? She's a good-looking woman."

"And you are a dirty old man."

"Watch that old stuff."

I chuckled. "Alright, you lecherous fiend. I've got some good news for you. Within another hour or two, you'll have glasses and a willing woman. Okay, I won't vouch for the willing. That's up to her, but she does have a history of it."

"Who are you talking about?" His eyes lit up.

"Angelique Carter, my dear reprobate. Henry got something for you from Upline, so he's sending it with her, and I asked her to swing by the house and get your glasses."

"Oh, great. I'll be able to see again. They won't let me wear my contacts. Listen, could you make a note to call the ophthalmologist for a new pair? I'll need a new back up."

"Sure thing." I dug through my purse for my notebook and added the note. Then I bit my lip. "George insisted on coming up. I'm hoping he'll meet me at the motel. In any case, he won't be here for a while." I looked at him. "Think we've got enough privacy to tell me what happened to you?"

Sid rolled his eyes but proceeded to tell me about how he'd been captured and moved.

"Actually," he said as he finished. "I'm still not sure how much time passed."

"Today is Tuesday," I said. "Henry had your car towed from the Mission Viejo tract and I got it back last night." I looked at him, feeling very worried. "We figured they wanted something from you. That's why they didn't kill you right away."

"I have no idea what," Sid said. "Why would they be asking about a yellow card? It doesn't make sense."

"It doesn't yet, as you are so fond of reminding me," I said with a shrug. "We go could go around and around on this or I could just get a deck of cards out."

"You don't have to stay glued to my bedside," Sid grumbled.

"I'll leave when Angelique gets here."

He chuckled. "Trying to protect the nurses from me?"

I rolled my eyes. "Sid, if they're willing, that's their business. Just do me a favor and don't press too hard and try and keep the shenanigans to when they're off-duty."

He let out an exaggerated sigh. "I'll try, mommy." Then he smiled warmly. "Why don't you get out that deck of cards?"

Angelique arrived around four and happily announced that she was free until Sid was ready to come home. I have no idea if Henry had given her that long or if she was taking it. I didn't care. Admittedly, that left me free to return to Los Angeles, which I nearly did, but I had told Sid I'd stick around, so I decided to stay. I had two keys for my motel room, and it had two beds. I told Angelique that she could share my room. She liked the idea. I gave her the extra key and went back to the motel.

Sure enough, George was there waiting for me. As he wrapped me into a warm hug, I began to think it wasn't such a bad thing that he'd come. We wandered around Ventura, had dinner, and George finally dropped me off at my room around nine.

Angelique was already there.

"You're back early," I said.

"I could say the same for you," Angelique said with a grin.

I yawned. "I'm really tired. I didn't sleep very well last night."

"I bet. As for me, visiting hours were over and I got

chased out.”

“How’s Sid doing?”

“Better.” Angelique shook her head and laughed. “He’s an amazing guy. You can tell that he’s feeling lousy with that concussion, but that doesn’t stop him.”

“Hm.” My thoughts began wandering.

I’d been mulling over what Sid had told me all afternoon. The yellow card was strange enough, but what I thought was more worrisome was that the thug assumed that any ID Sid was carrying was fake. We’d found out earlier that year that the target suspect was using paid thugs, so it was no surprise that Sid had been captured by a group of them. The problem was that paid help wasn’t always the most competent, which is why most operatives preferred to avoid using them, even for the dirty work. We weren’t entirely sure why this particular suspect was using them, but it was clear that he had told his “employees” about some of our basic protocols, including not carrying our actual ID when we were working a case. That begged the question of how much the contact (or suspect) knew about Operation Quickline.

“Lisa?” Angelique asked.

“Hm? What?”

“You’ve been in outer space all evening. What are you doing? Planning your wedding?”

“No.” I blushed. “I should be, shouldn’t I?”

“So I’m told. Sid said it was in April.”

I felt a quick pang of jealousy, which surprised me. I pushed the feelings aside. Sid had every right to tell Angelique. It was just weird that he was still talking to her about things.

“Yeah,” I said. “George was asking me about it again today. We’ve got to go look at the reception site where Mama made the deposit. He’s so excited about it. He wants to know what colors we’re going to have and which flowers.” I sighed suddenly. “And I can’t think of anything I want.”

“You’re kidding. I’ve had my dream wedding

planned since I was a kid."

"Oh, I planned mine, too." I shook my head. "It was just a long time ago and… I don't know. It just doesn't seem right anymore. George wants a big wedding, and I suppose he should have it. I just hope Mama's got enough money in her special account."

"Nice how they're expecting us to get married," Angelique grumbled. Her mother had been pressuring her to get married for years and it drove Angelique nuts.

I winced. "It's not like that. Mama does expect me to get married because that's what people do. But she started the wedding account for a different reason altogether. When my sister and I were each born, she started two savings accounts. One was for college and the other was for our weddings. Her daddy was a drunk and there just wasn't much money. She'd gotten a scholarship for college, but there was nothing left for her own wedding and she was so embarrassed that she swore she would never let that happen to her daughters."

"Wow."

"Is your mom still on your back?"

Angelique sighed. "Not as much, but not for a good reason. I mean, it's a good reason, but not a very happy one. You know how I kept joking that my sister-in-law Sadie was psychotic? Well, it turns out, she probably is. They think it's manic depression. Jeff's not entirely sure because her family is acting like it's all his fault and cutting him out of everything. The good news is that he's got custody of the kids and will probably get to keep them after the divorce is final. It's just that as it was all blowing up last month, Jeff and Mom got into this massive fight, and Jeff blamed her for pressuring him into marrying Sadie. And Mom was so upset, she asked me if I thought she had pressured Jeff, and I couldn't say no. So, she's mad at me for not telling her what she wanted to hear, but she can't really get on my back about not being married because of Jeff."

That led me to ask about Angelique's nephew and niece and we compared notes on babysitting nieces and nephews and how incredibly fun, but exhausting it is, and it was actually pretty late before we ended up going to bed. And while we may have stopped talking, I didn't stop thinking, mostly about how George wanted six kids and wanted them right away and how much I did not want six kids and definitely not any of them right away. I had no idea how I was going to get George to go along with me on that. George was not very good at hearing me sometimes.

June 27–July 1, 1984

The next morning, it hit. I was getting dressed. Angelique had the radio on, and it started playing "Sad Lisa." Out of nowhere, it seemed, a heavy black mood seeped through me like a dark, suffocating mist. I felt depressed and annoyed for no apparent reason. I covered it up, barely speaking to Angelique. She didn't notice. She was half-asleep, too.

It was nine-thirty when I called George's room to leave a message that I was going to breakfast and then the hospital. George, for once, was awake and met me at the diner next door to the motel. I worked hard at not letting my mood show and smiled as George chattered. I ate pancakes, bacon, and eggs, while George congratulated me on being able to eat so much and not gain weight. Then, when the waitress brought the check, he not only grabbed it out of my hand, he started getting syrupy again.

"George, will you please?" I snapped. "I feel like I'm getting diabetes."

"What?" George was completely baffled.

"I'll talk to you later." I got up and grabbed my purse.

"Lisa, wait. I gotta pay the check!"

"I'm going by myself. Good-bye." I stomped off and drove to the hospital.

Sid was shaved and not nearly as pale. He had the back of the bed almost upright and sat looking moodily at a magazine. He looked up as I closed the door.

"There you are," he said, his voice grim.

"What's the matter?" I tried smiling, still determined to hide my mood.

"The message Upline sent." He inched himself a little higher on the bed. "Apparently, our thugs seemed to think I was a floater."

A floater is a supervisor over a specific color line in the business. Henry is Sid's and my floater. They typically work as a two-person team. Henry had until his partner had been killed shortly before I was recruited.

"What made them think that?"

"The yellow card. Upline didn't say, but it sounds like it's a code of some sort."

"Oh, great. It sounds like we've got another leak in the system."

Sid shrugged. "To some degree. The funny thing is, they don't seem that worried about it. We were told to stand down and keep away from Henry as much as possible, but not to completely avoid him, either."

"And I'm guessing we have no Need to Know."

Sid sighed. "Lisa, that's how this business works. You know that."

I did, too, and understood why, but that didn't mean I liked it.

"Oh, I know. Except when it gets us into trouble. Like last summer. Remember that? And last winter, too. I almost got arrested because everyone was playing so close to the chest." I began pacing. "This is ridiculous! I feel like we're being set up as sitting ducks again."

"Lisa," Sid said softly.

"Well, I'm sorry. I don't like being used for target practice."

"Lisa." Sid grabbed my hand as I went past and held it softly. "What's wrong, honey?"

"What? Besides being set up for target practice?"

"Besides that."

"Nothing," I said a little too quickly.

Sid gently pulled me to his side, then gently lifted my chin to face his brilliant blue eyes.

"Is this a blue funk?" he asked softly.

I pressed my eyes shut, then nodded. I've had them since I was fifteen, and only two or three times a year. For some reason, it's the last thing I think of when it does hit. Sid had sat through two that he knew of. I'd had one that neither of us recognized until much later, but that one hadn't been terribly typical. He was the one who named it blue funk.

Somehow, he shifted himself over on the bed to make room for me and patted the empty space next to him.

"Come here," he said. I balked. "Come on."

"Sid, you're not feeling well."

"I'm fine. Believe me, Lisa, if I could make love yesterday, I can certainly give you room to cry on my shoulder today."

"But..." I looked at him, feeling utterly helpless. "I feel so stupid."

Nonetheless, I sat down on the bed and allowed him to put his arms around me. The sniffles started and I tried to force back the tears.

"Go ahead and cry." Sid gently squeezed me.

I did, for no reason at all, but that was the nature of the mood. Sid just held me and let me sob. There wasn't much else he could do. We both knew it was physically caused and that I just had to ride it out. The next day would be just as bad, although the depression would be replaced by really awful cramps.

I cried for fifteen minutes solid and Sid held me for at least another fifteen.

"Think you can face the world again?" he asked when I finally shifted away.

"Yeah. I think so." I wiped my nose with a tissue.

"Good."

"How are you feeling?" I asked.

"A lot better. The headache is mostly gone, although it does feel like it could come back at any second. The other aches and pains seem to have disappeared into the night. I won't be up and around for several days yet, but I don't feel so bad."

I smiled. "I'm glad."

"Even better, if I'm still feeling better this afternoon, the doctor says I'm going home tomorrow."

"Oh, good."

"I'll still be bedridden through the end of the week, but I'm on my way to hale and hearty once again." He paused. "If you don't mind, though, I should probably send you back to L.A."

"Why?"

"I'd like to update Henry. Yeah, I get it about the need to know thing, but you're right about too much being a mess."

"I think Henry's already figured it out. Or figured something out." I paused, feeling guilty for no real reason. "I called him Monday. I had to."

"Of course, you did."

"He found your car at that tract in Mission Viejo and took me along to check it out." I smiled. "I liked your signal for me."

Sid chuckled. "I thought you would."

"Anyway, the salesman at the tract said that an FBI agent had asked to use the house you were in for an operation, and he described the agent as the contact. Only when the salesman described the scar, Henry seemed to recognize it."

"Huh."

"And when I told Henry that we figured he was being kept in the dark on the case, he not only agreed but said that he now knew why."

"As in our contact is somebody Henry knows."

"Yeah. And if he's that close to whoever it is, then it's no wonder he doesn't want us that close, either. In fact, he said as much on Monday. He knew we'd figure something out, but he doesn't want us to act on anything without orders from Upline."

Sid nodded. "And Upline just ordered us to lay low." He shrugged. "Can't be helped. But I still think we should at least touch base with Henry. I don't think any of us want to be sitting ducks."

"I agree," I said, blinking my eyes. "Listen, I'll also get Conchetta to fix something extra nice for you."

"Thanks. Go ahead and take some aspirin

tomorrow and don't feel like you can't stay in bed."

I shook my head. "Staying in bed doesn't help. I just brood about it." I got up.

"Whatever." He took my hands and gently pulled me down and kissed my forehead. "You take care now."

"I will." I smiled softly at him. "And no molesting nurses unless they're off-duty."

"I'll do my best." Sid's grin was full of mischief.

"That's what I'm afraid of." I started for the door, then turned back. "Thanks, Sid."

"You're welcome, sweetheart. See you tomorrow."

When I got back to the motel, Angelique was already headed for the hospital. George, however, knocked on the door to the room almost as soon as I got in. When I opened the door, he pulled me into his arms and almost smothered me with one of his fabulous kisses.

"George!" I groaned when I could and tried to pull away.

"I'm so sorry about this morning," he said, holding me even more tightly. "I didn't know, Lisa. I didn't want to hurt you. I really am sorry, my dearest love."

"What are you talking about?"

"Sid just called me. He told me about how you were feeling. I'm sorry, Lisa. I didn't know."

"Of course, you didn't," I snarled, pulling out of his arms. "That was the idea."

"You're mad again." His face sagged and my heart softened a little.

"Not at you."

"Don't be mad at Sid. He was only trying to help."

"I'm sure he was."

That didn't mean he wasn't also gloating. I racked my brain trying to remember if I'd told Sid where we were staying. [You hadn't, but Angelique had - SEH]

"Look, George, I've got to get back to L.A., and I've got a ton of errands to run. How about if I call you tonight?"

I was a little surprised when George agreed. He

left me alone, and I packed quickly. I called the hospital to make sure Angelique knew that I was leaving, which she did. Then I went to the front desk to arrange to have Angelique sign for the final bill and to have it put on my credit card, only to find out that George had put the bill on his card. I reminded myself that George was just trying to be nice, but it still rankled.

I made it back to the house in Beverly Hills in record time. Conchetta was glad to hear that Sid was coming home and promised to make something extra special for him even before I could suggest it. My next move was to lock myself in Sid's office and use the special phone line that we only use for our side business to call Henry. I told him about what had happened to Sid, plus the contents of the message from Upline.

"Henry, we're not asking who this guy is," I pointed out. "We just don't want you to be any more of a sitting duck than we are."

Henry chuckled. "We're not, Lisa. This can be a pretty ruthless business, but nobody is going to burn a good asset. It just doesn't make sense to."

"But..."

"Lisa, don't worry about it, okay? Yeah, I get that it's a little nerve-wracking that this guy is still loose and that we don't know what all he knows. But what I'm hearing is that it's not nearly as much as he'd like to think. Sometimes, we just have to trust that other folks are going to do their job, and ninety percent of the time, they do. Sid got us some good intel. We'll see where it leads. In the meantime, you and Sid stay focused on getting him healthy again. Okay?"

"Okay," I said.

There really wasn't much else I could do. I tried to be thankful that Sid had come out of the ordeal okay and that he'd provided some good information. Henry was right. I just had to trust that whoever else would be on top of things. I still felt some niggling worry, but chalked it up to my mood and let it go. I spent the rest of the afternoon working on my sewing projects.

It was barely seven when my private line rang. It was George.

"How is my beautiful woman feeling?"

I bit my tongue. "George, I've just got to ride it out, so can you just let me alone, please?"

"Why didn't you call?"

"It's only seven."

"I was afraid something was really bothering you."

"Yes, there is, but it's nothing you or anyone else can do anything about. Why don't I call you tomorrow night? I'm not going to be feeling like talking to anyone before then anyway."

"Why are you avoiding me?"

I rolled my eyes. "Will you please? I'm not avoiding you. I just don't feel like dealing with people right now. Do you understand that?"

He sighed. "No, I don't."

"Well, you'll have to try. It's part of how I operate."

"But my dearest—"

"I'll talk to you tomorrow, George."

"I do love you, Lisa, more than anything. You do know that, don't you?"

"Yes, George, I know. I love you, too. Goodnight."

The next day was the worst. Sure enough, the cramps arrived. No matter what Sid said, aspirin didn't help, so I didn't bother. Worse yet, George showed up, bearing two vases filled with roses. One had been left on the doorstep the day before and I hadn't seen it because I had come in through the garage. I had George put the vases in my office. I also asked him not to send so many flowers. George asked how I was feeling. I asked George to leave. George said I should be in bed and asked if he could bring me something. I decided that we definitely had a communication problem.

Sid and Angelique showed up around noon, and the only thing worse than George hovering over me was watching Angelique stare at me sadly. The good news was that she insisted on playing nurse to Sid. I was happy to let her as I was feeling too rotten, myself.

Besides, she had to get herself settled in. She was moving in again. I was skeptical about how long it would last, but at least, she was doing all the running and fetching, not that there was that much of it.

My pager vibrated a couple times, but I couldn't do anything about it with George hanging around. Finally, around four, I convinced George that I needed a nap and that he should go to Bible study without me that night.

"I don't mind missing," George said.

"I need to know what's going on," I said. "We've got camp coming up."

"Oh, that's right."

"And I'll probably be asleep after you're done, so please don't call or come over."

George looked at me, and I guess he saw something in my eyes that meant he shouldn't push it.

I was about to try to check in on the pager when Angelique wandered into my office. She was good and depressed.

"Why do I let myself in for this?" she asked me. "I'll never be anything more than a friend to him."

"Then move out, Ange. He doesn't need that much taking care of."

"I can't. I love him."

I shook my head. "He'll never be able to return it. He just doesn't know any better. Sid has no concept of what love really is."

"Oh, he does. He may not know it, but he does."

"Ange, I know him very well."

Her laugh was sardonic and sad all at the same time. "Lisa, you're not facing the truth any more than I am. That man is so hung up on you, it's not even funny. He was calling George when I got to the hospital yesterday, to tell him about your bad mood."

"He was just gloating because he had one on George."

"He was, but not much. He was very worried about you."

"Well, we're good friends. George realized that."

Angelique shook her head and wandered off.

I finally got to check in on the pager and all it turned out to be was a notice that we were down until further notice. That made the next two days aggravating, at best. As far as Sid was concerned, he was still bedridden and bored silly. Angelique had returned to work on Thursday, which meant that I needed to keep Sid occupied. The good news was that there were a few phone interviews that Sid could do from bed. There were two articles that needed edits, and he was able to do that, as well. But he was bored enough by Friday morning that he hand-wrote an article, which meant that I would have to type it into the computer. The only reason that task got put on hold was that Sid had a doctor's appointment that afternoon and I had to drive him.

The doctor told Sid that he could walk around a little, as he felt like it, and Saturday, Sid spent wandering the house. He kept joking that there was only one way to keep him in bed and Angelique was too tired.

Actually, Sid was the least of my problems. George had returned early Thursday and hovered, talking about nothing but the wedding and asking me how I was feeling. He kept coming over on Friday, brought me dinner that night, then hung around all day Saturday, too, asking about the wedding and what he could do to make me feel better.

"George just can't get it through his thick skull that this blue funk thing only lasts two days," I told Kathy Deiner and Esther Nguyen Sunday after mass.

The three of us were commiserating over a late brunch. I had told George I needed to get back to the house to take care of Sid. Jesse, fortunately, picked up the hint from Kathy and got George to spend the afternoon scouting locations to shoot headshots for actors.

"It's not like he's stupid," Kathy said.

"Not stupid," said Esther. "He's just stubborn."

"The worst of it is," I continued. "I feel guilty because I want him to leave me alone a little. I mean, he treats me like a queen, sends me flowers all the time, says all sorts of sweet, romantic things. He acts in a way that most women dream about. And I feel like a total jerk because I want him to lay off a little. I never dreamed I could get sick of long-stemmed red roses. But now that I've got an office full of them, I'd like to see another kind of flower. I tell you, the last three days have been the pits. Thursday, the last thing I wanted to deal with was another human being, and there was George. I know you're going to hate me for saying this, Kathy, but he kept bugging me about the wedding. We should do this, Lisa. We should do that, Lisa. I have got a major case of the cramps, a sick boss coming home with a jealous girlfriend, a pile of overdue work, and nothing he's suggesting feels right to me. Then Mama called and asked me if I'd checked out the reception site she'd put the deposit on and got annoyed because I haven't yet."

"Go ahead and complain, Lisa," said Kathy. "It sounds pretty grim."

"And it gets worse," I said. "Friday, George came over with a pile of bridal magazines. Kept asking what I thought of all the bridal gowns and flowers and the like. I finally told him that if he wanted to talk wedding that badly, he could call my mother. You know what that clown did?"

"He called your mother," Esther said.

"You got it," I said. "While I was at the doctor's office with Sid. They talked for two hours. Mama was ecstatic. Then he brings dinner over Friday night, which really made Conchetta mad because she'd already made dinner. And then last night, we're eating back at the house with Sid and Angelique, and George had the nerve to ask Sid to give an opinion on some of the dresses in the wedding magazines."

"I can't believe that George would rub it in like

that," Kathy said.

"He wasn't rubbing it in. He is simply blissfully unaware that Sid is a little put off track about this whole affair. Of course, Angelique is sitting there cheering George on. I'm dying of embarrassment. Sid, naturally, won't give a hint that he's bugged. So, I guess it's not entirely fair to expect George to know what's going on. But you'd think he'd see that something's not right."

"That I believe," Kathy said. "Jesse says George has a tendency to see and hear only what he wants to."

"I'll vouch for that," I grumbled. "Now, I've got Mama, George, Sid, and Angelique all planning my wedding."

"I wish they were planning mine," Kathy said.

"I wish they were, too." I looked at her. "At this point, I'm beginning to wonder if I want to get married."

Kathy put her hand on mine. "Oh, Lisa, don't let me drag you down."

Esther snorted. "The wedding is the worst part. I used to work at that bridal shop. I saw more fights at that store. I know why the divorce rate is so high. Nobody can survive the wedding."

"I'd sure like to try," Kathy said with a deep sigh. "I mean, I understand why Jesse doesn't want me supporting him. That's an important thing for him. And even if it weren't, I can't tell him to marry me and let me support you or I'll go find someone else. There is no one else and I'd never follow through. I'm just too far gone in love with that man. I can't believe I'm acting like such a fool."

"Did you tell him that George is going to give him the condo when we get our new place?" I asked.

"Not exactly," Kathy said. "I did get him to compromise. As soon as he can put a roof over my head, i.e. pay rent, we'll get married. So the sooner George moves out, the better. Lisa, I don't care about your wedding plans, but I'll be more than happy to see you two house hunting."

"Hah!" Esther snorted. "You two think you got

trouble. At least, you asked for it. If you really wanted to, you could tell George and Jesse to get lost. I can't tell my father to get lost. He's driving me nuts. Ever since he got that residency at UCLA Medical Center, he has to live with me. It's great. I'm looking for a new roommate, got a nice two-bedroom place, so he moves in. Because I'm a woman, I get to clean up and cook. I got better things to do and he's a slob. Some doctor."

"Doesn't he have a private practice?" I asked.

"He just got his license for here. He had a private practice back home." Back home was Vietnam for Esther. Her family had fled about eleven years before, toward the end of the war. "We come here and he can't practice. He has to get license first. Only he can't speak English good enough for the test."

"I always thought his English was really good," said Kathy.

"Not medical English. He had a terrible time with that. Anyway, he finally learned it and got on at UCLA and moved in with me. And you know what he did yesterday? He told my two brothers to move in with us. Did he ask me first? No. That's all I need. You know how small my place is, two bedrooms or not."

"At least it will cut down on your rent," I said.

"Not a chance." Esther shuddered and shook her head. "My two brothers are stupid. Dimh is an actor and Phuong is an artist. They're not making any money. Dimh was doing okay when they were still shooting MASH. He'd get parts as a refugee or Chinese soldier. But any fool could tell he was Vietnamese. Anyway, they're going to start a Vietnamese theatre. They want me to help them translate Death of a Salesman into Vietnamese. They're stupid!"

"Isn't there any traditional Vietnamese theatre?" I asked.

"Maybe. I don't know," Esther said. "I just got a bad feeling they're going to hit me up for money. Well, they aren't going to get any from me, I can tell you. I don't care how much my father yells. Just 'cause they're men. Well, phooey on them."

That wasn't exactly what Esther said. Her command of the English language is exceptional and includes pretty much the full canon of cuss words.

"Watch your language, Esther," said Kathy.

"Stuff it, Kathy," Esther replied without rancor. "Who are you, anyway? Sarah Arnold, I mean, Williams?"

"Let's not start fighting," I said. "I've got enough turmoil with George and Sid."

"So do I," grumbled Kathy.

"Boy, do I," Esther said. "I wish I could find an excuse to get away from them for a while."

"That does sound nice," Kathy said.

"It sure does." I thought it over. "You know, Wednesday is the Fourth of July. How much time do you guys have off?"

"I just found out I got two weeks' vacation at my job," Esther said, brightening. "Of course, I got to save one week for Catalina. I got the Fourth off, but that's it."

"I'm in the same boat," said Kathy. "Although, I could probably get Thursday and Friday off, too."

"I bet I could, too," Esther said. "What about you, Lisa?"

"Well..." I pressed my lips together. The writing work was still behind, but Quickline was down and there was no reason to believe that it still wouldn't be the following week. "I can swing it. Sid can just lump it. Let's go somewhere just the three of us and the first person to mention a man gets fined."

"Oh, that sounds good," said Kathy. "But where?"

"I'd like to go camping," Esther said. She's basically cheap. [Uh, pot and kettle here, kiddo? - SEH]

"That does sound like fun," I said. "I know. I've been wanting to go four-wheeling down in Baja since I got my truck."

"Camping?" Kathy was skeptical. "In Mexico?"

"I done it before," said Esther, grinning. "It's a lot

of fun."

"The only problem is that somebody is going to have to sit in the jump seat. It's not all that comfortable."

"I'll sit in it," said Esther.

"I don't know about this," said Kathy. "My idea of roughing it is no room service."

"Have you ever been camping?" Esther asked.

"Well, no."

"Then you gotta try it at least once," Esther said. "It's settled. We're going to Baja. Just us girls and no men."

"You sure we'll be safe," Kathy asked, still not convinced. "I mean, aren't three women alone asking for trouble?"

"One woman alone, probably," I said. "Two women, maybe. Three women, I think we'll be fine. Besides, we know how to take care of ourselves."

"We'll bring a gun," said Esther. "Anybody here know how to shoot one?"

"Didn't you used to shoot skeet, Lisa?" Kathy asked.

I frowned. "Yeah, but I don't like the idea of pointing guns at people."

"I was just joking," Esther said. "Look, I'll arrange the campsite and route. Lisa, you take care of your truck and get the equipment together. Kathy, you get the food and supplies. But don't buy anything without checking with Lisa or me. We leave Tuesday night."

"I'd rather leave Wednesday morning," I said. "The traffic won't be as bad and I don't want to set up camp in the dark. Esther, see if you can get a beach site. It might be hard because of the holiday."

"Sure thing."

I went home feeling very pleased with myself. Better yet, Sid and Angelique were off getting Nick from the airport. George hadn't found out I was home. I had the whole house to myself. I reveled in it for a full fifteen minutes. The Sid, Angelique, and Nick came home.

I did find some time before dinner to tell Sid about my plans for the holiday.

"Have fun," he said with little enthusiasm. "Just remember to get it okayed Upline first."

"Oh. Right." I bit my lip. We normally had to get clearance a week before we went outside the country. "Should I call Henry?"

"No reason not to." Sid seemed pretty distracted.

"You okay?" I asked.

He frowned. "Just bugged."

"Rachel?"

"That's some of it." He sighed. "I had to call her while I was in the hospital, and I raised my concerns about Nick being left alone all day and night. So Nick tells me this afternoon that he can only stay through Friday because he's going to be spending the rest of the summer at camp."

I swallowed. "How's he feeling about that?"

Sid shrugged. "He thinks it could be fun, but he's not thrilled. He says he can take care of himself, but I get the feeling that he doesn't like staying home alone nearly as much as he says."

"I would imagine not," I said.

"It's the other thing he said that really bothers me. He thinks his mom is trying to turn him against us. She kept saying how camp will be so much more fun than being with us, and that if we really wanted him, we'd let him stay with us all the time."

"You've got to be kidding."

"I wish." Sid shook his head. "I just don't get what her game is."

"I think I know. She's punishing you because you won't let her manipulate you. Poor Nick."

Sid looked at me. "You think she's that petty?"

"No," I said. "But I do think she's that neurotic."

"Whatever. The one bit of good news is that whatever her game is, it seems to be backfiring. Nick is not at all happy with her."

I looked him over. "Anything else bothering you?"

"Getting knocked off the case. I'm getting the feeling Upline is worried that the contact saw me."

"But he's not going to know your real identity."

"For which I am grateful." He shrugged. "There's nothing we can do about it, anyway."

"I suppose not." I paused. "I'd better call Henry."

I went into Sid's office to make the call. Henry wasn't thrilled. It turned out our entire line was down, which made it really hard to deny my request. We set up which radio channels I would use to check in and what codes I would need.

"How are you doing?" I asked.

"Not great, but can't do anything about it," he said. "I just kind of wish I was going with you."

"I wouldn't mind, but this one is ladies only."

He chuckled and we hung up.

I was about to go out to the garage to check my little pickup and figure out what all I would need for the trip when I almost ran into Angelique, who was sniffling. I could hear music coming from the library, so I guessed that's where Sid and Nick were.

"Are you okay?" I asked.

"Just depressed over the same thing, as usual," she said. "I swear, I've had it with men!"

A thought hit me.

"I've got to make a couple phone calls first to okay it with my other girlfriends," I said. "But how would you like to forswear the male sex for a few days over the holiday and come four-wheeling in Baja?"

"Four-wheeling, huh?"

"It'll be rough. The first person to mention a man gets fined. And it will be crowded in my truck."

"Don't worry about that." Angelique grinned. "I should be able to borrow my brother's jeep. He keeps telling me to. That sounds terrific."

"Let me talk to Esther and Kathy. I don't think they'll turn you down."

Kathy and Esther were very happy to have Angelique and even happier when Angelique confirmed that she had her brother's jeep, too. The plans were coming together perfectly. I made my lists of what I needed, then skipped all the way to my room.

Monday morning, we got a call from Upline. I needed to go to Las Vegas to look at some videotape to see if I could identify our contact. Sid couldn't go because he wasn't yet cleared to return to work after his injury, and also, they were worried about him being recognized. I was instructed to change my appearance, which meant my blonde wig and makeup, which I took with me.

I put on the wig and the makeup at the airport while I was waiting for my flight. It seemed a little ridiculous that I had to go all that way just to look at some video, but that was the job, at times.

I met my counterpart, Blue Moon, at the Las Vegas airport. He was a smallish man, of nervous mien, or so it appeared. He drove me to an industrial park only a few minutes away from the airport.

"I was on the team when they nabbed Big Red," he said, referring to Sid's code name. "I want to grab this schmuck so bad my teeth hurt." Blue Moon glanced over at me. "I heard he came out of it okay."

"He did," I said.

"Good."

By that point, Blue Moon was pulling into a parking space in front of a box-like building with a white stucco exterior and dark glass doors at even intervals in the wall.

He pulled me into a spacious room filled with player pianos. Three of the walls held shelves filled with long red and white boxes. Several of the pianos had boxes scattered on their tops, and piano rolls falling out of them.

"Welcome to the Code Factory," Blue Moon told me as I looked around.

"Impressive," I said, trying desperately to hold

onto my cool exterior.

I'd heard about the Code Factory before. Its name notwithstanding, it was mostly about breaking codes and the crew had a phenomenal record.

"Wasn't this one of the groups that got scuttled when the Yellow Line went down last summer?" I asked.

"It just changed lines," Blue Moon said with a chuckle. "They weren't going to let this place go."

I didn't doubt it. Blue Moon led me into the inner office where a VCR was hooked up to a small TV. Videocassettes littered the desktop. A second man and a woman looked up as Blue Moon and I entered the office.

"Meet Little Red," Blue Moon said, jerking a thumb at me. "This here is Blue Nun and Blue Shield."

Oddly enough, Blue Nun was the man and Blue Shield was the woman. They nodded at me, then Blue Shield pressed a button on the VCR.

"There was a break-in here last night," she said. "The video caught this man going through the file cabinets. We think he might be our suspect, but as you can see, it's a little hard to see."

I watched the grainy black and white video as the man opened drawer after drawer. He looked pretty ordinary, but then I spotted something.

"Stop!" I yelped. "Can we back it up a little?"

Blue Shield pressed the buttons and the video slowly went in reverse.

"There," I said.

Blue Shield ran it forward, frame by frame.

"That's it," I said, pointing it out on the screen. "That's the scar, down the outside of his left hand."

"Good," said Blue Moon.

"But that doesn't answer why he was here," I said.

The others shrugged, but I suspected at least one or more of them knew why.

Radio static suddenly filled the tiny office.

"Blue Nun, we've got the suspect holed up in a

house northeast of your location."

Everyone in the office tensed. Blue Moon pressed a button on a microphone next to the TV.

"Give us your location."

The address made no sense to me, but to the others, it was crystal clear.

"Let's go," said Blue Shield.

Blue Moon grinned at me and nodded. We ran for his car while Blue Nun and Blue Shield ran for another one. It didn't take long to get to the address from the radio. It was a small ranch-style house, badly in need of paint. Another car pulled away as our two cars pulled up. Blue Moon put on an all-over ski mask and pulled his gun.

Now, I want to point out that my fellow agents are incredibly brave and have amazing skills when it comes to a wide variety of espionage-related activities. However, apprehending suspects is not something we do very often. In fact, leaving someone hog-tied for the normal authorities is about the extent of it, and that's usually because we were already fighting with the suspect, not because we were trying to arrest him or her. So when I write that Blue Moon went charging up the driveway to the front door of the house as if he were leading the charge up San Juan Hill, it's not that he was being stupid. He just wasn't very good at that kind of extraction because it wasn't what he did.

I scrambled after him, terrified that he was going to walk right into the contact's fire. That didn't happen, thank God. Blue Moon crashed through the front door, and I covered him. We all but fell into a large, empty living room. Blue Moon went running for the kitchen. I heard a window scraping open from the back and slid down the short hallway.

I rolled into the bedroom where I thought I'd heard the window. Sure enough, the contact was just outside the back window. He lifted his revolver and I ducked behind the door. The gunfire roared and two bullets slammed into the door jamb. I eased myself out from behind the door. The contact ran across the huge, barren backyard toward the back fence. Blue Moon came running into the yard from the kitchen. I didn't take any chances and fired. The contact faltered, but got over the fence a second later and disappeared. Blue Moon chased after but returned a moment later.

"We, uh, probably should have waited a moment later to cover the back," he gasped.

"Yeah. We should have," I said.

Blue Shield and Blue Nun came running up and reported that the contact had, indeed, gotten away.

We hurried back to the Code Factory before the police could find us on the scene, although Blue Nun made sure the house would be watched. At the Code Factory, I looked at the others.

"So, what would the contact be looking for?" I asked.

Blue Shield sighed. "We don't know. He was going through the files for our visible business, which would have made sense up until last summer. We used to hide things in plain sight. It was just easier that way. But last year, there was that leak. I don't know if you heard about it."

"Yeah." I couldn't say so, but Sid and I had been instrumental in plugging that particular leak.

"Anyway, when we changed lines, we found a way to better hide our sensitive files." She sighed again. "Moon, why don't you drive Little Red back to the airport?"

Blue Moon nodded and away we went. He apologized over and over for screwing up the apprehension, which was really annoying. There wasn't anything I could say. He had screwed it up. Once at the airport, I made sure he'd left, double-checked for tails, then bought my flight home. While waiting, I sulked and sank ten dollars in change into the slot machines. Not my brightest move, as the slots at the Vegas airport are notoriously stingy.

I got home in time to give Sid a quick report before

dinner. We agreed that it was curious, but that there wasn't much to be done. Nick talked extensively about his day over dinner, then George arrived to take me to the teen bible study.

We got back around eleven. George helped me into the house as I was pretty queezy.

"I'm proud of you, Lisa," George said, as we stumbled through the hall to my rooms.

"Ugh." I held onto my stomach. It figured he'd be proud of me.

"Really. I am. It was a valiant effort."

"George, you've said that five times in the last hour. I don't care how valiant it was, I still lost."

"But second place—"

"I hate second place!" I yelped.

Sid came slowly down the hall from the rumpus room.

"Lisa, are you alright?" he asked.

"Just suffering the effects of my ruinous eating habits," I said. "And I don't want a lecture."

"We had the pig trough tournament tonight at the youth group," George explained.

"George, shut up," I groaned.

He continued without mercy. "Lisa did really well. She was up against high school football players. Didn't even bother with the ladies' competition. She almost beat Jeff Childs. He's huge, too. He just barely won."

"By three lousy seconds." I sniffed. That hurt worse than my stomach. "Goodnight, George."

I shrugged George away and went into my outer room. A few minutes later, Sid knocked on the door.

"Are you dressed?" he asked.

"Yes." I hadn't left the couch.

"Can I get you anything?" he asked as he came in.

I shook my head. "Don't bother. I've got Pepto in my medicine cabinet. I'll get it in a minute."

"Okay. Do I want to know what a pig trough tournament is?"

"A pig trough is a double banana split," I replied.

"A long time ago, it was determined that to eat two pig troughs in one sitting was no big deal for Jeff Childs, Father John, Frank, me, and a few other young men, all of whom play football. So we decided to see who could eat two pig troughs the fastest."

"That competition being tonight."

"Mm-hm. Don't tell me I deserve what I got. I know I do. I guess the thing that really irritates me is that I could have beat Jeff a couple years ago." I snorted. "A couple years ago, my stomach would be giving me this much trouble. I'm getting old, Sid."

He chuckled. "You have no right to make that statement until you are on my side of thirty. Of course, if you'd learn to take care of yourself..."

"Sid, please. I just can't handle a health lecture right now."

"I only lecture because I care."

"I know. I appreciate that."

"Alright. I'll spare you. I guess I can forgive an occasional binge for the sake of competition. My sympathies on not quite making it. I know how you feel about second place."

"Thanks."

"By the way, what was your time?"

"Twelve minutes, forty-eight seconds."

"Pretty impressive. Makes it all the more frustrating, doesn't it?" Sid came over and began massaging my shoulders.

"Yeah." I shook my head. "George thought it was terrific."

"I get the feeling that George would have thought it was terrific if you had come in last place."

"He would." I made a face. "It's funny. I used to think it'd be wonderful to have someone think I could do no wrong."

"It is rather draining to be put on a pedestal, isn't it?"

"Yep. I'm going to have to talk to George about that."

"Do that," Sid said, then gently kissed the top of my head. "Goodnight, Lisa."

As he moved away, I caught his hand and squeezed it.

"Goodnight, Sid."

The next morning, I took Nick with me to buy the camping gear that I didn't already have. He had recorded "Sad Lisa" off my album onto a cassette tape and played it at least three times on my truck's tape deck while we were out. We didn't get back until well after lunch. Sid left the office and the two went back to piano lessons in the library while I tried to get caught up on the writing work. Nick was picking it up, though slowly, and was trying to learn "Sad Lisa." I have to give Nick a lot of credit for sticking with it. He was usually too hyper for anything like that. But he was determined to learn how to play that song and banged away at it for over three hours, at which point, both Sid and I told him that was enough.

George came by in time for dinner, then hovered as I tried to pack.

"Why can't I go with you?" he asked for the third time as I hauled my clothes out to the duffle bag on the cutting table in my outer room.

"I told you, George. It's women only." I glared at the collection of shorts, t-shirts, bras, underpants on the cutting table.

"But, Lisa, you shouldn't be going by yourselves. It's too dangerous."

"We're not going by ourselves. There'll be four of us." I looked at him. "Both Angelique and I have taken self-defense, and Kathy and Esther can keep their heads. We'll be fine."

"I don't like it. You're going to be in Mexico, you know."

"Someplace you go all the time," I pointed out as I shuffled around tops and bottoms.

George blushed as I set out a stack of bras. "Your

Spanish isn't so good."

"Neither is yours, George. Will you quit worrying?"

"I can't help it. I love you." He put his sweet teddy bear face.

I stopped and had to smile at him. "I know, George. I love you, too. I just... I don't know. You've been so overprotective lately, hovering all the time, and flowers every other minute. I don't understand."

George looked puzzled. "But, Lisa, we're engaged."

"So? I'm still the same girl you were dating. It's not that I don't appreciate it. It's that you're overdoing it. It's like Nick and 'Sad Lisa.' It's my favorite song and I love it, but I'm getting tired of hearing because it's on all the time."

"I guess." George looked down at his feet. He looked at me, then pulled me into his arms. "It's just that I love you so much and I'm so excited about getting married. I want to be with you all I can. Yesterday, you were gone and I missed you. Lisa, you are literally the woman I've always dreamed of marrying. I knew it the night I met you. I've been so patient waiting for you. Now that I have you and will always have you, I don't want to be away from you. Do you understand that?"

I sighed. "I suppose I do. But do you understand that I need room to breathe? I'm not the clinging vine type. I'm too independent. That's why I'm going to continue working after we're married."

"If you really want to." George took a deep breath and let it out. "I do want you to be happy. I still don't like it. I was us to be able to share completely. I'm so glad I don't have to work, we can do everything together. Complete oneness and unity. That's what marriage is all about."

"That doesn't mean glued to each other." I slid out of his arms and went back to perusing the list I had set beside the duffle bag. "We can be apart sometimes and still share completely."

"But you don't."

I stiffened. "I share."

"No, you don't. Like yesterday. Where were you all day? You never said. I had to ask Sid."

"What did he say?"

"That you were in Las Vegas doing research."

"That's where I was." I moved around to the other side of the cutting table.

"Then why didn't you tell me?"

"Because I didn't want you following me there." I glared at him. It was a lot closer to the truth than I'd really wanted.

George stepped back as if I'd hit him in the stomach. I blinked back tears.

"I wouldn't have done that," he said, obviously very hurt. "All you had to do was ask."

"But I did ask, at least twice, when I was in Ventura, and you still came."

"Didn't we have fun?"

"That's not the point, George." I took a deep breath. "It's that you don't listen, and so, when I need to do things, I can't tell you what I'm doing. It's why I didn't tell you where we were going camping." I hadn't, initially, told him that I was even going, let alone where. But George had found out about the trip from Jesse, who, of course, had been told by Kathy. "I don't know where you got this cockamamie idea of marriage meaning two people glued to each other, but it's not my idea of marriage. I love you, George. You're sweet, you're kind, you're a good man. And if I'm your perfect woman, then why can't you just let me be who I am?"

George looked away. I could have sworn there were tears in his eyes.

"Jesse said I was getting a little pushy."

"You were." I went over to him. "George, I didn't want to hurt your feelings. I get that you're excited and I'm glad you are. It was just too much, is all."

He shrugged haplessly. "I just want everything to be perfect for us."

I slid into his arms. "It doesn't have to be perfect. It just has to be us."

"This is why I love you, Lisa," he said softly.

We kissed and I felt such a strong rush of love for him. We lingered for several minutes, then George left and I finished packing my bag and began the process of packing the truck.

The trip was an incredible success. I suppose I should have been a little more concerned when I checked in with Upline at a payphone near the Mexican border and Kathy gave me a funny look. But I was with friends, I was having fun, and I was more relaxed than I'd been in a very long time. We didn't even do that much four-wheeling, only to where we'd set up camp. We spent most of the time sunbathing, swimming, eating, talking, and even reading.

Until Friday evening when Kathy began longing out loud for civilization, and the others agreed that it was time to head back to San Diego and find a hotel. That was going to be a bit tricky for me. Technically, I wasn't supposed to change plans like that. So, I found a moment to get into my truck's glove box and tapped out a signal for my Upline person. I got the signal back to radio near midnight.

Fortunately, we'd all bedded down by that point. I slipped out of the tent and slipped over to my truck. I opened the door, got in and shut it as quietly as I could, then put my key in the lock and turned the battery on. The radio was in the glove box and looked pretty much like your basic Citizens Band radio, but was a lot more powerful.

"This is Little Red to Red Base, come in," I said into the mike.

"Red Base to Little Red, we copy." The voice on the radio blasted out loud.

I quickly turned it down. "The civilians want to change plans. We're headed back to San Diego in the morning. Over."

"Copy that, Little Red. Thanks for the update. Over."

"Over and out." I reached over and turned the radio off.

I slipped back to the tent as quietly as I could. Kathy was awake.

"What were you doing in your truck?" she asked sleepily.

"Just checking something," I said. "It's okay."

Kathy yawned and went back to sleep. I started breathing again.

We got back into San Diego in the early afternoon, got a couple rooms next to each other and that first delicious shower after camping. By that time, it was getting close to six. Angelique said she knew of a really good Mexican restaurant, not far from the downtown FBI offices, but by the time we got there, the wait for a table was at least an hour.

"I'm starved!" I groaned.

"You're always starved." Esther grinned.

"Well, I'm hungry, too," said Angelique.

"It's not going to be any better anyplace else," Kathy.

That we had to agree was true. Kathy gave her name to the hostess and we went into the bar to wait. Fortunately, there was a table near the back. I grabbed the chair facing the room and then noticed Angelique was checking out all the men.

We ordered a pitcher of margaritas and Esther added a round of tequila on the side.

"They always make the margaritas too weak," Esther said.

"Uh, guys," Angelique said, hesitantly. "Would you be terribly upset if I broke off and returned to the hotel a little later?"

I pressed my lips closed.

"Ange!" Kathy said, her voice dripping with mock outrage.

"Ange, Ange, Ange." Esther shook her head. "I say we throw the book at her. She is really violating the pact. She's not only talking about a man but threatening to go off with him. Despicable."

"How low can you get?" Kathy asked.

"I stand convicted. Guilty as charged." Angelique laughed. "My deepest apologies, and to make it up to you, I'll not only stay, I'll pay for the drinks."

"I move we reinstate her," Esther said promptly.

"I second the motion," I said quickly.

"All those in favor, say aye," Kathy said with a grin.

Which we all did.

The waitress arrived with the pitcher, glasses, a big basket of chips, salsa, and a plate of serrano chiles. Angelique tried the salsa and pronounced it far too spicy for her. I tasted it and shook my head.

"Not near spicy enough," I pronounced, grabbing a serrano.

"And speaking of spicy," said Esther. "Can we talk guys now?"

"Why?" I asked and Kathy began shaking her head.

I should have known better.

"Because I want to know, is Sid Hackbirn really as sexy as they say?"

Kathy looked at me reprovingly. Angelique laughed.

"What do you think, Lisa?" Angelique asked me, still laughing.

I stammered. "Me? I'm not sleeping with him."

"We know that," said Esther, dunking a chip.

"So. That doesn't mean you don't know how sexy he is," Angelique said, toying with her glass. "You're closer to him than any of us. You can't tell us you don't want to sleep with him."

"Yeah, I can," I said, then blushed. "Okay, I've been tempted. But I want a real relationship. I don't want to have to wonder what he's saying to someone else or if I really am the best or whatever. I want a real commitment, and we all know Sid is simply not up to that. I deserve a real commitment. We all do."

"Yeah," said Angelique thoughtfully.

"So, Ange, is he really that good in bed?" Esther demanded.

"You're not going to get her to give up until you spill," Kathy said.

Angelique laughed, then sighed. "Okay. Yes, he is that good in bed. He has this way of making you feel like you're the only person in the world and it's incredible."

"Too bad he can't sustain it," I said. "But that's the tragedy of his upbringing. He wasn't taught about relationships and has no clue how to make one work."

"Sadly, that's true," said Angelique. "In fact, that's why I've never really understood you two. I mean, I can see you're friends, but I just don't understand how he kept you around long enough to become friends."

"Oh, he told me upfront he didn't have time for virgins with standards," I said, munching on another chile. "But I was working for him and he got dependent on that, and then he realized he'd lose me if he did get me into bed. And we both had to work at it. I didn't have a lot of respect for his values, either. We eventually worked it out and that's how it happened."

"Blech," said Esther. "I didn't want a goopy answer."

Then she said something so obscene, I'm still blushing about it. Kathy, at that point, gave up trying to keep Esther in rein, and the whole conversation devolved rapidly into a discussion on meeting one's more intimate needs. I couldn't even begin to keep up, and the worst of it was, I was getting hot under the collar and hearing Sid laughing his fool head off at my naivete. The only thing that saved me was that my pager went off. I excused myself and went to the restrooms, where there was a payphone on the wall.

I listened at both the men's room, then the ladies' room doors and didn't hear anything. I dialed the phone number on my pager and gave the receiver code.

"I saw that you were down here," the man on the

other end said. "We're calling everyone in. That suspect you guys on the Red Line have been after, we've got orders from Upline to bring him in, and we're doing it tonight."

"That's good news."

"We need you to meet us in thirty."

"Uh, no can do. I'm with civilians and they'll notice it if I take off."

The man cursed. "What are you doing with civilians?"

"My line is down, remember? I'm on vacation."

He cursed again. "Look, is there any way you can get your pals to this restaurant? It's a popular one with the Feds in the area."

"We're already here," I said, mentally snarling at Angelique for suggesting it.

"Great. We'll need an extra lookout in case it goes sideways. Say you saw a friend and went running after, if you need to."

"Hmmm. Alright. We should be getting seated at any time, though, and it's really crowded."

"That's one of the reasons we want to do it there. Can you stay in the bar?"

"No promises," I said, thinking of George and his complaints about me holding out on him.

There wasn't much the man could do. I couldn't blow my cover. I hung up and went to the bathroom. When I got back to the table, the hostess was standing there with an apologetic look on her face.

"What's up?" I asked.

"It's going to be another hour," Esther grumbled.

"I'm afraid we have a couple large parties tonight and people aren't leaving," the hostess said.

And Sid wonders why I pray.

"Is there any way we can have dinner in here?" I asked.

The hostess smiled in relief. "Of course. I'll get you some menus."

She returned quickly and we took even less time

to order.

I kept an eye on the crowd as the conversation between the others lumbered over other areas. Even as I did, I began to feel a little resentful. Sid and I had become exceptionally close because of Operation Quickline. It's how we survived and that was not something I could share with George. I didn't even want to, really, not because I would have minded working with George, but because of what I was watching out for: danger. I didn't want to expose George to that. I didn't want to expose anyone I cared about to it. Operation Quickline had become a barrier between me and everyone I loved, and at that moment, it made me angry.

As our dinners finally arrived, the mood in the bar shifted very subtly. Angelique noticed it first.

"I wonder if something's about to go down," she said, looking around.

Esther looked around the bar, too. I spotted at least two men and a woman I'd seen from drops and the like.

"What do you mean?" Kathy asked.

"It's a weird vibe, like the guys in the office get when they're about to go on a major operation." She nodded at one of the two men. "That guy there has a gun."

"Should we leave?" Kathy asked, looking a little forlornly at her plate.

Angelique scrunched up her face. "Nah. It's probably not going to happen here."

No sooner had she said that when the contact slid into the bar from the back. His eyes flitted everywhere and I put my head down as he looked our way.

"I think I know that guy," Angelique said, nodding at the contact. "Now what's his name?"

"Oh, they're going after him," Esther said.

The three Quickline agents surrounded the contact and squeezed him between themselves. The contact was having none of it. He struggled and yelled.

The agents drew their guns.

"Get down!" I hollered, diving under the table as the bar filled with screams.

Angelique kept down but started toward the struggling group. Terrified, I scuttled after her and caught her when she just a few feet from the struggle.

"What do you think you're doing?" I hissed at her as a tall table went over, spewing glassware and margaritas everywhere.

"I know him. He's a good guy."

"But you're not an agent and there's three of them and only one of you!" At that point, I realized why they'd needed me at the restaurant. If Angelique knew the contact as a good guy, then he was probably a Fed, which meant there might have been other Feds mistakenly defending the contact, thinking he was their colleague.

The Quickline agents took advantage of the chaos to subdue the contact somehow and spirit him out of the bar. Seconds later, FBI Special Agents filled the bar, taking statements. I dragged Angelique back to our table.

"What did you think you were doing?" Esther screamed at Angelique. "Did you want to get yourself killed?"

"But he's one of ours and he's just been kidnapped." Angelique started crying.

"Did you want to get kidnapped too?" Esther demanded, her fury making her face red. "They had guns. I don't see a gun on you. You think they were going to stop just because you said so? You think you were going to put them out? You watch too much TV!"

"Easy, Esther," Kathy said, more out of force of habit than anything else. She was trembling all over. "Oh, my god, that was scary."

"Yeah," I said, my voice strangled. I did not want to think about what could have happened to these, my dearest friends.

"What are we going to do?" Angelique cried.

An older man in a suit approached, showing his badge and ID.

"Evening, ladies," he said gently. "We need to get a statement on what you saw."

"He's a good guy," Angelique sobbed. "And they just took him out of here."

"I'm afraid he wasn't," the older man said.

"Let me see your ID," Angelique demanded.

The man handed it over. Even in the dim light of the bar, it looked good. The name on it was Charles Wyzecki.

"You're Charlie Wyzecki?" Angelique asked.

"Yes, ma'am. And you are?"

"Angelique Carter. I work for Henry James in the L.A. office." Angelique grabbed her purse and dug her own ID case out. "I know that guy they dragged out of here. I just can't remember his name."

"It's always hard when it's one of our own," Wyzecki sighed.

"But what about due process?" Angelique asked.

"He'll get it. He was just stealing a lot of sensitive information, so we have to debrief him first so that we can present a case without betraying secrets."

Angelique shuddered. Wyzecki got each of our statements and our names and addresses in a remarkably short time. The restaurant offered us replacement meals, but we were too shook to really eat them. Or, rather, the others were. I ate even more than usual, but as I pointed out, being upset made me eat more.

We returned to the hotel after that. Angelique and I were sharing a room. She was still very upset.

"You just think you know somebody," she sighed after we'd climbed into bed. "Not that I knew this guy that well. But he was around a lot. And, you know what, it was something involving covert operations. Sheez."

"Really?" I asked, hoping she wouldn't start asking questions about Sid or me.

"Yeah." She sniffed. "I'm sorry I spoiled everything."

"You didn't spoil anything," I said. "Who knew something like this would happen? I mean, come on. Agents taking some enemy in a crowded bar? How often does that happen?"

"Given some of the phone calls I've gotten, probably more often than you might think," Angelique said. She paused. "I've been thinking, too. About what you said about Sid and what I deserve. You know, you're right. I deserve better than what I've got with him."

"Good. Um. Please don't tell him I said that, though."

Angelique chuckled weakly. "I wouldn't dream of it." Another pause. "Your friends are pretty special."

"All my friends are pretty special, Angelique."

"That's me, too, huh?"

"Yep."

"Good. Thanks." There was an even longer pause. "I'd kind of like to stay friends with Sid, too. You think that's possible?"

"I don't know. It depends on how easy you find it to stay out of his bedroom. As we both noted, he's pretty tempting."

"Maybe I'll go cold turkey for a while."

We laughed softly and it wasn't long before I could hear Angelique's soft breathing as she slept. I fell asleep fairly soon after that.

We spent Sunday goofing off in San Diego, shopping and generally trying to relax after the night before. Around five, we found a payphone at another restaurant, nowhere near the local FBI offices. I called George, Esther called her father, Kathy called Jesse, and Angelique called Sid. The message was essentially the same: We were going to leave San Diego when we were darned good and ready and not to wait up for us.

That being said, it was only a bit after eleven when I finally pulled my truck into the garage in Beverly Hills. Angelique had gone back to her place and would pick up her things later. I was surprised to find that Sid was still up.

"I hope you had a good time," he said as he helped me unpack the camping gear, which we stowed on the side of the garage for the time being.

"Very nice," I replied. "Somewhat more eventful than we expected, but still good."

"Terrific." He looked over the gear, then nodded toward the door. "We need to talk."

I yawned. "Now?"

"Yes."

"Okay."

I followed him into the house. He led me to the office.

"We've got some good news, bad news," he said as we went. "They captured our contact over the weekend."

"I know. I was there," I said. "Angelique wanted to go to this restaurant near the local FBI office, and guess where they wanted to stage the bust?"

"Oh, great."

"Angelique was pretty messed up. She recognized the contact and thought he was a good guy."

Sid's eyebrow lifted. "Does this have anything to do with why she went to her place tonight?"

"Ummmm. Possibly?" I winced.

Sid looked at me for a moment, then shrugged. "Whatever. We will be hosting the prisoner after the debriefing until they can get the charges together."

"Okay. Any idea when that's going to happen?"

"Not really." Sid sighed. "And that's the bad news. You need to go to San Francisco tomorrow to finalize any travel arrangements."

"San Francisco?"

Sid shrugged. "I don't understand it, either. But I have to be here to pick up our contact when he becomes available, so that leaves you."

"Alright. How long do you think I'll be gone?"

"The meeting is set for two. You've got an eleven-thirty flight. With luck, you could be home for dinner. But I wouldn't count on it."

"Okay." I frowned. "George is not going to like

this."

"He already knows you're going."

"He called you again."

Sid shrugged. "After you called him to let him know you were coming in late tonight. He wanted to be sure I didn't worry."

"Does he know where I'm going?"

"Yeah."

"Terrific, Sid. Do you realize he'll probably follow me up there?"

"Even if you asked him not to?"

I sighed. "I don't know. I had to get on his case pretty hard about the Baja trip. But that doesn't mean he actually heard me. I'm a little worried that he decided to call you after I told him I'd be late."

"What the hell." Sid waved his hand. "Get him to delay his arrival until tomorrow morning. Then why don't the two of you hop over to Tahoe so he can meet your folks? You can afford to."

I looked at him carefully. "Why do I smell a touch of something rotten in the state of Denmark?"

Sid smiled, oh-so-innocently. "If you are implying that I have ulterior motives, then rest easy. Mae called this morning so Darby could talk to Nick before he left." (Mae is my older sister and Darby is her son. Darby and Nick are the same age and good friends.) "Before the boys talked, we got to chatting and Mae let on that your folks are a little concerned that they haven't met George yet."

I glared at him. "And there is not even a hint of sadistic glee on your part at the thought of George meeting my father?"

Sid and my daddy just barely got along. By all accounts, it was because Daddy was jealous, which made no sense whatsoever.

"Well, it will be interesting to see how they get on," Sid said. "But I do not doubt that there will be no problems. George is a fine, upstanding, well-intentioned, young man. In short, he is everything I

am not. He and your father should get along famously."
Sid smiled then turned to the office door. "I assume you
are very tired after your little trip. Time for both of us
to get some sleep. Goodnight, Lisa."

I sighed. "Goodnight, Sid."

[I will interject here. There was a certain amount
of glee at the thought of George meeting your father,
but not sadistic glee. When Mae suggested that I set up
the meeting, I was a touch put out.

"Why?" Mae asked. "Daddy will love George."

"Nice of you to rub it in."

Mae laughed. "For someone who says he knows
my baby sister so well, you are not getting it."

"Getting what?"

"How stubborn Lisa is and how if Daddy wants
her to do something, she'll turn around and do the
opposite."

I chuckled. "You're right."

"Besides, Daddy doesn't like you because he's
jealous of you. He is not going to be jealous of George."
She paused. "Get it?"

"Yeah."

Unfortunately, when Angelique called to let me
know she was moving out again, she suggested that I
try to break you and George up and go for you, myself.
Which I absolutely, in no way, was going to do. But,
damn, I wanted to. - SEH]

The next morning, George called me right at eight, which given his tendencies to sleep in, meant a lot. He wanted to come up with me. I asked him to meet me the next morning. We compromised on meeting for dinner that night at the hotel where I was planning to stay. He was very excited about driving up to Tahoe the next day to meet my parents.

I sat back in my desk chair. Something was up. George's behavior was definitely odd, but at least I could pinpoint a reason for it. He was trying to make up to me after our fight before the Baja trip. Sid, on the other hand, was back to playing the distance game. The night before, it had been more like usual with him. That morning, however, he was gruff and didn't say one word more to me than he had to. He wasn't mad, at least, I didn't think so. I decided it was time to find out.

I slid into his office. "Hey."

"Yes?" he said without looking up from the computer screen. I couldn't tell what he was reading.

"We've got to talk."

He sighed and turned to me. "About what?"

"I don't know." I shrugged and flopped into one of the chairs in front of his desk. "You seem off. Did you talk to Angelique?"

Sid's eyebrow lifted. "Yeah. She called last night. She's moving out." He looked at me. "Which I'm assuming you already knew."

"Yeah. How are you feeling about it?"

"Fine." He was.

"Then it's not her that's bothering you."

"I never said it was."

I sighed. "Then it's something about George."

"What about him?" Sid went back to reading his screen.

"I don't know, Sid. That's why I'm here. You're avoiding me again. I think you've been avoiding the whole issue."

"I don't think I have." Sid paused, pressed a few keys, then went back to reading.

"Not on the surface, maybe. But we're not really talking about it. You keep dancing around the issue and I don't know how you really feel about it."

"What difference does it make, Lisa? I have no right to interfere. I've set it up like that and you've made your commitment."

"Sid, you're my friend and a very important person in my life. If we're to continue that friendship, I need you to be open and honest."

Sid sighed, but he turned and faced me. "What can I say? As your husband, George will be taking my place in many ways. How do I feel about it? Not good. What do you expect? But at the same time, I do respect you, Lisa, and it is your choice."

"But you're acting like you feel a little jealous."

"A little?" Sid's eyes bore into me. "Lisa, I feel a lot jealous." He suddenly got up and prowled around the room. "More than jealous. I feel incredibly envious." He paused and looked at me. "Do you realize, my dear woman, that when George marries you, he will be getting from you the one thing I have wanted from you more than anything else?"

"This isn't just about the sex."

"It's a big part of it." Sid resumed prowling. "It's just... Look, I have nothing against George. He's a nice guy. A bit of a goop, to use Nick's terminology, but a nice guy, nonetheless. I once heard him say you were too good for him, and I must admit, I'm inclined to agree. But I want you to know that I'm not trying to break you guys up. I want to respect your choices, Lisa."

"I know, Sid, and I appreciate it."

"I want you to be happy." Sadly, he landed on the edge of the desk closest to me. "I just don't think you will be with George."

I couldn't help feeling a little defensive. "And if I disagree?"

Sid got up. "Well, you wanted my opinion."

There was more to it than that. I knew Sid well enough for that to be plain. He continued prowling. I got up and stopped him.

"What do you want, Sid?"

He turned away. "What do you mean?"

"What do you want? What do you want me to do?"

"What I really want you to do. Deep down." He looked up at the ceiling as if he couldn't breathe.

"Yes."

"Alright." Sid turned back to me, his bright blue eyes fixed on mine. He gently, oh, so gently, took my hands in his. "I want you to dump George." He paused and swallowed. "And I want us to become lovers."

"Lovers?" I stepped back.

"Yes," He stepped closer. "I want you to move into my bedroom, Lisa. Permanently. I'm offering a lifetime commitment. I'm willing to go that far."

My heart stopped and I blinked.

"They why not get married?" I heard myself say.

Sid's hands slipped from mine and he began prowling again. "You know I don't believe in marriage. It's a crock."

"Are you saying that what Mae and Neil have is a crock? Or my parents? Or any of a dozen other couples I could name?"

"No, but it's not the piece of paper that does it."

"But it does make a difference, and probably even to you. In fact, I suspect the whole reason you don't want to marry me is not because of your principles but because you'd have a hard time justifying any infidelity."

"It wouldn't mean anything, Lisa."

"Yes, it would and we both know it."

"Alright." Sid held his hands up. "You're saying no. That's that. We'll forget I ever said anything."

He looked so forlorn. I blinked back tears and took

a deep breath.

"I'm not necessarily saying no," I said softly.

He watched me as I began to prowl.

"I also have my feelings to consider," I said.

"And?"

"In your case, they're very strong."

He looked away. "Not strong enough."

"Sid." I walked over to him and softly brushed his arm. He turned to me, his brilliant blue eyes questioning me. "What you are asking me to do is something very hard for me to justify. But I'm going to try."

"I don't understand."

"I'm going to think about it. I'm going to think very long and hard and pray about it."

"Really?" Sid's eyes lit up with hope.

"Yes. I'm not making any promises. I can't."

"I understand, Lisa. I don't know that this will be easy for either of us." He took my hands and gently pressed them to his shoulders. "But I do think we will make very good lovers."

I smiled. "So, do I. That's why I'm considering it."

"I'm glad."

Tenderly, Sid placed his hands on my shoulders and his lips on mine. My arms slipped up and around his neck. His arms gently held me against him. As we pulled away, my hand rested on his shoulder, his soft hand playing with my hair. He held me as if I were the only person in the world for him, and I suspect that, for the first time in his life, I really was. [It was always you, but, no, that was not the first time. - SEH]

I looked at him uncertainly. He took my chin in his hand and gently, with just a spark of passion, kissed me again. I had touched his passion before and it had frightened me. This time, strangely, it reassured me.

"Sid, I..." I looked at him and then pulled away. "I— I've got to get going. I've got to pack and..."

I hurried to the doorway, then stopped and slowly turned to him.

"Sid, I don't know what's going to happen, but I

think that until I tell you otherwise, I'd better consider myself still engaged to George. I don't want to tell anyone about this. It's not you. I just don't want to upset George unnecessarily."

"That's perfectly reasonable," Sid said. "I'll see you whenever."

"Alright. I'll see you." I fled.

[And I celebrated. Yeah, I know. Not the most appropriate response, but that's when I knew you were not going to marry George, and that was the most important thing. Yeah, I wanted you as my lover, but even if you couldn't, I knew it would happen eventually. But marrying George, that scared me like nothing else. I was afraid that you were running away from me and that if I meddled even the least bit, it would drive you right into his arms. That would have been a disaster for you and a longer wait for me. - SEH]

I left Los Angeles in a storm of mixed emotions. At that point, it seemed like it was Sid or George. I loved George, there was no doubt about that. He was very sweet, practically adored the ground I walked on. Yet Sid was also very sweet and while he did not adore the ground I walked on, he had told me once that I was the best thing that had ever happened to him.

I leaned back in my seat on the plane as it took off and remembered the incident. Sid had compared me to losing his virginity. I had been insulted until he reminded me just how much sex meant to him.

This wasn't about the sex, though, at least, not all of it. Sid wanted me for our lifetimes, a huge concession for him. Or was it? We already lived together. We already had a strong commitment, thanks to Quickline. Admittedly, it had happened because we both thought that I could not be reassigned. If we hadn't, Sid would never have let himself get backed into a situation where he was forced to communicate honestly with me. By the time we'd found out that I could be reassigned, our relationship was well on its way. In fact, it was very much like a marriage. About the only thing missing was the sex.

Only now, Sid was asking me to add that dimension. I caught my breath. Angelique had been right. I definitely knew how sexy Sid really was. There was a gentleness about him that was special, and warm, and very exciting. Sid aroused me like no other man could, even George.

Poor George. As much as I loved him, I had to admit, he had no grace. He was like a warm, cuddly teddy bear, and about as awkward, too. As far as I knew, George was still a virgin (and that was something else I should have asked before agreeing to marry him). Even if he wasn't, that didn't mean he'd be any good at lovemaking. Sid had told me more than once that good sex didn't just happen, that it was a skill. I wondered how much time it would take for George and me to learn that skill.

The plane landed at the San Francisco airport. I rented a car there and drove it to the hotel downtown. I must have been out of my mind driving in that city. L.A. is bad enough. San Francisco is twice as crowded and has all those hills, besides. I was glad I'd gotten a car with an automatic transmission.

As I fought my way through the traffic, I couldn't help thinking about Sid again. He'd grown up there, somewhere near the Haight Ashbury neighborhood. He'd taken me there before but I didn't remember where it was. He had done all the driving that trip and I hadn't paid that much attention to where we were going.

I did remember what a hassle parking was. I was glad to pay the valet at the hotel, which is saying a lot for me. I stuck to public transportation after that. I checked in and found that I only had a few minutes to get to the Fisherman's Wharf, where the restaurant where I was to have my meeting was.

I was a good fifteen minutes late when I approached

the desk at the restaurant.

"I'm supposed to meet Mr. Faber-Lloyd here," I told the man at the desk. "My name is Miss Frye."

"Miss Frye?" The man smiled. "Yes, Mr. Faber-Lloyd is expecting you. Right this way, please."

Mr. Faber-Lloyd, a corpulent and elderly man in a cheap dark suit, was not alone at the table. The woman who sat next to him was petite and beautifully turned out. She had fluffy short hair and a pert nose. The last time I had seen her had been in Paris when Sid and I had been on a particularly difficult job, the only occasion I'd had to go overseas so far. She kept her face bland, but I could see that she recognized me.

"So, you're Miss Frye," Mr. Faber-Lloyd said, giving me the once-over. He was slurping up the broth of a pot of cioppino, a seafood stew that was the local specialty.

"Yes," I said, sitting down in the empty chair. "And who is your guest?"

Like most restaurants on the Wharf, the room featured huge picture windows overlooking the San Francisco Bay. The table was at the corner of the room, and both Mr. Faber-Lloyd and his guest had gotten the two chairs with their backs to the wall.

"This is Mrs. Ellis," said Mr. Faber-Lloyd. He glanced at her, then me. "Although, I get the feeling you two know each other."

"Darling," said Mrs. Ellis with a smile. She was eating a salad decorated with tiny shrimp. "You know we don't discuss those sorts of things." She looked at me. "I understand that your people have picked up that nasty, fence-walking pest."

"If you mean the guy that was busted Saturday night in San Diego, then yes," I said, eying her warily.

"Dearest," Mrs. Ellis said. "You needn't be quite so modest about it."

"No modesty," I said. "It wasn't me."

"Well, the bugger is captured, that's what most counts." Mrs. Ellis buttered a small bit of bread and popped it into her mouth. "Mmm. I do love this local sourbread."

"I was told there were travel arrangements to be made," I said.

Mrs. Ellis' eye flew open wide and she glared at Mr. Faber-Lloyd. "Travel arrangements. Good lord, don't you people bloody talk to each other?" She turned her gaze to me. "No, my darling. I'm afraid we need to get some evidence swapped out."

I tried not to gasp, but it escaped anyway. Swapping out evidence happened when the real evidence was too sensitive for the public forum of a courtroom. The only problem was that swapping the real evidence with something as damaging but not as sensitive generally meant a break-in.

"Oh," I said. "I didn't bring my tools."

She glared again at Mr. Faber-Lloyd. "We've got a major operation planned for tomorrow morning to capture one of the associates of your fence-walking pest. We must get the evidence swapped out or it will be a disaster."

"I get that," I said. "But I see no reason why you need out of town talent to do it."

She rolled her eyes and looked at Mr. Faber-Lloyd. "Our friend here is being followed. And I..." She winced. "I have other reasons for not engaging in the actual swap."

"And there is no one else in the Bay Area who could possibly do this," I said, glaring at her.

Apparently, there was because Mr. Faber-Lloyd began looking very cross.

Mrs. Ellis looked at me and smiled. "Of course, there are. We wanted you, and/or your partner."

"I'm so glad you wanted us," I replied, without any hint of warmth. "I suppose it won't do any good to ask why."

"No," said Mrs. Ellis, smiling. "But I am glad you asked. You said you didn't bring any tools. What will you need?"

"What am I breaking into?"

Mr. Faber-Lloyd jumped in. "It's a jewelry store on Pier Thirty-Nine, lower level." He pulled out a small map of the pier, which had been refurbished some years before as a tourist shopping area. "You'll need keys. I've already put those in your purse."

"What about lock picks?" I asked. "Keys will help, but I'll need something if I run into something you didn't expect."

"They're on the ring with the keys," Mr. Faber-Lloyd said. He pointed to a spot on the map. "Here is where the burglar alarm for that block of stores is. That key is on the ring I gave you. It's basically a circuit breaker box. Each store has its own switch, so if somebody wants to work late, they can without calling in the cops on it. The target store switch will be the third on the left. Do not override all the alarms or that will bring in the cops. Are we clear?"

"Third on the left," I repeated. "Should be."

"Now, you're going to want to stage this as a regular burglary, otherwise our targets might get wise and pull out before we can bust them."

I sighed. "Of course. What do you want me to do with the jewelry I steal?"

Mrs. Ellis chuckled. "Why not wear it, darling? You'd probably look better in it than most of their clientele."

I shook my head. "Not my style."

Mr. Faber-Lloyd cleared his throat. "Most of the really valuable stuff gets put in the store vault when they close, anyway. You'll probably find some watches and rings in the cases, but that's it. They have regular locks on them, so they should be easy to get into and clear."

"Okay," I said. "But where's the evidence and what do I swap it with?"

"There's a file labeled November 1983 in the back room file cabinet. That's where the evidence is. I also put a plastic bag in that purse of yours. Put the file in there. There's a possibility we can get some latent prints off of it, in addition to the contents, themselves. I put the stuff to swap in the bag."

I sighed. "Now I just have to find an all-over ski mask in the middle of July, not to mention a dark hooded sweatshirt and my other tools."

"I saw a nice variety of knit caps in a store over that way," Mrs. Ellis said, nodding toward the front of the wharf. "You should be able to get the sweatshirt there, as well. As for tools, I'm not sure."

Mr. Faber-Lloyd nodded his head. "There's a couple hardware stores in Chinatown, up on Grant. Not sure what you'll need, though. Just be remember the third switch down on the left for the burglar alarm, and you'll be good. You've got keys and no one is going to be investigating any burglaries after tomorrow's operation, anyway."

"I only have to get out of there before tomorrow's operation," I said, a little glumly.

"You'll do quite all right," Mrs. Ellis said with a smile. "And we'll make sure there's some backup." She favored Mr. Faber-Lloyd with an irritated glare.

I gave her a quick irritated glare of my own to register my disapproval and got up.

"I'd better get going, then," I said, feigning a bright tone.

"Good luck," grumbled Mr. Faber-Lloyd.

I left the restaurant. As Mrs. Ellis had indicated, there was a souvenir store across the street that sold all kinds of knit caps and sweatshirts and the like. Fortunately, San Francisco gets pretty nippy at night, even in the summer. I even found an all-over knit cap. I couldn't find any zip-front hooded sweatshirts that didn't have anything printed on them. Although, I did find a nice black one with "San Francisco" embroidered in shiny gold thread on the upper left front. I figured I could pull those threads out and mentally added a seam ripper to my list.

I checked my watch. It was just after three o'clock.

George would be at the hotel at six. I didn't have a lot of time but went first to the Pier to check things out.

I really liked Pier 39. Both times I'd been there, I'd been with Sid. Sid isn't big on shopping and Pier 39 isn't quite up to his income and tastes but he loves watching me. At the same time, I drive him nuts. I'm always falling in love with things, which amuses him no end, then refusing to buy them, which he can't understand at all. It's not like I'm broke.

I could almost hear Sid's gentle chuckle as I looked at a pair of small emerald earrings at the jewelry store that I was going to break into. I couldn't help feeling irritated that he was haunting my thoughts so completely. Well, I had promised to think about his proposal. However, I had something more immediately important to think about.

I looked around the store for about five more minutes, noting where the two video cameras were. Given what was going to happen the next day, a video recording of me doing the burglary wasn't going to make much difference. As I left the store, I got that creepy sensation that meant only one thing. I had a tail. Mrs. Ellis had said Mr. Faber-Lloyd was being watched. The tail must have shifted to me, which meant ditching it would only identify me as an operative. That meant browsing the pier a while longer, as if I were, indeed, a tourist.

As I did, I couldn't help thinking about those emerald earrings. George would have simply bought them, in spite of my protests. Sid would have just groaned. He might have gone back later and bought them, depending on how close it was to a holiday and how much I really was in love with them. Sid could tell if I really wanted something or not. He was generous but he was also selective about it. George just spoiled me randomly and had a definite talent for overkill.

I ambled down to the street and caught a bus to Chinatown. I settled into my seat, then looked out the window. We passed one of those flower stands that are all over San Francisco. I remembered the first time Sid and I had gone to San Francisco. We'd gone for the fun of it, supposedly. But the case we'd just wrapped up had both of us dealing with our respective youths, and Sid had decided to share some of the places of his past with me.

We'd been walking around downtown that afternoon when we came across a flower stand. Sid bought me a small bouquet and presented it to me with a small bow. Then, for a joke, he took a couple of the blossoms and put them in my hair. I didn't connect the gesture to the '60s song about San Francisco until later, but it was exactly the sort of thing Sid could and did pull off beautifully. We had such a lovely afternoon, only to end up fighting after dinner. I don't even remember what the fight was about.

I thought about what Angelique had said and Sid's inability to sustain a relationship for more than two weeks. I had been with him longer than anybody. He fought with me. He wouldn't fight with Angelique or anyone else. He wouldn't bother. He'd just wait until they got fed up and took off.

I was so absorbed in my thoughts that I almost missed my stop. I came back to earth with a start and got off the bus at the last second. No one got off after me, so if someone had been following me that way, I had shaken him. Which, as I thought about it, was exactly what I did not want. I checked around me and didn't see anything worrisome.

I had landed in the heart of Chinatown. The sidewalks were crowded with tourists and also with locals. That was the nice thing about the neighborhood. Real people lived there, so while the shops carried a lot of touristy stuff, there were shops with stuff for everyday life. Painfully aware of time slipping past, I window-shopped, buying the occasional trinket, some silk fabric, and a seam ripper, when I finally found a hardware store.

There I got a gift set of screwdrivers, a set of wire-cutters, a flashlight and a navy blue canvas backpack. It was just past four-thirty when I got to the street again. I continued down the street, shopping and trying to figure out how to get back to the hotel without a tail. I wanted to change clothes before George got there and George would be on time.

That was a very nice thing about George. He was not only very prompt, he was because it was only kind and respectful of others to be so. George recognized everyone as his equal or better. He was a very humble man, in a very healthy way. Sid's ego was phenomenal.

The gun in my back took me completely by surprise.

"No screaming now, sister," hissed a rough voice with an accent I didn't recognize. "Just come along with me."

His hand on my arm tightened, and he pulled me into an alleyway. He was a small man, wearing a nice wool suit. He slammed me face-first into a wall. I whimpered and kept struggling. He clipped me on the head with the butt of the gun. The blow dazed me enough to knock me to my knees. Confident that I was down, the man turned back to my purse. I had only a second, but I pulled myself together and sprang at him. He dropped the gun and my purse and staggered. When he came at me, I was ready and his groin went straight into my knee. He doubled over and I put him out with a solid blow to the back of his neck. I grabbed my things and ran.

By the time I was certain that I had lost my tail, I was hopelessly lost, myself. It was just after five, too. There was only one other option. I stopped in the lobby of a skyscraper and found a payphone. I dialed home and Sid answered on the first ring.

"Sid? It's me," I said. "We've got trouble"

"What's the matter?"

"Those travel arrangements aren't. It's an evidence swap and I picked up a tail from the meeting. Is there any way you can come up here tonight and help me with the break-in?"

"No, I can't." He sighed. "There's a big meeting tonight. We're going to set up the prisoner transfer to the Feds."

"Oh, damn!" I bit my lip, trying not to cry.

"What's the matter, honey?"

"Nothing and everything. I'm lost. I don't know how to get back to the hotel."

"Alright," he said soothingly. "Where are you?"

"Gill and Columbus."

"Gill. Hmm. Not sure where that is, but you're on Columbus. That's good."

He proceeded to give me the directions.

"Okay. I got it," I said when he was done.

"You going to be alright now?"

I swallowed. "Yeah. I'll be fine. The tail's gone and I can handle the break-in."

"Of course, you can."

"It's just... Well, the Brits are back. I mean, she is, whatever her name is. The one we met in Paris."

"Oh. Her. Huh. That makes sense."

"It doesn't to me. Anyway, she specifically requested us for this little job."

"That does not make sense."

"She said the San Francisco guy was being followed, and I'm guessing they passed a tail onto me."

Sid sighed. "Okay. Listen, why don't you call me when you get in after the break-in? I'm not worried about you, but things do go wrong and I'd like to bail you out as soon as possible."

"Well, there will be back up. What kind, I have no idea."

"That's something, I guess. Either way, don't forget to call."

I smiled, in spite of myself. "I won't. Thanks."

"You're very welcome, honey."

I hung up. I followed Sid's directions and even caught a bus that got me to Union Square. The hotel was just south of there, plus there was a Macy's on the square, itself, and I still had a couple more items to purchase, namely, a pair of black jeans or work pants, and a pair of black leather gloves. By the time I had gotten my shopping done and myself back to the hotel, it was, sadly, just after six. I hurried up to my room, then called George from there.

"I'm so sorry," I said when he'd picked up. "The meeting ran long. I couldn't help it."

"Oh," he said. I could tell he was feeling a little irritated. On the other hand, I was there on a business meeting and if that ran long, he couldn't really complain. "Well, that's okay. Our reservations are for the eight o'clock seating."

"Eight?" I yelped. My stomach gurgled. It had been a long time since I'd eaten last.

"Yeah. It's one of those dinner shows," George said, very pleased with himself. "Then we can go out and see the town at night."

I have to give George his due. If I hadn't had to break into a jewelry store before midnight, that plan would have sounded like a lot of fun. That was one of the things that George and I had in common, we were both night owls. Sid was an early bird from the word go and expected me to go along with it. Admittedly, if Sid had been planning the evening, there probably would have been dancing, which George absolutely refused to do.

"That sounds like fun, George," I said. "Great. That will give me time to get a shower and clean up a little."

"Oh."

"Okay. Maybe not. What were you expecting, George?"

"I wasn't expecting anything." He sighed. "I was just looking forward to seeing you is all."

My heart melted. "Oh, George. That's so sweet. I'm sorry. It's just been a really, really tough day. The interview went so badly. Then I got sent on a wild goose chase, and the final meeting was a complete waste of time and it wouldn't end and it wouldn't end."

I could almost hear George biting his tongue, and had to hand him even more credit for that, given how little he wanted me to be working at all.

"That's too bad," he said softly.

"Thanks. Listen, why don't we compromise? We'll go to your dinner show, but make it an early evening. In the meantime, I'll get dressed as fast as I can and then we can have drinks and hors d'oeuvres in the bar downstairs."

"That sounds good," George said.

So I took a quick shower, patched up my scrapes as best I could, then put on a dress and headed downstairs. George was waiting for me and had ordered a bottle of what turned out to be pretty decent bubbly. As I walked up to the table, George scrambled to his feet and pulled me into a warm, loving hug. I snuggled in until he hit the spot on my scalp where I'd been hit earlier that day.

"Ow!" I jumped away.

George looked panicked. "What's the matter?"

"Nothing," I said, sitting down. "I just hit my head there today."

"You've got a scrape on your cheek, too."

I sighed. "I fell. Okay? You know what a klutz I am. Only one more thing to make a lousy day really lousy."

"I'm so sorry, Lisa." George settled into the padded chair next to mine.

The bar, like the rest of the hotel, had a comfortable feel. It was a little worn around the edges, but in the dim lighting of the bar, especially, I could see Dean Martin, Frank Sinatra, and the rest of their buddies, plotting things as they hovered over their martinis.

"We could have stayed up the street," George said.

I munched on some of the peanuts from the dish on the table. "I like it here. The service is extremely good and way more personal than up the street. The rooms are just as nice. And it doesn't cost an arm and a leg."

Given that my parents are in the "hospitality industry," I tend to look at hotels differently than most people.

"The service isn't that good," George grumbled. "I tried to send some flowers to your room and they couldn't find it."

That was because I was traveling as Janet Donaldson.

"That's good," I said, munching on more peanuts. "They weren't going to let just anybody know I'm here. That's more secure."

George looked at me, then nodded. "Oh. I hadn't thought of that."

"Come on." I grabbed a menu. "Let's order some appetizers."

"We're supposed to get appetizers at the show," George said. "I don't want to spoil our dinners."

I laughed. "George, when was the last time something spoiled my dinner?"

He laughed, too, and we ordered some nice appetizers. I don't remember what they were, but I do remember enjoying them. It was a good thing, too, because dinner was a complete disaster. The show was one of those living history things, only the history was not accurate, and everyone in the place was simply going through the motions. The food was pretty awful, too. Intermission came none too soon and I told George that I was leaving.

"What do you mean?" he asked, scrambling after me as I headed to the front of the theater.

"I'm not staying," I told him.

"But we have more dinner."

"I know. I don't want it. And if I don't want it, doesn't that say something?"

He frowned. "I suppose."

"George, it's not your fault. Okay?" I put my arm on his. "How were you to know this place sucks as badly as it does?"

"They're doing their best, Lisa."

I rolled my eyes. "No one in this place is doing his or her best. That's one of the reasons it sucks so badly. The show is awful. It has nothing to do with real history, not to mention the way it keeps bashing Mexicans. I was embarrassed for you."

"You get used to it, Lisa."

We'd hit the street by that point. I looked around for a taxi.

"I see absolutely no reason to get used to that," I said, waving my arm as a cab came around the corner.

"And you don't see that it's even more embarrassing for me to leave something like that in the middle?"

I paused. He had a point.

"I'm sorry, George," I said. "I have to respect that you feel uncomfortable leaving early. But you did promise me an early night and it's already ten. I get the embarrassment thing. I really do. But those feelings are what scammers use to keep you in their control. And that place is a scam. I'm not blaming you. How else would we have found that out except by going? And you know how I love stuff like that usually. So, it was very sweet of you. But if I had to stay there one more minute, I would shoot someone."

George nodded and waved for a taxi. This one stopped for us. I don't know if it was my eloquence that had won him over or the fact that at least two other couples were also on the street complaining even more loudly and stridently than I was. Either way, we got back to the hotel before much later. I kissed George good night in the lobby, then went to my room, ripped the stitching out of the sweatshirt, and changed clothes, putting the tools and keys that I'd gotten into the daypack. I slid out of the hotel and back onto the street, trying desperately not to think about Sid.

But as it happens when you're trying not to think about something, that's exactly what you end up thinking about. And it wasn't as though the evening had been an entire loss. George and I had said grace over dinner, which I loved. That was something I'd never be able to share with Sid, who had been raised an atheist and who did not understand prayer. George loved me. Sid couldn't. George would be exclusively faithful to me. Sid probably would not. He probably wouldn't see too many other women, but if I wasn't around, he wouldn't wait for me. He'd just need to get his hornies out and it wouldn't mean anything more than that. Still, George was going to marry me. Sid wasn't about to.

That was the big problem. Sid was willing to make a lifetime commitment and to him that was marriage. Could I accept it as such? I knew that after seven years or so, the government would, and there was always the possibility that I could eventually get him to validate our vows.

The cab ride down to the area near the Pier took me past the theater. I winced. I probably should have been more sympathetic to George's embarrassment, but if Sid had gotten conned that way (and it was very unlikely that Sid would), he wouldn't have waited until intermission to leave.

I had the driver let me off at that parking garage across the street from the Pier. The streets weren't empty by any means, but things had slowed down for the night. The Pier, itself, was only minimally lit. I slid into the shadows, put on my sweatshirt, and all-over hat, pulling it down over my face, and put on my gloves. I made my way around the shops until I found the panel that I'd been told about. The light over it had been broken, for which I was grateful. The second key I tried on the panel worked and I found the third switch on the left and switched it off. Now, all I had to hope for was that it had done what it was supposed to do.

I was two stores away from the jewelry store when I heard footsteps. I pressed myself flat into the shadows of a doorway. A corpulent security guard was trying the door of the jewelry store. I recognized the silhouette and smiled. Of course, he couldn't break in, himself. He'd be an immediate suspect. He started my way, then stopped. I don't know if he saw me or not, but he turned and went the other way.

I waited a couple more minutes, then hurried over to the jewelry store. As I unlocked the door, I noticed the red gleams of light on the back wall near the ceiling. It looked like the cameras were live and recording. Whether someone was watching them live, that was another question. That kind of surveillance is pretty darned expensive, but I had to assume that someone was watching. To cover as much of the store as possible, the cameras had been trained so that they only caught people from the waist up. Keeping low, I slid in the door and shut it quickly. I held my breath and listened. No alarms were going off, but that didn't there weren't any. I had only a very few minutes.

I hurried to the back as fast as I could while crouched over. There was a curtain between the front and the back office, which I pulled as fast as I could. It wasn't light-proof, so I pulled my penlight from the front pocket of the day pack. The desk, which had been built onto the side wall, was surprisingly neat for such an establishment. Shelves above the desk held bound catalogs and other ledgers. There was a four-drawer file cabinet next to the desk. I started my search there and came up with nothing.

Some people supposedly get a high off of being someplace they're not supposed to be. I am not one of them. I was breathing so hard, the front of my knit mask was soaked. It began to itch, too. Despairing, I looked up at the ledgers, then down at the desk. There was a drawer with a lock on it under the surface of the desk. I got my lockpicks out and had the drawer open in a jiffy. There was the file. I pulled it out, swapped the evidence, and then put out my penlight. Squeezing my eyes shut to get them used to the darkness, I opened the curtain and, again crouching, slid along to the first case with something in it. I got my lockpicks out again and swept the contents of the case into the day pack.

I'm not even sure what I'd gotten. The worst was that I saw: wires coming from the case. A silent alarm. Just what I did not need.

I didn't worry about the cameras at that point. I ran to the front of the store and let myself out, not stopping to lock it. It wouldn't matter. I could see red lights flashing at the street end of the Pier. I slunk along the other way. It was a dead-end, but I was hoping I could sneak past the police while they were looking at the jewelry store.

No such luck. The cops worked their way down both sides of the pier. There was only one way out. After sliding my day pack over my shoulder. I climbed over the railing and onto the huge wooden braces under the Pier. It was slippery going, at best, as I crawled my way toward the cement bulwark and land. I had about fifty feet to go when something tugged at my pack. I turned and felt my way behind me. One of the straps had gotten caught in the cross brace.

I straddled the brace, gently working the strap back and forth. It was good and jammed. I could hear a policeman above me call to the other cops that they should check the second floor of the Pier. I looked up and saw his feet through the cracks in the boards above me. The wind whipped up and my teeth began to chatter. I worked at the strap some more and debated getting out my box knife. The strap suddenly came free and I was thrown off balance and fell into the water.

It was so very, very cold. I've run around in sub-zero weather in my jammies before and this was still colder.

"What was that?" one of the cops yelled as I came up for air and clung to a pier post.

I yanked the mask off of my head and let it sink into the water. A light shown down on the water next to the Pier. I made my way to the other side of the pier post as silently as I could.

"I don't see nothing," another cop yelled.

"It was probably a seal," said another voice. It was

Mr. Faber-Lloyd. "We get a lot of them around here."

I spit out some seawater and shivered. If Faber-Lloyd was my back up, then I was in deep trouble. I swam to the next post, then realized I could touch the bottom with my head above the water. Slowly, I made my way up the bulwark. What probably saved me was that the higher up I got, the more sheltered I was from the icy wind off the water. When I could finally go no further, I crawled to the edge of the pier and looked over the bulwark to the sidewalk. The red lights of three police cars were still flashing, although only one cop was standing by the cars. He didn't seem to notice or care that a petite woman with fluffy short hair limped along the sidewalk nearby, looking at something in her hands. I had to do something.

My hands were trembling so hard, I could barely open the day pack's front pocket. I got the penlight out but almost dropped it. I took a deep breath and held it long enough for my hands to stop shaking. Then I flashed the light twice in the woman's direction. Her head popped up and she looked around. I flashed the light again and she nodded. A minute later, she waved me toward herself. I looked back at the Pier. I couldn't see anybody looking down from the railings. In fact, I couldn't see anybody at all.

I scuttled across the top of the bulwark, then climbed onto the sidewalk in the first dark spot I could find. Mrs. Ellis was there in a second and embraced me.

"Good God, you're wet!" she whispered.

"Sorry." My teeth were chattering again. "I fell into the water."

She held me closer and waved. "No worries. I've got a car here. Let's get you into it right away. I do hope we have a blanket."

The black limousine pulled up and a chauffeur bounced out and held the door open for us. Mrs. Ellis didn't say anything, but the chauffeur immediately knew what was wanted and as we got in, he got something from the trunk of the car. A second later, he handed in two towels and a fluffy blanket. Mrs. Ellis quickly began drying me off, but it didn't stop the shivering. I was chilled to the marrow of my bones.

As the car pulled away, Mrs. Ellis stopped rubbing me long enough to pour a glass of brandy from the small cabinet in front of us.

"How did you find me?" I asked.

"Tracking device on that ring of keys we gave you," Mrs. Ellis said with a smile. "I could have explained, but you left in such a huff."

"I didn't have time," I said, trying to get the shivering under control. "I had to get the place cased, buy tools and clothes and meet someone at six."

"Busy girl. I thought you were merely annoyed with our lunch partner. Heaven knows, I was."

"Idiot. He is, I mean. Didn't mention the video cameras on the site. And it turns out there was a silent alarm on the cases."

"Oh, dear."

"I hope it didn't mess up tomorrow's operation."

"Actually, it's the best of all circumstances." Mrs. Ellis poured me another bit of brandy. "If our targets had come in this morning to find just that file gone, they would have gathered their jewels and fled. But now, the store is crowded with police officers. They don't dare flee without taking the contents of their safe. They are well and truly caught. Which is a very good thing for our side."

We soon pulled up in front of my hotel. I was not particularly surprised, even though I hadn't told Mrs. Ellis where I was staying. We got my key from the day pack and Mrs. Ellis rushed me inside the lobby, explaining that her cousin had fallen off a boat in the dock. I was soon in my room, still shivering, but alone. I called Sid, praying he wasn't involved with anyone at that moment. Sid will pick up the phone no matter what he's doing or what state he's in while doing it. I didn't get a chance to tell him everything because I was still shivering from my swim. He caught on, asked, and then sent me to take a long, hot shower.

"And, Lisa," he said. "I'm really proud of you. That was one hell of a tough job you pulled off."

"Thanks, Sid. I really appreciate it, but I really need that shower."

"We'll talk later."

I hung up and stripped and got the shower going. The hot water hurt, at first, then it finally started to work its magic. Sid's words, too, helped warm me like nothing else. When he praised me, it meant something because he didn't offer it willy nilly, for every ridiculous little thing. I turned off the water, dried off and got ready for bed. As I slipped under the covers, I think I knew that I was not going to marry George. I was still fighting it. Lord, how I fought it. But deep down, there were feelings that as hard as I tried, I could not deny them.

George never knew. I was desperately afraid of hurting him, as I knew it would. In the end, I didn't get the chance. But considering why I didn't, I would have much rather had that awful conversation. Then again, he wasn't the one who suffered. I was.

No matter where my head had been the night before, I woke up the next morning determined to make my problem a simple choice between Sid and George, with George having the edge. After all, George wanted to marry me and be faithful. Sid was happy to give me a lifetime commitment but could not promise fidelity. Perhaps it was the three and a half hours I was going to be riding in a car with George that did it.

Actually, it turned out to be four hours. George was up early enough that we were able to get on our way by nine-thirty. Only he insisted on driving the entire way and drove like a snail. Having had to engage in the occasional car chase, not to mention ditch a tail or two, it's only fair to concede that my driving habits are not the same as most people's. I do not have Sid's lead foot, but, well, I'm not exactly a slowpoke, either. I could have driven us to South Lake Tahoe in less than three hours easily.

On the other hand, George insisted on being a polite, conscientious driver, and that was a good thing, I told myself. He even asked me for directions as we came into the South Lake Tahoe area.

I was basically born into the hospitality industry. My parents had owned a small motel in South Florida, where they come from, then sold it and bought the Tahoe property when I was around two-years-old. I'm not sure when, exactly. Either way, it was before I had any real memory. The resort in Tahoe is a little off the beaten track. The main lodge faces a side road, and with it are the staff buildings and the laundry (which I knew all too well). Behind all that, for about five acres, are rows of cabins. After the last row of cabins, is the back of my parents' house. That house faces another, smaller road.

That was the road I directed George to and he pulled up into my parents' driveway. A minute later, Murbles and Richmond, my parents' two very large mixed-breed dogs, came running up, barking their fool heads off, as usual. George looked worried, but I got right out of the car. The dogs danced around me as I greeted them.

"How are my sweet babies?" I crooned. "Come on. Settle down, guys. How are my sweet little puppies?"

"Lisa?" asked George on the edge of whining. "Are you sure those dogs are safe?"

"Are you kidding?" I said, laughing and petting the dogs. "These are my babies."

Murbles, sadly, was showing his age. He was around nine years old at that point. Richmond was six or so. I'd found him abandoned during a trip home when I was in college. I suppose they were intimidating, but when George refused to get out of the car, I got a little disgusted. [Odd how I feel some sympathy for George - SEH]

"George, they're sweethearts," I said, getting a hand on each of their collars. "Come meet them."

George got out of the car. He walked up slowly to the two dogs.

"Now, just reach out a hand and let them sniff you," I told him.

George did. Murbles sniffed, then whined and loped back to the house. Richmond wanted to sniff George's crotch, as well, and I pulled him back.

"Lisle? That you?" Daddy came around the side of the house.

Daddy is a huge man with a stern face and huge eyes. His voice is deep and gravelly and has a strong Southern accent. He, like my Mama, calls me Lisle after his mother, who was German.

"Daddy!" I hollered.

Leaving George to fend off Richmond, I ran to my father. He gave me a big hug, then the two of us headed for the house porch.

"Lisa Jane!" Mama came out of the house and onto the porch.

She's as small as Daddy is big, bright and pert like a little Southern sparrow.

"Hi, Mama!" I called, then turned. "Come here, George, and meet my folks."

I could see Daddy sizing up George as they shook hands. Daddy didn't really smile or say anything, but that's his way. Daddy's very jealous of the men in my life. He really doesn't like Sid. They only get along because they have to.

Mama bubbled all over George, but then, that's Mama's way. There are very few people in this world that Mama doesn't like. As far as she's concerned, everybody is just as good and innocent as she is, even Sid. Well, she knows what he's up to, but she won't talk about it and usually acts as if he isn't.

It was hard to say what my parents thought about George. They were very nice to him, but there was something funny about it. For one thing, Daddy wasn't jealous. I figured George would get his approval, but he didn't quite. George was the first man that I had dated that Daddy wasn't jealous of. Mama was as nice as ever but had stopped talking wedding.

We had lunch in the kitchen. Mama had made sandwiches. It was a nice, casual lunch, the conversation being light and not really of any substance. Then George blew his big chance to score points with my mother by not offering to help clean up. It was no big deal, and Mama certainly did not fault him for it. But as she shooed us away to look at the rest of the resort, I could tell she was not impressed.

I took George to the horse barns. Daddy kept a small herd for the guests to ride, which meant these were the sweetest tempered horses you've ever seen. Sid was not fond of horses, but he accepted that I was and let it go at that. George kept trying to protect me from them as if he was scared they were going to do something terrible.

But what really did George in was the call to the main lodge. George, Daddy, and I were down there chatting with Miles Weaver, the desk clerk, when the phone rang.

"Plugged toilet in number twelve, Bill," Miles told him after speaking to the guest who'd called.

"Alright," Daddy grumbled.

"Daddy, I'll get it," I said cheerfully. "Are the tools in the same old spot?"

"Same place as always, Lisle," Daddy said with a grin.

"Come on, George," I said, and headed for the back of the lodge.

"Why don't you call a plumber?" George asked as he followed.

"For a plugged toilet?" I snorted. "A plugged toilet is nothing and plumbers are expensive."

"But you shouldn't have to do that."

"Why not? I'm capable." I got out the plunger, the snake, some rubber gloves, and a couple wrenches.

"Lisa, you're a woman," George said.

"I noticed. What has that got to do with anything?"

"You don't know the kinds of things that go down those places."

I laughed. "Oh, yes, I do, George. I've unplugged many a toilet in my time."

"But my wife does not do such menial things."

I stopped and glared at him. "I am not your wife yet, and if you want me to be your wife, then you'd better get used to the idea that I am going to do what I darned well please, as long as it's not immoral or illegal. Furthermore, I do not like the concept of woman's work or man's work. A person works according to God-given talent and not sex. Nor is there is any such thing as menial work. I am not too good to unplug a toilet or sweep streets or whatever. Are we clear?"

George stepped back. "Okay, but I still don't like this."

"Fine. Then do me a favor and either shut up and

help, or go up to the house and cry on Mama's shoulder."

George opted to help, but he didn't last too long. The people in cabin twelve had small children, which gave me a clue as to what was wrong. I asked the parents if anything was missing. The mother looked frantically at the array of toys strewn across the room's floor and shrugged. George looked as though he was about to say something, but I nudged him in the ribs.

We went into the bathroom, where I put on the rubber gloves and got to work. George waited just long enough for me to stick my hands in the toilet, then decided that he'd meet me up at my parents' house. Okay, it was a pretty sick mess, but nothing that terrible.

It's not like I don't understand that plumbing is gross. Sid couldn't handle plumbing, either. His toilet got plugged every now and then. The first time, Sid had asked me to call the plumber, rolled his eyes when I insisted on taking care of it, myself, and then let me do my thing. The other three times, he offered the plumber, shook his head and let me get on with things, and thanked me for saving him some trouble. No complaining. No chauvinism. If Sid didn't like something, he expressed himself quietly and usually with a remedy for the situation. If my idea was better, he'd do that. There was a give and take with us that I was beginning to wonder if George could understand.

It didn't take long to retrieve the toy that had been flushed down the toilet. The parents were horrified that one of their little darlings had been the cause of the mess. I just laughed and pointed out that most kids waited until vacation time to act up and that they wouldn't believe some of the antics my sister's kids had gotten up to.

Mama had apparently been telling George the same thing when I got back to the house after cleaning up in the lodge.

"They just can't help it," she was saying as I walked into the kitchen. "Oh, Lisa, there you are, honey. Would you go tell your daddy it's time to put on the coals?"

"Yes, Mama."

"George, why don't you help me with the salads?"

I didn't hear George's response, but I couldn't imagine him being much help.

I found Daddy out by the big barbecue grill and smoker in the gated side yard next to the house.

"Mama says it's time to put on the coals."

"Okay." Daddy immediately bent to the task. "Where's George?"

"Mama wanted him to help with the salads."

Daddy chuckled. "Yeah. She said he needed a bit of training."

I was about to ask in what, but Mama and George came along just then. Mama held up a pitcher of dark tea and held a six-pack of beer. George was laden down with a covered bowl and a big picnic basket overflowing with napkins, place settings and more food.

"I made some sweet tea for a treat," Mama announced, putting the pitcher on the picnic table next to the grill.

That was odd. Mama almost never makes sweet tea because it is really loaded with sugar and no one else in the family really likes it. It's even too sweet for me, and my sugar habit is legendary. George was clearly getting his baptism by fire. Mama also pointed out the beer, which she put in the cooler next to the table, along with a bottle of white wine that she got from the basket.

Daddy put the hamburgers on the grill while Mama and I laid out the table. George got a beer for himself and one for my father and the two chatted while Daddy cooked. We ate, talking aimlessly about nothing, and when we'd finished, I bounced up with Mama to clear the dishes and help clean up. Mama told George to talk to Daddy and she and I went back to the house.

As Mama got the water going in the sink, I put the leftovers away, then got a towel. I could see that she looked a little down.

"You don't seem happy," I told her.

"Oh, I'm alright," she said with a sigh.

"Come on, Mama." I grabbed a dish from the drying rack and put my towel to it. "You were so happy about me and George getting married and now you're not. What's going on?"

She looked at me. "When you called about getting engaged to George, I thought he could make you happy." She paused. "And that you were finally over Sid."

"I thought you liked Sid."

"I adore Sid. He is the sweetest man I have ever met since your daddy." She blinked her eyes. "But he is never going to marry you, and I do not want you wasting away your life on a man who will not marry you."

"But I'm happy with Sid." My gut leaped as I realized how true that was. "It's not wasting my life away if I'm happy, is it?"

She blinked and smiled at me. "That's all I want, Lisle, baby. You know that."

"I do, Mama." I went back to drying plates and glasses. "I mean, it's not perfect. And we may be coming to a compromise of some sort."

I watched for her reaction.

"A compromise is always good," she said, finally, and frowning. "A little security would be even better." She shrugged and scrubbed at a spot on the over-sized spatula Daddy had used. "Of course, these days, even being married ain't that secure."

"True enough," I said. "Who's getting divorced now?"

"The Shakespeares." Mama rolled her eyes. "She finally got tired of him cheating on her. Said she could run the business better than he could and wanted her chance to try. Back in my day, we put up with that kind of nonsense because we didn't have the opportunities you have now. That's why I raised you girls to be self-sufficient. So you won't have to be stuck like the women were when I was growing up." She shuddered.

The screen door creaked and George wandered in with the cooler.

"Bill asked me to empty this," he said, smiling.

Mama grinned at him. "You can put everything in the fridge, George. Lisa, why don't you go see what's keeping your daddy?"

"Sure, Mama." I dropped my dishtowel on the kitchen table and went outside.

It was only eight, and the summer sun was just barely touching the tops of the pines. There was a little forested area just beyond the yard, with a little clearing just beyond that. I knew I was supposed to be looking for Daddy, but I suspected Mama wasn't that worried about it and wouldn't begrudge me some time to digest the conversation we'd just had. I walked through the trees to the clearing and took a deep breath.

There was no question about marrying George. I was not going to. I couldn't. But what to do about Sid? Mama hadn't exactly given her blessing on me moving into his bedroom, but I could tell she wasn't going to have a conniption over it, either.

Actually, it wasn't just about moving in. Sid was not some fairy-tale come to life. He could be a royal pain in the butt. He was vain, stubborn. His values were often counter to mine. On the other hand, I shared things with Sid that I shared with no one else, things that had nothing to do with Quickline. Sid shared with me in the same way. We weren't just best friends. In fact, we were as emotionally intimate as he wanted to be physically. Our communication was stronger than some married couples I knew, and these were good marriages.

I looked around the clearing, remembering the fall before. Sid and I had talked there. He had gone to a great deal of trouble to get Motley for me, even though he hadn't really wanted a dog. He kissed me then, not on my forehead, but full and warm on the lips. I chuckled as I savored the memory.

George, I had to concede, was almost better at

kissing than Sid was, possibly why I hung onto being engaged as long as I had. The trouble was sweet romantic kisses, no matter how delicious, were not enough for me. I needed a real relationship. I needed Sid.

When Sid kissed me, it was special. A lot of the time it was because he had no other way to express how he felt about me. Only what would happen when the kissing became commonplace, when the lovemaking became commonplace? I didn't think that would happen. I could see the initial thrill fading, but not the deeper emotions between us. They were too strong already. We had gone way past infatuation. We'd been together too long and had worked too hard. Ours was an exceptionally, incredibly good relationship. Surely that meant something?

I heard leaves crunching in the trees behind me and saw my Daddy headed my way. He smiled as he entered the clearing.

"Am I interrupting anything?" he asked softly.

"Not really," I said. "Just thinking."

"I'm guessing not about George."

I shrugged and looked at him. "How do you feel about him, Daddy?"

"I like him alright. He's a fine young man." Daddy sighed. "Kinda feel sorry for him, though. I don't think he knows you ain't marrying him."

"I haven't said I'm not." I pursed my lips, feeling more than a little piqued that Daddy was reading my mind.

Daddy chuckled ruefully. "Aw, Lisle. Let's just be honest. We both know who you're pining for and it ain't George."

I sighed. "I'm sorry, Daddy."

"What for?"

"For liking Sid and not George. You hate Sid."

"I don't hate Sid."

"You don't like him."

"I like him fine." Daddy looked away into the trees.

"I just worry about him, is all."

"He's not going to do anything."

"He ain't going to intend to do anything, and that's the problem." Daddy sighed. "I can just see you and him getting all het up and you ending up doing something you're rather not and feeling guilty about it. That kind of guilt is hell on a relationship." He looked at me closely again. "On the other hand, I remember somebody getting into a pretty big snit reminding me that it's her life and her decisions."

"Oh, that." I couldn't help laughing softly. I had taken Daddy to task pretty strongly. My gut twisted. It was time to tell him what Sid had asked for. I just couldn't figure out how to begin. I hadn't even told him that I lived at Sid's house, which I suddenly realized was the perfect place to start. "Um, Daddy, since we're being honest, there is something I've got to tell you. About where I'm living."

"You mean at Sid's house?"

I gaped. "How did you know? When did you know?"

"Janey told us when they were up here last Easter." Daddy looked at his feet. "I kinda wish you'd found a way to tell us yourself."

"I've been wanting to for ages!" I yelped. "I didn't want to do it over the phone. But Mae wouldn't let me every time we were visiting."

"Now, don't blame it all on your sister."

I kicked at the ground. "I most certainly can. You know how she is about starting fights during the holidays. And last fall, you were already mad enough at Sid."

The light was fast starting to fade, so I barely caught the grin on Daddy's face.

"At least, that's out in the open," I said.

"Bill? Lisa?" Mama's voice echoed through the little forest.

"Guess it's time to come in," Daddy said, turning toward the house.

"Daddy." I touched his arm. "Are you okay about

Sid and me?"

His long arm wrapped around my shoulders and he squeezed me next to him.

"About okay as I can be about anyone hanging around my little girl." He cleared his throat. Arm in arm, we walked through the trees. "I tell you, Lisle, you sure know how to pick 'em. George is a nice boy, but he's soft. He looks like he could stand up okay, but he's a wimp. On the other hand, that damned boss of yours, and his city sheen and fancy ways, you'd think he was a wimp. But he could knock the snot out of George. He's one tough customer. I tell you, Lisle, if he wasn't so close to you, I could almost like the man."

Mama was calling us in to play games. We tried playing poker. Daddy is really good at it. He's even won a few tournaments. He taught me, so it's really a lot of fun to play with him. Mama enjoys it, but we can read her like a book. George didn't get the game at all, so Mama had us call it quits fairly early, before Daddy and I could take George to the cleaners. We moved on to Monopoly. In short, it was an excruciating night. Thank God, Mama kept us busy and sent us to bed early so that we could return the rental car and catch a flight out of Tahoe airport.

As we left the next morning, Daddy hugged me and whispered in my ear.

"Best get on with it," he said. "Waiting won't make it any easier."

"I know," I sighed.

But I couldn't dump it on George on the way home. It would make traveling together too hard, not to mention not wanting to cause a scene on the plane. We got the car returned and made it onto the plane just in time. George burbled on about how much he liked my parents. I looked out the window and tried to figure out when and how I was going to tell him. George didn't seem to notice that anything was wrong. Of course, I sighed, he was not very good at telling when I was not listening to him. He was not very good at listening to me, period, which meant if I didn't do it right, he'd probably think we were having a fight and wouldn't get it.

My thoughts drifted back to Sid. I was still undecided about what to do about his offer. I really didn't want to hurt his feelings, but I wasn't entirely comfortable with moving into his bedroom, either. If I was concerned about hurting George's feelings, I was even more worried about hurting Sid. Then the plane landed and I realized I had to make up my mind soon.

While we waited for our luggage at the airport, George told me that that following week, he was meeting with his lawyer to change his will in my favor. I told him it was far too soon to do that and I didn't want his money, anyway. George went to get the suitcases. George wanted us to meet in Westwood for lunch since we both had our own cars at the airport. I agreed, telling myself that I was going to break it off there, public place or not.

As we finished eating, I got my nerve up.

"George, we need to talk."

He sighed. "Yes, we do, Lisa." He reached over the table and grabbed my hands. "Look, I know you like to keep things to yourself, but it's really getting to be a problem for us. I think we need to go to counseling together so we can learn how to communicate."

I pulled my hands away. "George, you need to learn how to listen."

"I listen. You don't talk. Your parents aren't like that, so I don't understand what's going on. I think counseling will really help us."

My parents weren't part of a top-secret espionage agency, and there was no way I was going to tell George what was really going on.

"I'm not going to counseling," I said.

"It will be alright. You'll see."

"George—"

He got up and grabbed the check. "Lisa, no more. We're both tired and getting mad. Let's each go home and we'll talk about this tomorrow."

I was so shocked, I sat back and watched him go. The waitress offered dessert and I ordered it. I don't remember what I ordered, I was so confused. George, I decided, could wait for another time. I still had to face Sid.

The weird thing was, having my parents more or less okay with me moving in with Sid did not make it easier to. It was hard because Sid and I obviously had the kind of relationship most couples wish they had. But something wasn't quite right about moving in and I couldn't figure out why for the life of me. After I finished and paid for it, I went to the back of the restaurant and called Sid.

"I'll be home in about twenty," I told him.

"Great. I'll be waiting for you."

"Good." I hung up.

The odds were decent that Sid had figured out something was up, but it couldn't be helped. He obviously heard the garage door opener going, because he was near the garage door when I came in. He was wearing a sport shirt and tight, very dark-blue jeans.

"Hi," I said, lugging my suitcase inside.

"Hi. How was Tahoe."

I swallowed. "Interesting."

"Here. Let me get your case."

He bent and as our hands touched on the handle, it was as if I felt a spark run through me. I could feel my heart beating faster. I looked into his sweet, gentle eyes. He moved in closer. My eyelids shut as his soft lips gently caressed mine. The suitcase thudded onto the floor. I was utterly drawn into him. Our arms wound around each other. My lips returned the kiss with equal fervor.

Our lips parted and Sid looked at me, one of his eyebrows slowly rising. I couldn't help it, I kissed him again. This was about more than simple passion. This was about something deeper. I couldn't help wondering if Angelique had felt this way kissing him. Then all I could think of was my father pointing out how guilt was hell on a relationship.

Sid felt me cooling first. He pulled away a little and kissed my forehead.

"Can't, huh?" he asked softly.

I shook my head. "I'm sorry. I'm afraid I'll feel guilty and then resent you, and that's not fair or right. I can't do that to you, Sid."

He sighed but laughed lightly. "I know."

"I'm so sorry."

He held me a little tighter. "Don't apologize for being who you are. You had to be honest with me. I expected nothing less."

"I didn't want to hurt your feelings."

He laughed softly again. "You didn't hurt them."

I pulled away a little and looked him in the eyes.

His shoulders lifted a touch. "Sure, I'm a little disappointed. But hurt? No. Frankly, I expected this." His hand brushed my cheek. "Nothing's changed."

"We're still friends, then?"

"Yes." He almost choked. "If I had thought for one second that my proposal would change that, I would never have made it. Lisa, I value our friendship above everything else in my life. I can't give you up."

"I can't give you up, either, Sid."

His hands cupped my cheeks. "Lisa, when we come together—"

"If we come together."

"When we come together, it will be with joy or it will not happen." His eyes held mine. "That much, I can promise, and you know I'm not going to go back on my word."

Smiling, I reached up and kissed him, then sighed. "I wish I could."

"I know. We'll just have to wait, is all." He held me close to his chest and kissed my hair.

"You achieved one of your objectives," I said, sinking into his hug. "I'm not going to marry George. I can't."

"Lisa, it was never my objective to break the two of you up." He paused. "I mean, I wasn't trying to offer you an alternative."

I laughed and pulled away. "I know that. You were very clear that you wanted me to be able to make my own choices." I paused and looked at him. "Anyway, I haven't had a chance to tell him yet. It's not going to be as easy as you would think."

"Hurt feelings?" Sid asked, his eyebrow lifting.

I winced. "Some. But the other part is his problem with only hearing what he wants to hear. I have got to find some way to make it absolutely crystal clear that the wedding is not happening."

Sid winced also. "You've got a point. Why don't you give your Father John a call? He might have some ideas."

"You're right." I grinned at him. "What a great idea. Thanks."

"Good." Sid smiled. "Why don't you get unpacked? Skip the business wear today. We need to be ready in case our house guest causes any problems."

I picked up my suitcase. "He's here, then?"

"In the special guest room. One of us should probably be awake at all times." Sid grinned. "And, naturally, we got a bunch of writing work in, including one editor request for another miracle."

Namely, an editor was up a creek and needed us to turn something around extra fast. Those jobs were a pain, but they did put us in debt to the very people we needed to assign us more work.

"That sounds like fun."

Sid shrugged. "It's an easy one to crank out. We've also got interviews to figure out."

"Okay."

"See you in a couple."

"See you in a couple." I turned and went into my little suite of rooms and finally started breathing again.

Things had not only gone better than I had hoped for, I was in love. I stopped. In love with Sid? Motley was right there and demanded petting, which I did automatically. Was I really in love with Sid? I was. I was in love with a man who could not love me back, exactly the scenario my mother was worried about. But then I remembered my answer. I was happy with Sid. I thought it over. I was, without question, happy with Sid. So, it didn't make any difference whether or not Sid could return the feelings, which as I thought about it, was why I was not now in his bedroom. When Sid could return those feelings, and it seemed we were slowly headed in that direction, then we would consider the sex. Until then, I would just have to love him silently.

I grimaced. That part sounded pretty nauseating. Unrequited love, pining away. Blech. I was not a Victorian romance heroine. On the other hand, I was perfectly content as a single person. I wasn't going to be pining away. I could wait for Sid to get his feelings together, and if he never did, that was okay, too. I was happy with the way things were. I thought it over. Nope. I was definitely happy, a little on the blissful side, but happy.

[So was I. By that point, I think I knew what was holding you up, and it was the one thing I couldn't promise. I still didn't understand why my fidelity was so important, but I was okay with the concept of being faithful. I just didn't think I could be, and I was terrified of what would happen if I broke that particular promise. - SEH]

When Sid came to get me in the pre-dawn hours of that Thursday morning, I was pretty shaky. It wasn't Sid, though. We'd settled in the afternoon before and cranked out a lot of work, including a pretty darned good article for the miracle. Things weren't quite back to normal. In some ways, they were better. In other ways, a touch more awkward. But working together was fun again, and that made me happy like nothing else.

No. My problem was George. I'd fortunately been on the phone doing an interview when George left a message on my answering machine. In typical George fashion, he was calling to let me know that he'd made an appointment for us with a counselor, and then he went on to reassure me that these sorts of things were normal for engaged couples, and that he stilled loved me and that we would be so very happy together.

Later, George had come over to pick me up for teen bible study, and Sid had convinced him that I was stuck at the library doing research and then was going to meet a friend who'd dropped in from out of town. I was actually in bed. Our prisoner swap was scheduled for four a.m. and I needed to get some sleep before spelling Sid at prisoner watch around eleven. That's when Sid told me that George had asked me to call him in his studio that night. It should have registered, but it didn't quite.

Instead, I spent my hours on watch writing notes, with one eye on the tiny TV set on Sid's desk. The video surveillance camera had been installed in the holding room a year before after we'd been bamboozled by another such house guest. The houseguest slept, moving just often enough. I tried to keep my mind on my notes but couldn't help brooding about George. It was a relief when Sid showed just after three, yawning, but freshly shaved and every hair on his head perfectly in place.

He wore a dark, long-sleeved polo shirt over his jeans, his shoulder holster with an FBI Model Thirteen revolver in it and held an all-over ski cap in his hand. I was similarly dressed and got my cap off the desk. Each of us was wearing a transmitter under our shirts, with tiny earpieces in our ears.

"How are you doing?" Sid asked softly, as we made our way through the hall to where the prisoner was.

"Okay," I said. "Let's get this done."

We put our masks on and got the prisoner from the room. He was wearing surgical scrubs and nothing else. Sid cuffed his hands behind his back and blindfolded him, then we took him out to the garage. Sid rode in the back of my truck with the prisoner. We pulled up in the alley where the transfer would take place. A short way down was a spot between two larger buildings where the middle building wasn't as deep. Just before I turned my headlamps off, they picked up the black sheen of a carbine.

I slid my mask back on (I'd taken it off to drive), then tapped the transmitter.

"Red Team to Team Five, we are in position with the prisoner, over," I said into it.

"Team Five to Red Team, we have eyes on you. Proceed with the transfer."

I got out of the truck, went around to the back and raised the shell's back door, then lowered the truck bed gate. Sid had nudged the prisoner down the bench seats I have in the back there. I drew my gun, and taking the prisoner's arm, pulled him out of the truck.

"Hey! What's going on!" yelled an all-too-familiar voice.

Before I could wonder how or why George Hernandez was there, the prisoner suddenly crashed into me, knocking me to the ground.

"He's popped the cuffs!" said Sid's voice in my ear.

The prisoner whipped off the blindfold.

"Hey! Stop that!" George hollered again.

It seemed as if George was running in slow motion toward us as the prisoner lifted what had to be Sid's gun and fired. George crumpled.

"No!" I screamed.

The prisoner was off and running as the Team Five leader continued cussing and directing his agents. Sid helped me up and pushed me into the truck's front passenger seat.

"You hurt?" he asked.

"Don't think so," I gasped. I turned, but Sid was already scrambling around the front of the truck to the driver's side.

Sid tossed something in my lap, turned the engine over and peeled out of the alley.

"We're clear!" he hollered into his transmitter and whipped off his mask.

He looked at me and I slowly removed my mask, too.

"He'll get help just as fast," Sid said softly.

"We've got a civilian down!" one of the Team Five members, called into his transmitter.

I could hear them calling for an ambulance, then Sid signed out for us and the transmitters went silent.

"I'm sorry, Lisa." Sid glanced at me, then pressed his lips together. "What the hell was he doing down there?"

"Oh, hell." I suddenly started sobbing. "He has a studio and darkroom downtown. I didn't know where it was, but he and Jesse apparently spotted a prisoner transfer a couple months ago and the two of them have been watching off and on ever since. Oh, my God. This is my fault! George told me the night before you went missing and I was going to message it Upline, but then you didn't come home and I forgot."

"Don't be ridiculous." Sid glared at the freeway in front of us. "Prisoner transfers happen all over the place. You had no reason to believe we were in the same alley as George's studio. Besides, you don't even know if that's what George and Jesse saw, and even if you did, you had no way of knowing that George would be there or stupid enough to confront armed people in masks."

"You said he wanted me to call him in the studio tonight."

"Yeah."

I looked over at him and knew that he'd been thinking the same thing as me. I looked down at my hands and noticed what was on my lap.

"Is this?" I asked.

"George's camera." Sid glanced over at me. "I didn't think I'd want to risk it."

"I wonder if he got any shots."

"Doesn't matter. That's why we do these things in masks."

When we got home, Sid and I went into the office. Sid called Henry and I tried to clean up my notes. Sid put the camera in safe underneath his wastepaper basket. It's hidden under the carpet and really hard to see that it's there. Sid cursed as he twisted the combination dial. It was not an easy safe to open. Dawn light slid in through the windows. Motley whined from my bedroom.

I went and sat in my desk chair. A minute later, my sweet dog was in my lap, begging for some petting.

"When do you think we'll know how he's doing?" I asked Sid, finally noticing that he was pacing in front of my desk.

"I have no idea. Probably before lunch."

I nodded. "Where's the mail?"

"Lisa, it's not even six. It's way too early."

I stared blankly at the computer screen. "I've gotta get some work done. We're already way too behind."

"Lisa." Sid pulled me up from my chair and held me close to him. I hung on, not daring to let go.

"I'm so scared, Sid. What's going to happen to him?"

"Probably nothing. They ran a security check on him a long time ago and he came out okay. It depends on what he saw or thought he saw."

"If he saw something that IDs me, then at least he'll know why I was holding out on him."

"Does that mean you want to marry him now?"

"No, Sid. I couldn't." As I held him even tighter, I almost told him why.

The waiting was agony. Sid never left me the whole time. He tried to get me to take a nap on the living room couch. We were both exhausted, but neither of us could sleep. We picked at breakfast around seven-thirty, then I insisted on trying to get some work done. The only thing we managed was to get the miracle article ready for the postman when he came by at ten.

After that, Sid took me into the library and gave me my knitting while he worked through Chopin's Twenty-Four Preludes. At a quarter to twelve, there was a phone call. It was just a salesman. I hung up angrily.

Conchetta made lunch and we ate in silence. There was nothing to be said. For once, my appetite had left me and I barely finished half a tuna salad sandwich. After lunch, Sid took me back to the living room sofa, only this time, he gave me a back rub.

One-thirty and there was still no word. We tried watching TV, but even PBS was too inane. One-forty, the phone rang. It was Mae wanting to know if George, Sid and I would like to come for dinner that Sunday. I told her I didn't know and would call her back later. George definitely would not be coming, but I couldn't tell her that yet.

At two o'clock, Sid got fed up with watching me prowl restlessly around the house. He sat me down at the piano and tried teaching me to read bass clef. I think he was trying to jolt me into thinking about anything but George. Ten minutes into the lesson, the doorbell rang. I checked through the one-way glass on the door. It was Jesse.

Sid squeezed my shoulder, then headed for the office, leaving me alone for the first time that day. I put on a smile and tried to look as if everything was normal.

"Hi, Jesse. Come on in." My voice felt strained with the feigned cheerfulness.

Jesse didn't notice. He stumbled into the hallway, just barely in control.

"Lisa. We gotta talk," he said.

"What's wrong?" I asked. Coldness gripped me as I began to realize the news would be worse than I thought. "Come on into the living room."

Jesse followed me and numbly sat on the couch.

"It's... It's George, Lisa." Jesse's hands were shaking. "He was at the studio last night, pulling an all-nighter. The cops don't know how, but he got shot."

"Oh, my God. How is he?"

Jesse looked at me, the tears spilling onto his cheeks. "He's dead, Lisa."

I tried to catch my breath. I hadn't expected that. Or maybe I had but was trying not to face it. I couldn't breathe. I couldn't hear. I couldn't speak. I couldn't cry. All I could see was George running in slow motion toward me and the prisoner lifting that gun and firing.

"Dead," I whispered. The sobs began slowly and I grabbed at any thought that even seems like it made sense. "George... I... His parents. What about his parents?"

"They were with him," Jesse said. "I mean, they were in the hospital waiting room. He was in surgery all morning. I guess it happened around four or something. He only died a couple hours ago. The hospital contacted his family. His sister just called me. I came right over. I mean, I called Kathy first. I'm sorry. I was so shocked, I didn't know what else to do. She's calling everybody else. I think we're supposed to go to his folks' place tonight."

We got up. Jesse started out. I stopped him. We fell into each other's arms, sobbing uncontrollably.

Somehow, Jesse pulled himself together first. He sniffed and took some tissues from his pocket. He gave me a clean tissue and used one, himself.

"Listen," he said softly. "George is with God now. He's happier there."

"That's right," I said. "We ought to be happy for him."

"I'm just gonna miss him." The tears slid once again down Jesse's cheeks.

"That's plenty to cry over," I said. "But we'll be okay. God knows what He's doing. It's better this way.'

Jesse nodded and wiped his face and nose with his tissue.

"I gotta get back to Kathy," he said. "You gonna go out to the Hernandez's tonight?"

"Yeah. I'd better. What time?"

"I think six or so. I'll call you. Or Kathy will." Jesse looked at me. "I'm so sorry, Lisa."

"I'm sorry for you, too," I said.

"Thanks."

Jesse left. I closed the door behind him, not making much sense of what was going on. Sid was there, standing quietly behind me.

"Sid..."

"I know," he said, reaching over to hold me. "I heard."

He held me as I cried.

"I'm here, Lisapet," he whispered and kissed my hair. "I'll always be here."

My sobs eventually abated. Sid led me into the library and gave me my bible. I thumbed through the Psalms while Sid played. There was some comfort there, although not as much as I wanted.

"Sid," I said slowly. "I don't how to say this."

Sid stopped playing. "You're concerned about the state of my immortal soul."

"Kinda." I winced. "Not entirely. I have to believe that there's some plan in place for truly good people who don't happen to believe. It's just that..." I sighed.

"It could just as easily have been you this morning instead of George."

"And it could just as easily have been you," said Sid, turning back to the keys. "You and I face that all the time. It's the reality of our work."

"I know. It's just that George is with God and he's happy now."

Sid shook his head. "Amazing how easy it is for you to assume he made the grade when he was such a pain in the butt to you."

I shrugged. "It's what I believe in. Life after death. Heaven."

"Yeah. I know."

"I'm sorry. I shouldn't have brought it up."

Sid sighed, then turned on the bench toward me. "I think I'd be worried if you hadn't. Lisa, please don't ever apologize for being who you are. You're bugging me right now because you care. You wouldn't be you if you weren't concerned about whether I'm going to Heaven or Hell."

"I didn't say I was worried about that," I said. "I just don't know what I'd do if it had been you this morning."

"And I don't know what I'd do if it had been you. So, we're even on that score."

I almost blurted out how I felt about him. He looked at me thoughtfully.

"Are you ruing lost opportunities?" he asked.

Normally, this would have been said with a slyly lecherous smile, one that never failed to arouse me. But not this time. He seemed genuinely concerned.

I thought. "Not really. You?"

"Always." He chuckled lightly, then looked down at his hands. "Sorry. That came out wrong."

"Sid, you shouldn't apologize for being who you are any more than I should."

He smiled at me. "You're right. But while I would love it if you did, I really do not want you talking yourself into doing something that will make you feel guilty later."

"I know. It's what Daddy said he's most afraid of happening to me."

"He told me the same. I told him that I refuse to do that."

"By the way. He likes you better than he liked George."

Sid's eyebrows rose.

Frank and Esther came by around four to offer support, however, dubious it turned out to be at first.

"It's like everyone is paying attention to George's parents and completely forgetting about you," Frank grumbled. "And you're the grieving widow."

"Me?" I looked at him puzzled.

"Well, you were going to marry him. Just because it hadn't happened yet doesn't mean you're not grieving," Frank snarled.

Something caught at my throat and I burst into tears. I heard Esther cursing Frank out for being an idiot.

"You okay?" Sid asked.

"I'm such a fraud," I sobbed. "I was going to dump him. Now, what do I do?"

"No kidding," said Frank, bemused, as Esther whacked him. "Come on. Jesse thought she might be getting ready to."

"That doesn't mean she didn't love George," Esther snarled. "How is it you're so smart and you act so stupid sometimes?"

"I do love George," I said softly.

Sid put his hand on mine. "Then that's what you go with. You didn't take dumping him lightly."

"I wanted to be sure he understood that I was," I said.

"I know that one," said Esther. "George don't always listen so good."

"And I knew it was going to really hurt him, so I wanted to be as fair and kind about it as I could," I said. "But I do not want to be the grieving almost widow. It's just not right."

"So don't say anything," said Esther. "George's family is not going to care."

"But what about the Bible Study and the Teen Group?" I asked.

"They're not going to care," Esther said. "And do you really care that much about what they think?"

"Sort of." I looked at Sid. "What do you think?"

"I like how she asks him," Esther hissed at Frank.

"Sheez, Esther, and you talk about me being insensitive," Frank retorted.

Sid laughed. "I think Esther's got a point, honey. I mean, you probably don't want to advertise that you were about to dump George. But you did love him, and you are definitely grieving, so I would say that means you're not a fraud."

I nodded.

Sid ended up asking Frank and Esther to stay to dinner, which they did, and then the four of us drove out in Sid's BMW to Malibu to the Hernandez house.

It was a miserable visit. Mrs. Hernandez immediately fell on me, proclaiming me her last chance at grandchildren. While I strongly suspected that she was using that as a cover for her real grief, it felt very uncomfortable. It was as though I were merely a prop for her scene. Mr. Hernandez was distant and angry and George's siblings bickered bitterly amongst themselves.

The worst was how they treated Jesse and Kathy, or, rather didn't treat them. They basically ignored Jesse and Kathy.

"You are George's best friend," I gasped at Jesse as I handed him and Kathy each a glass of wine. "How can they ignore you like this?"

"It happens," said Jesse grimly.

"They have never treated Jesse well," said Kathy, sending an ugly glare at one of the uncles, who seemed pretty bent on getting drunk.

Kathy and Jesse left shortly after that, and Sid

and I gathered up Frank and Esther and left, as well. We let Frank and Esther out of the car on the driveway, then Sid pulled into the garage. As the two of us went into the house, Sid shook his head.

"Well, that put a new perspective on George," he said.

"I guess so," I said.

Sid gently stroked my cheek. "I know it won't be easy, but do try to sleep," he said. "Our bad guy is still out there and I'll bet anything we're going to get called in on finding him."

"Probably." I sighed. "Sid, I do want to thank you for being here. It means a lot to me."

"You're welcome." He reached over and gently kissed my forehead. "Goodnight, Lisa."

"Goodnight, Sid."

July 13-14, 1984

The next couple days went by in a weird blur as if I were watching myself from someplace else. Friday morning, Sid got me up at the usual time, but not to go running. Instead, we took a drive in Sid's BMW up the coast.

"Where are we going?" I asked with a yawn.

We were dressed in our running clothes, but it didn't seem like we'd be running.

"We've got to get rid of George's camera," Sid said. "It would place us at the scene."

"Oh."

He glanced over at me. "I don't know that I should be bringing you."

"I'll be fine." I took a deep breath. "It sounds terrible, but it's really all for the best. I've been praying about it, and that's what keeps coming up. George never knew that I couldn't marry him and was spared a lot of pain. There would have been a lot of awkwardness at the bible study and in the teen group because not everyone would have understood. I know George would have thought I was being terribly unfair. It's definitely better this way."

Sid nodded. "By the way, Henry had a team go in and clear George's studio. Standard operating procedure."

"I understand."

We ended up driving past Ventura before we found a stretch of coast with a good, rocky stretch and that was deserted enough to get rid of the camera without causing comment. It was summer, and the beaches were filled with campers and surfers. Sid had already destroyed the film in the camera. We got to a bluff overlooking the ocean and Sid was about to toss the camera when I held him back.

"May I?" I asked.

He handed the camera to me. It was a very nice Canon SLR. It seemed a shame to destroy it, but the numbers etched onto the bottom identified it as George's. We couldn't afford to have it connected to us.

I took a deep breath and threw. It sailed out over the bluff and crashed onto the rocks, then bounced into the water below. Sid slid his arms around my waist.

"You are a very strong woman, Lisa," he said, his voice soft, but carrying over the sound of the surf.

I felt the tears running down my cheeks. "Am I? I don't feel like I am."

"You are." He kissed the side of my head and gently squeezed me.

Then, after we got home, there were the phone calls. Mae calling to offer her support. Daddy calling. Sid, at first, thought he'd messed up and tried to pretend that he was at my place. But Daddy called him on it. Then when Sid gave me the phone, Daddy asked if he and Mama should come down. I told them no.

Somewhere in there, one of George's sisters also called. The coroner had already released George's body and the funeral arrangements had been made, with a rosary on Sunday night and the funeral mass on Monday morning, at the Hernandez's church in Hollywood, not our own.

"That was awfully fast," Sid said.

"The funeral arrangements?" I asked.

"No. That they released the body so quickly." Sid shook his head. "Something's up."

We found out what the next morning at breakfast. Sid cursed as he looked at the front page of the morning newspaper.

"What's the matter?" I asked.

Sid held up the paper. The article was on the bottom half of the page, on the right.

"Family Claims Cover-Up in Shooting," read the headline. I reached for it, but Sid chose to read it aloud, instead. The gist of the article was that the

Hernandez family had been given conflicting accounts from the police and the FBI about what had happened to George. The police had told them that George had been involved in a gun battle with a suspect, then the FBI said that he'd stumbled into a hostage situation that the agents had been attempting to diffuse. The Los Angeles Police Department had confirmed that there had been a gun battle with a suspect, and one of Henry's underlings confirmed the hostage story. Neither side would comment on the discrepancy. The coroner's office would not confirm that the autopsy on George had been rushed, but the police spokesperson had expressed surprise that the body had already been released.

Sid dropped the section onto the table.

"I'll bet Henry is fit to be tied about this," he said. "Somebody must have slipped up."

"But who?" I asked. "And why couldn't they have just said what happened without naming any names?"

"I'm sure it's that our contact is still at large. Henry is hoping that he'll go back to one of his safe houses. The contact can't have gotten far in downtown L.A. in just surgical scrubs and bare feet."

"I hope Henry is alright."

Sid sighed. "I'll give him a call when we're done eating."

I finished the fruit salad Conchetta had made the night before. She had offered to come in that day, but I had thanked her and said no. There wasn't that much she could do, and if we needed food, I knew of a good restaurant that could deliver quickly.

Sid found Henry in his office at the FBI. Thanks to the news story, Henry was being deluged with requests from the media. He did tell Sid that the underling who had released the report about George's death had based it on what the agents involved had told him and that those agents had told the L.A.P.D. officers who showed on the scene the same thing.

"Then why did the police say something different?"

I asked Sid.

We were sitting in the library again, with me trying to knit and mostly ripping stitches out instead.

"We don't know," Sid said. "The only other thing Henry told me was that we were to sit tight, avoid talking to reporters, and to absolutely not go after the contact ourselves."

We found out why there were two stories between the police and the FBI when the reporters started calling. We had put it on the answering machines that I was not going to be making any comments, but that didn't stop them from leaving messages. One of them wanted me to comment on the report from the police that identified the two bullets the coroner had recovered as coming from an FBI-issue gun.

"No kidding," I said as the recording finished. "It was your gun."

Sid looked at me with an odd frown. "And you had dropped yours."

"I did?" Squeezing my eyes shut, I shook my head. "I was on my backside. And all I saw was George, then the contact raising a gun and shooting him."

Sid shook his head. "Your gun landed next to you on the pavement. I grabbed it before I got George's camera."

"I don't remember that part."

"No surprise," Sid grumbled. He looked at me. "It was a complete mess."

Okay, Sid used a seriously obscene term instead of mess. I blushed.

"So, now what?" I asked.

Sid didn't really get a chance to answer. The doorbell rang and when we looked through the glass, it was pretty clear the two men on the doorstep were cops. Sid opened the door, inspected their IDs, then helped the two officers into the living room, and sat next to me on the couch. The two detectives both wore polyester suits and were taller than average. Detective Bryce Skipman, according to Sid, was the significantly thinner of the two. The other was Earl Fredericks. He had a rather avuncular feeling about him, but not enough of one for me to let my guard down.

"Miss Wycherly," Fredericks said. "We hate to bother you at a time like this, but we need a few questions answered."

"I understand," I said.

"As I'm sure you've heard by now," Skipman said. "There are some discrepancies surrounding your fiance's death."

"Such as?" I asked.

"Well, the fact that it was a major FBI operation and we didn't know about it was pretty unusual," Skipman said. "Usually, we know when they've got something big going down, and this operation was pretty big based on the number of agents they had there."

"The thing that bothers us, though," Fredericks continued, "is that the bullet was probably fired from a Smith and Wesson Model Thirteen."

I looked at Sid, who shrugged, then back at the detectives.

"Okay. What's a Smith and Wesson, what was it you said?" I asked.

"Model Thirteen," Skipman said. "It's the standard revolver carried by FBI agents."

Both he and Fredericks watched me digest that.

"So, you're saying that George was killed by an FBI agent," I said.

"Looks like," Fredericks said. "And the FBI won't let us have any of the guns the agents were carrying so that we can determine who fired the bullet."

"Did they say why?" I asked.

"Nope," said Skipman. "All they say is that they're conducting an investigation of their own and will we please butt out. But we've got two stories about what happened and a bad feeling that somebody is not being on the level with us."

"I see," I said.

"What we need to know, Miss Wycherly," Fredericks said. "Is did your fiance have any connection to the FBI that you know of, or did he get into trouble with them some way or other, or was he involved in something that might have been under investigation by them, or was he acting like he was trying to hide something in any way?"

I shook my head. "No on all counts."

"Was there anything unusual in his behavior?"

"Not really," I said.

"Okay," Fredericks said. "One last thing. According to Mr. Hernandez's sister, he was complaining that you were holding out or hiding something from him."

I caught my breath and thought fast.

"I wasn't." I blinked my eyes. "I mean, it wasn't anything connected to the FBI. It's just really personal." I looked at Sid.

He reached over and laid his hand over mine.

"It's okay," he said. "Why don't you tell them?"

I glared at him for a moment, then faced the detectives and swallowed.

"Sid knows by accident," I said, trying to buy a little time. "I was trying to find a way to tell George, but these things are not easy to talk about."

"What things?" Fredericks asked, looking a little on the eager side.

I glanced at Sid again. "I... I... I was abused as a child. By a man I trusted. I couldn't tell George." I sniffed. "He was so loving and I couldn't tell him that I was terrified of having sex with him." I blinked back tears. "I just couldn't tell him. I know I should have, but I couldn't."

Skipman and Fredericks looked at each other and Fredericks nodded.

"That's very brave of you, Miss Wycherly," Fredericks said, soothingly. "We appreciate your honesty."

"You won't tell anyone, will you?" I asked.

"Of course, not," said Fredericks.

The detectives got up and Sid saw them out.

"Well," Sid said as he returned to the living room. "Your flair for melodrama has saved us again."

I shuddered. "I feel like such a fraud. Sid, this is turning into a nightmare."

He said down next to me and put his arms around my shoulders. "I wonder how much the police have?"

"Who knows?" I said, snuggling into his embrace.

"The thing that really bothers me is that I caught some definite antagonism toward the FBI," Sid said. "That's not normal around here."

"Huh?" I asked.

"L.A. area law enforcement and fire agencies are usually pretty good about working across jurisdictions," Sid explained. "And in the past, that's included the Feds. I'd better call Henry. He deserves to know about this."

From what I heard on my end of the phone call, Henry was curious about what was in the official police report. Sid offered to go get it. Henry (apparently) said no. Sid said that the odds were against him getting caught. Henry ordered Sid not to go after it. Sid hung up the living room phone and looked at me.

"Henry said not to get that report," he said.

"That's what it sounded like."

"Except that I really want to see what's in it."

"Sid, if Henry said no, he's probably got a good reason."

"Which is why I'm not going after it," said Sid with a sigh.

The doorbell rang again and this time it was Kathy and Jesse. I let them in and we all sat down in the living room, with Jesse and Kathy on the couch and Sid and I each in a different chair.

"Lisa," Jesse began slowly. "Kathy and I have to go make a statement with the Hernandez family in a bit." He swallowed. "There's just one thing stopping us." They both looked at me.

"I don't understand," I said.

Kathy took a deep breath. "Lisa, we know something is going on with you." She nodded at Sid. "And with you, too. We just don't know what. You dodge people all the time. And that time we were on vacation, you made that phone call, supposedly to Sid, but you used a local number for San Diego. I saw you dial it, and there weren't nearly enough digits to be calling here. Then you lied to me about it. And Friday night, you got up in the middle of the night to talk to someone on a radio in your truck that I would have sworn you did not have. And you act weird sometimes. When people sneak up on you, you act like you're going to attack. Then Chip Weaver told me that one time he tried to follow you home in his car. He said you ditched him so fast, his head spun."

"And that's not the half of it," Jesse said. "When George died, he was doing that all-nighter in his studio. He'd seen the guys with the guns again. He called me to tell me. And he saw your truck. He was scared to death that you had driven right into whatever those guys were planning, so he went to warn you off."

All the air left my gut and I suddenly felt dizzy.

"I don't what George saw, but it wasn't Lisa's truck," Sid was saying.

"Then why is Lisa sitting there, looking like she's punch drunk?" Jesse demanded.

"It doesn't matter," I gasped. I took a couple of deep breaths. "It doesn't matter. Whatever George saw or didn't see, it doesn't matter."

"Yes, it does, Lisa," Jesse said. "The FBI is covering up George's death. Another one of us has gotten shot by a cop, and all they want to do is pretend it didn't happen. Or that George somehow deserved it, because he must have been up to no good. He was a Mexican, after all."

I saw the pain in Kathy's and Jesse's eyes and knew where it came from. How many times had Jesse been hassled by the police just for dropping by Sid's house? Sid had even bailed Jesse out of jail when he'd been arrested simply because he'd been waiting in his car for me to come out of the house. Kathy had a cousin doing jail time for a crime he didn't commit. They didn't talk often about these things, but I'd seen enough to have an idea of what they were up against.

"It wasn't like that," said Sid.

Jesse and Kathy froze.

"Sid, they don't want to hear that," I said softly. I swallowed. "The problem is, I can't tell you what's going on."

"Why the hell not?" Jesse bounced up.

"Because I can't," I said, sniffling.

"You don't want to know, anyway," said Sid, standing also.

"Sid!" I snapped. "Jesse, I can not tell you." I glanced at Sid, who was back in his chair. "We can not tell you."

"You're not telling me anything!" Jesse snarled.

I bounced up. "It's a better answer than George ever got!"

"I don't care." Jesse turned to go. "Come on, Kathy."

Kathy was looking at me and over at Sid. "Wait, Jesse."

He turned. "We're not going to get any satisfaction here."

"No," said Kathy. "But it's not their fault. They really can't tell us." She looked at me again. "What is it? Some sort of contractual thing?"

"Something like that," I said softly. I looked over at Sid. "There isn't much I could say, even if I could tell you guys. But I can promise you this much. It isn't a cover-up and it's not because George was Mexican. It's because the person who killed him is still out there."

Sid slowly stood. "Believe me, Jesse, if I thought there was even the slightest chance that the Feds were trying to cover some racist nonsense, I'd be yelling, too. I do accept that I don't necessarily see things the same way you do. But I'm doing the best I can here."

Jesse looked down at his feet and shook his head. I walked up to him.

"Jesse, you have reason to wonder about what happened to George and every reason to wonder about me," I said softly.

"But the gun, it was FBI," Jesse said.

"That's what they said," I replied. "I don't know what's behind that and I don't have any way to find out. It's possible that the person who killed George did because of George's race. I don't know. But I'm reasonably confident that the reason the FBI isn't saying anything is because they want to catch the guy, not cover up who did it. Not because they're blameless that way, but something else that I can't talk about."

Jesse looked at me, then looked over at Sid. "Are you sure?"

"As sure as we can be," Sid said.

"Alright." He sighed deeply. "Now what?"

I blinked back more tears. "Whatever you think best. If you need to make a statement, go ahead."

Kathy got up and patted Jesse's arm. "Come on, honey. Let's go talk this over."

She, at least, smiled at me as Sid and I walked them to the door.

When Sid and I were, at last, alone, I sank onto the living room couch, trying not to cry.

"Terrific," Sid complained. "Just terrific."

"I'm sorry."

"No!" Sid waved at me. "You were fine. There's just something that's not making sense."

I sniffled. "You're right. Why wouldn't they have put out an all-points bulletin, or whatever, to get this guy? I mean, being one of their own is embarrassing, but still, he's been debriefed. There's no reason not to put the public onto him."

"I can see not wanting to call attention to the espionage," said Sid, pacing. "But that's it, and given the press this case is now getting, it doesn't make sense not to put out the Most Wanted notice."

I shoved the heels of my hands into my eyes. "If only my brain didn't feel like it was stuffed with cotton wool."

Sid chortled in spite of himself. "I love it when you fall into British-isms."

"That's it!" I sat up straight. "Our British friend. What's-her-name? A12, at least, that's how we knew her when we met in Paris. Although Dragon called her Marian."

"Okay. I know who you're talking about."

"She was in San Francisco. You said that made sense."

Sid frowned. "Well, they were here last winter tracking this guy."

"What was it she called him? That fence-walking pest."

"In other words, a double agent." Sid began pacing the living room again.

"We know he was one of our own," I pointed out. "Angelique recognized him, even if she couldn't remember his name." I stopped.

Sid and I looked at each other, remembering the same thing at the same time.

"Henry knows him," Sid said, softly.

"Could that mean we know him? As ourselves?"

Sid shrugged. "I have no idea, but that would account for a lot, especially with them wanting us to lay low for so long. But then why did we get tagged to hold him until the transfer?"

"Or me get sent to San Francisco?" I frowned. "No, wait. They asked for me."

Sid sighed and looked at me. "Well, there's no way of knowing right now."

"You're right." I looked at my watch without seeing what time it was. "There's got to be something I can do. Maybe I should try getting some sewing done."

I started for my rooms. Sid followed. I turned on him.

"Sid, I appreciate you being here for me, but you

don't have to stay glued to my side."

He smiled and nodded. I went to my rooms. A little while later, I heard him leaving.

I suppose it shouldn't have surprised me. It had been several days, at least, since he'd last gone out. And it was ridiculous to assume that Sid would try to stay celibate when I couldn't move in with him. Still, my eyes filled at the thought of him and another woman. It wouldn't mean anything, he'd said. Funny, it still seemed to mean everything to me.

July 15–16, 1984

When Sid offered to go with me to mass the next morning, I nearly bit his head off. I also relented and was glad that he was there. It was just so awkward, with so many people coming up to me and telling me how terribly sorry they were. Jesse came up during the Sign of Peace and gave me a big hug, which helped a lot.

"You okay?" I asked him softly.

"As okay as I can be," he said. "At least, the Hernandez's aren't asking me to move out of the condo."

"He told me he wanted you to have it," I said.

Jesse nodded. "His sister, Marisela, told me that, too."

Marisela was George's sister that was closest to him in age.

Sid hung back. He'd gotten a couple evil glares. I later heard that there'd been a rumor that Sid had taken advantage of George being dead to finally seduce me. Given how guilty I was feeling then, I'm glad that I didn't know about that part. Still, it was frustrating to see the tight smiles as people greeted me, then Sid.

"You don't deserve it," I complained as Sid drove us to a nearby restaurant. Frank and Esther had invited us and Kathy and Jesse to go to lunch after mass.

"So what?" Sid answered. "They're petty, obnoxious people. I do not give a damn what they think of me and cannot for the life of me understand why you do."

He had a point, so I did not say anything more.

It turned out to be a nice lunch, then Sid and I had to get home before Mae got there. We had a quiet afternoon, then she and Sid put together a salad for our dinner. I still wasn't eating much and soon we headed out to Hollywood and the funeral home where George was. As we waited for the rosary service to begin,

I paced in the lobby outside the viewing room. I had already seen that it was an open casket, and that had me a little freaked. You see, I have this thing about corpses. I'm terrified of them, which sounds a little weird, considering the business I'm in. But it's actually because of that business. I got traumatized early on, and it's never gotten any better.

I was hoping that by waiting, we could sit in the back, but as soon as we entered the viewing room, we were ushered right up to the front row of pews. Kathy and Jesse were already there. The Hernandez family sat in the same row, across the aisle. Mrs. Hernandez wore a long black veil but managed to smile at me. Mr. Hernandez remained stiff and unemotional.

I tried looking everywhere but at the coffin ahead of me. Being right up front, I could see a little of George's nose and forehead. When Father John got up to the podium near the foot of the casket, I kept my eyes focused on him.

He looked so terribly sad as he cleared his throat.

"I want to thank Monsignor Cuestas for allowing me to be here and speak tonight," he said slowly, nodding at the priest sitting next to Mrs. Hernandez. He paused. "It is never easy burying someone who has left us before his time. It's worse when violence is what took him from us. I've done enough of those funerals in my time and will probably do more before I'm done. But George was also a friend of mine, as were many of the other kids I buried. I tell you right now, it does not get easier. I am here as a partner in your grief. I loved George."

Father coughed, then continued. "I met him as a young freshman at UCLA, where I was doing some campus ministry. He was eager, passionate, diving in deep into whatever was needed, and at the same time, always worried that whatever he was doing wasn't enough."

I felt my gut twisting again. Worse yet, out of the corner of my eye, I saw one of George's sisters glaring at their father.

"He used to ask me how could taking silly pictures help the poor?" John continued. "Then he did that series on skid row, which got us the funding we needed to build the Rossmore Family Shelter."

That had happened long before I'd met George. I'd heard about the series, but not from him.

"True, George could be stubborn, especially when he'd made up his mind about something."

I flushed.

"But he was one of the biggest-hearted men I've ever known, and that heart was permanently on display on his sleeve at all times." John cleared his throat again. "So we are here. We are here in our hurt and in our love for George. But we are here for more than that. We come to pray, to cry out, to yell at God, but mostly we come because we believe in something more than we have here down on earth. Yes, we are in pain because one of ours has been taken away, but we take comfort in that Christian promise of life after death, that we will one day be reunited with George. And so we begin. In the name of the Father, the Son, and the Holy Spirit."

The prayers went by quickly, and I was glad of that. We were hardly through the first decade of Hail Marys before Sid shifted in utter boredom. Still, it was all too soon before John was offering us the opportunity to come forward and pay our last respects. I balked. Kathy and Jesse needed me to move so that they could view the body.

"Come on," hissed Mae, giving me a little shove.

"I can't," I whispered.

"Lisa, please. It's rude not to."

"Mae," Sid growled. "Don't push her."

"I can't," I sniffed.

"Lisa, don't make a scene." Mae was good and annoyed.

I bolted from the viewing room, sobbing. I hit the lobby and stopped for a moment, uncertain which way to go.

"Lisa." Sid touched my arm.

The panic filled me again and I tried to run, but Sid held me close.

"It's alright, honey. It's alright," he whispered. "Go ahead and cry. You'll be fine."

It took a while to get myself back under control. I was still trembling when the viewing room doors opened. I pulled away from Sid and tried to find a tissue. He had one and I took it.

The crowd of teens, relatives, and other people slowly filtered into the lobby. I slid back to the wall and waited for Mae to come out of the viewing room. Sid went in to get my purse.

"I don't understand it, either," Mae was telling somebody as she left the room. "But she has gotten this phobia of looking at dead bodies."

"Hey, here she is!" called Frank Lonnergan's voice. He swept up and pulled me from the wall. "You doing okay? Sid told us about your phobia."

"Just feeling a little silly, is all," I said with a subdued sniff.

"Happens to the best of us. Come on. We're going to go to Jefferson's for a drink."

"Sure. Except that Sid drove."

"He's coming with us." Frank squeezed me around the shoulders. "You'll drop your sister off back home, then meet us there. Okay?"

"Okay."

I was looking for Sid when Father John approached.

"Got a second?" he asked.

"Yeah. You okay?" I smiled weakly at him. "I forgot that you and George were that close."

He shrugged. "It comes with the job. I've got a pretty good support system, though." He looked at me and winced, then checked to see if anyone could overhear us. "I, uh, wonder if you know anything about what happened to George. I want to know if I should be raising hell about the FBI or not."

I chuckled sadly. "I was there. We were doing a prisoner exchange. George saw my truck and came to investigate, and that's how he got shot. The prisoner popped his cuffs and stole Sid's gun. Ours are FBI issue, so that's how that happened."

"Crap." John blinked his eyes for a moment, then looked at me. "Don't tell me. You're feeling really guilty about now."

I shrugged. "A little. But Sid pointed out that there was no way we could have expected George to be there, let alone to come out and face off a couple of armed strangers. We were wearing masks, you see. Anyway, if you want to protest the supposed coverup, go ahead. It's not going to change anything."

John sighed. "Well, will I see you at Jefferson's?"

"Yeah. I'm glad you're coming."

It was a somber party, and I noticed Sid and John spending some time talking to each other. It didn't seem to be anything deep and they were both smiling by the end.

I wish things could have gone nearly as well the next day. The funeral mass was beyond dreary. There was almost no singing. An organist played the hymns rather badly, according to Sid and Frank. Monsignor Cuestas officiated and gave possibly one of the longest and most boring sermons I had ever heard. It was supposed to be comforting. All it did was make me fidgety. You'd have thought, given how long the Monsignor had known the family, that he could have made things more personal. The graveside service wasn't any better. Worse yet, at the end, Mrs. Hernandez screamed and threw herself over the casket. The weird thing is that it wasn't the most convincing performance I had ever seen. I mean, I want to be charitable, here, and she was grieving the loss of her only son. I'll leave it at that.

We did stop in at the Hernandez place afterward for the catered buffet lunch. But the food that was supposed to be hot was icy cold. The cold food items were limp and warm. None of it looked edible at all, and I set a pretty low standard for what constitutes edible. Sid and I were both relieved when our pagers began vibrating.

We made our goodbyes quickly and hurried out of there.

"I feel like such a heel," I said to Sid.

"Why? That was a disaster," Sid said.

"But they're grieving. You have to cut them some slack."

Sid rolled his eyes. "Cutting them some slack would be ignoring some mismatched place settings. Maybe a burnt crust or two. That was nothing short of a fiasco."

I sighed. Sid was right. Still, it seemed rather churlish to complain.

It took a few minutes to get to a payphone. Sid made the call. His eyebrows rose. He said yes and that we'd be there as soon as we could, but that we were looking at a good thirty minutes. Well, that's what it looked like he said from where I sat in the passenger seat of his BMW.

"What's going on?" I asked, looking at him anxiously.

"We've got a meeting," he said, sliding into the driver's seat and turning on the ignition. "And not just a meeting, but a meeting at one of the toniest restaurants in L.A."

"Really?"

"Yeah." Sid stayed focused on getting us around the curves of Mulholland Drive, but just barely. "Honey, this place is so exclusive, even on my pile, I have to wait six months for my reservation."

"That's weird," I said, frowning. "Could this meeting have been planned that far in advance?"

"I have no idea," Sid said.

The restaurant was rather humble looking from the outside. It was on Melrose Avenue, just before it got to the really trendy end. Inside, the tablecloths were white, and the plates were black, and the decor minimalist, at best. The room was open, and unlike other places, the tables were all well apart from each other. Two men in suits sat at a table, in an intense conference as they ate. Nearby, three men sat with an actress I recognized. She smiled but looked vaguely disgusted with them.

I saw Henry first, at a table in the far corner of the room but stopped short when I saw the pair sitting next to him. The top was set for five. She was fairly small, with fluffy short blonde hair. He was much taller and had a rather horsey face.

"Them," Sid grumbled.

I glanced at him. "Yeah."

Henry saw us and waved us over. She smiled at the waiter and we were barely seated before menus appeared in front of us, as well as glasses of water with a slice of cucumber, and individual bread plates, each with a perfect, light brown roll and a rosette of butter next to it.

"Sid, Lisa," Henry began, his voice and face neutral. "May I present—"

"Oh, let's do keep it informal," she said. "I'm Marian. This is Andrew."

When I'd last seen her, her name had been Mrs. Ellis. That had obviously not been her real name. I shivered because it seemed as though Marian and Andrew were, in fact, their real names.

"Nice to meet you," I said. I glanced at my menu and paled. Not because of the selection but because there were no prices on it.

"And it is our pleasure to act as hosts today," Andrew said, giving me the once over.

"That is very kind of you," Sid said.

Sid and I passed a puzzled glance between us. We started with cocktails. Sid opted for bourbon and water. I chose a martini. I don't usually like them unless I can get really good gin. I figured this place would have passable gin. Andrew whispered to the water, and when the cocktails appeared, the bourbon was in a snifter and a good bit darker than usual. The martini glass was frosted and icy. Andrew and Marian had large glasses of gin and tonic, and Henry also had a snifter, but with scotch.

Sid picked up his glass and sniffed.

"It's a lovely single barrel out of Bardstown, Kentucky," Marian told him. "I do hope you like it."

Sid's eyebrows rose and he sipped.

"It's amazing," he said. "Thank you for your kindness."

I sipped my martini. "Wow. That's really good."

"Yes, well, Henry told us you've had quite the trying morning," Marian said.

"I'm afraid so," said Sid. He looked at Henry.

"I told them about the funeral," Henry said. "And about Lisa's relationship to the victim."

"Our deepest condolences, dear," Marian said, then looked Sid over, then smiled at me. "Now, may I suggest we table more serious matters until we've enjoyed our lunch?" She smiled at me again. "In spite of this place's dreadful pretension, the food is very good."

It was, indeed. We had lovely radish salads as starters, then a clear bouillon with bits of crab and green onion in it. I had ordered the roasted duck breast with apricot sauce. Sid had chicken of some sort. I forget what the others had ordered. I know Marian enjoyed what she'd ordered because she sighed with exquisite pleasure when she tasted it. My duck was incredible, tender and rich.

The chatter was mostly about Los Angeles, what to do, what venues would be the most crowded for the Olympics, which were less than two weeks away, what would happen to all the traffic in the area. Finally, Sid asked the question that both of us had been wondering.

"So, what brings you two to Los Angeles?" He smiled as if he'd only asked as part of the pleasant banter.

"The Olympics, of course," said Marian. "You couldn't expect us not to come for that." She suddenly sighed, then put down her knife and fork and delicately dabbed at her lips with her napkin. "In any event, there are obviously enterprises of great pith and moment to discuss."

Andrew cleared his throat.

Marian tittered. "He does hate it when I quote Shakespeare."

"My dearest," Andrew said with bored affection. "I do not mind in the least if you quote Shakespeare. It is your misquoting of the good bard to which I object. It is enterprises of great pitch and moment. Not pith."

"Oh, dear. How careless of me," Marian said, her tone utterly lacking in contrition.

"The bottom line," said Henry quickly, "is that thanks to Andrew and Marian, we know where Len Powers is."

"Who?" I asked.

Sid looked at Henry. "Len Powers? You mean the guy in San Diego who was heading up the National Security Team?"

"Unfortunately," Henry said.

The National Security Team was kind of an inter-agency group that handled arrests by undercover agents and people who worked for groups like Quickline.

"How long have you known it was him?" I asked, feeling more than a little irritated.

"Only since we went to Mission Viejo together and you asked that sales agent about his description," Henry said. "That's when I knew who he was and why Upline had been keeping me in the dark. I'd worked with him too often. We'd had good reason to believe, based on some of the evidence you two dug up last winter, that we were dealing with someone in the agency."

"On our end, we had found out that there was a person in your FBI who was likely to be the source of our trouble," Marian continued. "The problem was that he was working both sides."

Henry glared at her briefly. "Which meant was that we had to be certain that he was genuinely selling us out."

"The problem with walking the fence," Marian interrupted. "Is that at some point or other, one side is going to expect you to prove your loyalty. It turns out that Powers pest had agreed to hand over your entire courier operation."

Sid frowned and looked at Henry. "Quickline?"

"Yes," said Henry. "The other side has been trying to bring that down since before last year."

"We're just couriers," I said. "Wouldn't they want a harder target, like missile sites?"

"They know where the missile sites are," Andrew said.

"And intelligence is only useful if it gets into the right hands at the right time," Marian said. "That courier network of yours is vital to all our interests."

Henry shifted. "Marian and Andrew and their people have seen to bugging the Rumanian consulate."

"We did that last winter," Marian said.

"We didn't get that much from it, though," said Henry.

"We all thought they found the bugs," Marian said with a laugh. "Very disappointing. They were very good ones. It turns out, however, that Mr. Mihaili, our Rumanian friend, is simply that cautious. More to the point, he is harboring our fence-walking pest."

"In addition," Andrew said. "It appears that they are going to ship him to Rumania very soon, probably before the end of the week. They are only waiting until Mr. Powers collects his dossier from where he's hidden it."

"Do we know where?" Sid asked.

"I'm afraid not," Marian said. "And Mr. Powers is not going to tell them."

"Why not?" I asked. "It would make it a lot easier for them to get what they want."

"Yes, one would think," Marian replied. "But there seems to be an appalling lack of trust all around. Mr. Powers does not want to simply tell Mr. Mihaili where the dossier is, as Mr. Mihaili will simply grab it, then do away with Mr. Powers. Mr. Mihaili, for his part, does not want to enable Mr. Powers to pick up the dossier, as he does not trust Mr. Powers to return with it. Nor will he let Mr. Powers retrieve the dossier under guard. We're guessing that Mr. Mihaili does not have the resources for a sufficient guard, and as we all know, to our sorrow, that Mr. Powers is quite the escape artist."

"One thing that is clear," said Henry. "It's that Powers does not want to be returned to Europe without that dossier. If he does, he's dead."

Andrew nodded. "We, and presumably Mr. Mihaili, are hoping that he will find a way to go after the dossier on his own."

"The problem is what if he doesn't?" Marian added. "We've got a potentially very damaging dossier laying around somewhere and no idea of where to find it."

"We have some idea," said Henry, reaching into his inside jacket pocket. "We found this in a corner of his desk in the San Diego office."

It was a large corner off of a piece of office paper with a line drawing of what looked like a lot of housing plats around cul-de-sacs. One was circled.

"A housing development," said Sid. He shrugged. "We know he liked using them."

"But why would he leave a valuable file someplace where he was squatting?" I asked.

Henry shrugged. "We're guessing that he didn't want the file on him, and left it someplace thinking he'd be able to get back to it in a short time."

That made sense.

"It seems like a pretty long shot," Sid said.

"It is," said Henry. "But it's the best lead we've got."

"It's the only lead we've got," Marian grumbled. "Besides trying to keep tabs on our slippery friend."

"Which we will do, of course," said Andrew.

"In the meantime, we get to go house hunting," Sid

said and then looked at Henry. "How much support do we have on our end?"

"Strictly Quickline crews," Henry said. "We can't afford to let anyone else see that damn dossier."

We finished lunch shortly afterward. Henry followed Sid and me back to Sid's place, where we got out a couple of Triple-A maps and the real estate section from the day before's paper.

I checked the answering machines while Sid and Henry started marking up the maps with what they found in the newspapers.

"All reporters," I announced when I was done. "But it seems like it's easing up. I don't think we got nearly as many calls today as we did yesterday."

"Good," said Sid. He turned back to Henry. "Alright, we can probably eliminate the Mission Viejo and Pomona tracts."

I stared at the maps. "Henry, last winter, when those two NST guys came after me when I was trying to make that secrets buy. That sting we were setting up?"

"Yeah?"

"Len Powers was their boss."

Henry looked over at me. "That's right. So?"

"Well, could it have been Powers that leaked the story about the FBI cover-up to the press?"

"Why would you say that?" Henry asked.

"Do we know who did?"

Henry thought. "Actually, no. I did talk to a couple of the guys. They're usually pretty straight with me. I did ask them if LAPD was the leak, and they said it wasn't. In fact, one told me that the Hernandez family got the tip through an anonymous phone call and they went after us and the LAPD."

"What's that got to do with what we're trying to figure out?" Sid asked.

"What if Len Powers was the person who tipped the Hernandez family?" I asked. "By creating a stir, it would make it harder for us to find him unless we made it public that we were looking for him. And us having to go public was exactly what he wanted."

Henry growled. "Lisa's got a point, Sid. He's always been pretty cocksure of himself. Wouldn't call in backup. Always knows what he's doing."

"Fine," said Sid. "But how does that affect what we're doing?"

"If he's that cocksure," I said. "Then we shouldn't eliminate the places we know he's already used. He could have gone back to them, assuming that we wouldn't check them twice."

Both Sid and Henry groaned. But they had to agree I had a point. We all went back to work, debating how far out to go and who would do what. The plan was pretty simple, but as it fell into place, a cold, nagging fear settled into my stomach. There was so much territory to cover, and no way of knowing if we were even guessing right about the housing developments. If we were wrong, it would be devastating.

We were on the road by nine that morning, headed to Mission Viejo in Sid's BMW, which meant that he was driving. Since Sid had driven there that first time, the month before, we had no trouble finding it again. The agents in the sales office were busy gossiping amongst themselves when we arrived.

Henry had told us he would send an alert to all the various sales offices in the area about a suspect posing as an FBI agent in order to use an empty house. Apparently, he had done it overnight. The cops had already brought a copy of the alert to the sales office we were in, and the staff could talk of nothing else. No surprise since the fake agent had actually been there. It was also the day off for the sales agent I had spoken with when I was there with Henry. So, Sid and I posed as house hunters rather than real FBI agents.

We oohed and ahhed through the model tour, recognized the model for the house Sid had been kept in, then were offered a chance to look the place over. It hadn't sold yet, so we took advantage of the situation, and spent over an hour searching every inch of it. Sid had talked the nice young woman who had brought us up there into heading back to the office so that we could discuss the pros and cons of the place in private. After we were done and convinced there wasn't anything to find, we walked down the hill, skirted the sales office and hurried on.

We ate lunch in Tustin, at a cafe we found, then went on to a housing tract there. I'd been kept briefly in a house at the tract the previous winter. That house had not only been sold, the new owners had been living there since May. The good thing was that we were able to scratch that entire tract off our list. Almost all of the houses had been sold and it was far too populated for our kind of squatters to find it useful.

From there, we went up to Pomona. We didn't get up there until the middle of the afternoon. We did the model tour, then tried to see some of the actual houses. The sales representative refused to let us. We left the sales office, then went ahead and drove around what streets there. Based on what we'd seen in the models and what Sid remembered about the house he'd been kept in, there were five possible houses.

The first two houses clearly weren't right. Something always gets left behind when the squatters leave, bits of tape, re-painted spots, stuff that no one would ever pay attention to, but still there. The houses had no sign, whatsoever, of any of that. The third house, we couldn't get into. There was a big "Sold" sign in the front yard, which was still dirt, and we could see workers through the windows. Sid felt the other two houses were more possible, but we didn't find anything. We left the tract in pretty low spirits.

Now, the truth of the matter is that both Sid and I knew darned well that the first day of a hunt like this was most likely not going to turn up anything. I have no idea why we were expecting to hit the jackpot straight out. Perhaps it was the tension of the day. [Or, in my case, a certain other tension. - SEH] In any case, by the time we got on the freeway to Los Angeles, we were snipping at each other. It didn't help that between the regular rush hour traffic and an accident near downtown, we were crawling by the time we got past the 605.

I checked the clock on the dashboard. "Great. It's almost six and we're not even to the East L.A. interchange. Sid, we've got to pull over."

"Don't tell me you have to go," he grumbled.

"No. I've got to get something to eat. We'll be lucky if we get to Beverly Hills by seven and I don't want to be late to Bible Study."

"There's no place to eat around here," he said, checking his blind spot to the right, nonetheless. "And besides, stopping now to eat dinner isn't going to make you any less late."

"I was hoping we could, for once, do a drive-through," I grumbled. "It's not like it's going to kill you."

"It's about respecting our bodies, Lisa."

I snorted.

"And let's not get holier than thou about what I do with my body," Sid snarled.

"I didn't say anything."

"By this point, you don't have to. My sex habits are not causing near the harm to my body that your junk food habit is causing yours."

[Had we but known that line of reasoning could have been debunked in a New York second by the AIDS epidemic. If I recall correctly, it hadn't really affected the straight community yet, although I know I had heard about it by then. And to think all I was scared of was herpes. - SEH]

"So you say," I said. "I'm still perfectly healthy."

"That you know of. Not to mention your blessed scriptures also tell you to take care of your body."

"They say a hell of a lot more about avoiding cheap sex."

Silent, angry tension blanketed both of us. I blinked my eyes and stared out the passenger window.

"It would never be cheap," he said, his voice so soft and hurt I barely heard him.

"I know." I kept my eyes fixed at the cars surrounding us. "I wasn't talking about me."

Sid let out a full breath of air. We continued on in silence. Sid was hurt, I could tell and I was just as hurt. The traffic on the Santa Monica freeway suddenly loosened up and Sid got off at Robertson. We stopped just long enough for me to get some rolled tacos. I held off eating them while I was in the car. When we pulled into the garage and got out of the car, Sid started for the inside door.

"Sid," I called. "Um, I owe you an apology. That

was a really cheap shot. I'm sorry."

Sid turned and looked at me. "I set you up for it with my own." He sighed and continued awkwardly. "So, I accept your apology and offer my own."

"Accepted. Friends?"

"God, I sure hope so." His smile was wan but genuine.

"I am."

"Good." He nodded. "Why don't you get going? You don't want to be late. I'll give Henry our report. Maybe find out who bought that house we couldn't get into."

"That probably can't hurt. See you tomorrow."

I so wanted to hold him and have him kiss my hair, but he was right. It was getting late and I needed to head out. As it was, I got to church a little early and ate my tacos in the truck.

As I walked in, Frank was at the front of the room, playing his guitar softly. He glanced at me, and as I got hugs from our friends, the tune slid into "Sad Lisa."

"You okay?" asked Esther, giving Frank a glare.

"No. It's fine," I said. "In fact, that's exactly how I feel right now. That song has been haunting me since—"

I choked. It had been haunting me since the night George had proposed. The proposal that had eventually pushed Sid into asking me to move into his bedroom, which I couldn't do, and George was dead and Sid was off probably getting laid and I was there at Bible Study feeling like a complete fraud because while I was grieving George, I wasn't missing a beloved fiance. I burst into tears.

I was about to run when Kathy and Esther slid their arms around me.

"That idiot," Esther grumbled, tears rolling onto her cheeks. "Why did he have to play that song?"

"It's okay, Esther," I said, sniffing. "I just need to do a little crying. We probably all do."

We did. Everyone in the group had been touched by George, and the tears flowed freely. He had been a very generous, loving man, filled with ideals and the passion to do good works. It was what I had loved about him. And I had loved him. Sid was right about that. I had accepted George's proposal because I loved him. I had found it hard to break it off because I was afraid that I was going to have to be cruel to get him to understand that we were not getting married. And I was afraid because I had loved him. The whole mess had been because I had loved George.

I cried, finally able to grieve for George's loss. Not just his death, which was still utterly terrible, but for the dream of the relationship that really never could have happened, even had Sid not been around. George had thought I was the woman of his dreams. He hadn't really known me, and that wasn't the spy business, it was me and who I am.

We were all getting a hold of ourselves when Dan Williams got us all going again by announcing that he was considering canceling camp because of George's death.

"George's death has really hurt all of us," he explained over the clamor. "I don't know that it's fair to the kids or to George's memory to go on as if nothing has happened."

"But George wouldn't want you to cancel camp," Jesse said. "He loved camp. It was his time to really be there for the kids, especially some of the tough ones."

"We can't pretend that George isn't dead or that we're not feeling it," I said. "But that doesn't mean we need to cancel camp. We and the kids probably need it more than ever. Why don't we dedicate this camp to George's memory? Say prayers for him and his family."

"And the bastard that shot him," grumbled Frank.

That caused another uproar. Dan finally got control of the meeting.

"Alright. We'll keep camp going," he said. "I don't want to talk about who shot George and who's covering it up or not. It's not going to change anything and will just divide us."

We went on to finalizing plans, assigning cabins, and doing a lot of the last-minute work that always needed doing before camp. We sang one final round of songs, then broke up.

In the parking lot, Jesse and Kathy came up to me.

"Want to meet us at Jefferson's in a few?" Jesse asked. "We need to talk."

"Oh, great," I said. "What now?"

"Nothing to worry about," said Kathy. "But we need to talk and I'd rather we did it away from everyone."

I entered the bar on pins and needles. Kathy and Jesse showed up about five minutes later. Jesse found us a table near the back. I slid into the spot with my back to the wall. Jesse and Kathy sat next to each other across the table from me.

"Well?" I asked.

Jesse took a deep breath. "Kathy and I have had quite the day."

"You alright?"

Kathy laughed. "More than. That's kind of the problem. In a good way."

"George's will was read today," Jesse said. "They called me in with all his family there." He blinked his eyes with a strained laugh. "George left everything to me. I mean his family got a couple things. But all his money. His condo. It's all mine. And his family isn't going to contest it. His dad told me that he wasn't going to object to his son's last act of kindness."

"After the way he treated you?" I gasped.

"I know." Jesse shrugged. "I don't get it, either."

Kathy sniggered. "I'm pretty sure Marisela and maybe one of his other sisters had something to do with it."

I had to snigger, as well. "Or maybe even George's mom. Wow. That's terrific, you guys."

"You sure?" Kathy asked, eying me.

I suddenly sniffed. "No. It's great. George told me the day before he was killed that he was going to change his will. I didn't want him to. I didn't want his money. I have my own."

Jesse's eyes narrowed. "Why do I suddenly get the feeling that wasn't the only reason?"

I shook my head. "Okay. I did love George. I really came to terms with that tonight. But... I was going to break it off. We really weren't right for each other. I'm too independent and he didn't get that, and..." I shrugged.

"Well, thank God you had come to your right senses," Kathy groaned.

"We were getting so scared we were going to have to talk to the two of you," Jesse said.

"What?" I think my mouth fell open.

"Honey, you and George were not right for each other," Jesse said. "Kathy and I were beside ourselves. We didn't want to say anything to either one of you. If we talked to George, he'd only get more bent on marrying you, and we didn't want you telling him and the same thing happening."

"You mean you didn't want us to get married?"

"It wasn't that," said Kathy. "Well, it was."

"George was living in one of his fantasies," Jesse said. "You know how he'd get that way. He saw how quiet you were, most of the time, and he liked how you would stand up for folks when someone was being mean. He also saw how strong your faith is and thought it meant you would fall in line."

"I knew damned well it was your faith that made you stand up to people," Kathy said. "And that you weren't going to fall in line for anybody at any time."

"Hey, I loved George like my own brother," Jesse said. "But you know how it is when you get real close to people like that. You still love them, but you gotta be honest about them, too."

"Yeah. Wow. I guess it's a really good thing that George didn't a chance to change his will," I said. "Although, he did say that he was going to sign the condo over to you, Jesse. I doubt he would have changed that. He really didn't want you left out in the cold. And I didn't want him to change it, so you don't have to feel guilty about me not getting anything."

Jesse chuckled. "Oh, there's plenty of guilt to go around." He sniffed suddenly. "I am glad about having some money, but I would much rather have George back. Having his money doesn't come near to compensating for losing him."

"You are such a good man, Jesse," Kathy said, covering his hands with her own and looking at him so fondly. She looked at me and grinned. "There's other news."

Jesse laughed. "See, I had promised Kathy that the second I could put a roof over her head, we were going to get married. We signed the probate forms, left the lawyer's office, and I took her straight to the rectory. We waited a whole hour for John to get free, but we got our date."

"Really? Oh, wonderful!"

Kathy nodded, her eyes filling as she grinned. "Yeah. We are finally getting married. We decided to wait until next April, though. We'd heard George complaining about how all the good reception spots were already getting booked."

"April, huh?" I bit my lip and tried not to laugh. "You didn't happen to get the twentieth, did you?"

"Yes." Kathy grabbed my hands. "You don't mind, do you? We can change it."

"Are you kidding? You two deserve that spot far more than I ever did." I suddenly thought of something. "I'd better call Mama right away. I wonder if she's asked for her deposit back."

"What do you mean?" Jesse asked.

"On the reception space that she booked." I dove into my purse. "I've got the address here somewhere. I'll call Mama first thing in the morning, find out where she stands with the deposit, and you guys can check the place out. If you like it, you can have it."

"Your reception space, too?" Kathy asked.

"Why not?" I put my purse aside, having not found the address. "I wasn't going to be using it, and it'll be easier for Mama to get a full refund if all they have to do is transfer the booking to you guys."

Kathy couldn't help it. She squealed with delight, then started crying again.

"I'm so happy," she said sniffing. "And it feels so awful that it's only because George died. What's a girl to do?"

"Be happy," I said, blinking back my tears. "I'm not going to say that George would have wanted it that way. But he did love you guys very much, and he did want your happiness. That's why he was going to sign over the condo to Jesse when he moved out."

"He loved you, too, Lisa," Jesse said. "He kept saying how much he loved how independent you were and how you thought for yourself."

I couldn't help chuckling. "Thanks, Jesse."

We talked about George and laughed about George and cried about George for another hour or so, then headed home. It was almost midnight by that point. Sid's car was in the garage when I pulled in. I checked the alarm box and realized that he'd gone out and had only just gotten back, himself. He'd also put a note on my door, asking me to buzz his intercom when I got in so he'd know I'd gotten home okay, and reminding me that we were going running at the usual time.

I buzzed Sid in his room, then went to get ready for bed, myself. Sid buzzed back to let me know that he'd heard me, but nothing more. I felt terribly sad again, then remembered what Jesse had said about George, about how you have to be honest about the people you love, and still love them. Sid was who he was. He'd been trained to think that free love was normal and that it was abnormal to keep sex for marriage. He couldn't change that and his appetite any more than I could change my training and my appetite. I still loved him, and while he couldn't return those feelings of love, he obviously cared enough about me to worry when he'd gotten home ahead of me.

That was quite a lot, actually. I had no idea how things were going to fall out, and when I thought about it, I was pretty content with the way things were. Oh, things were not perfect, not by any stretch of the imagination. But my relationship with Sid was still a darned good one and there was even room for a little bit of hope.

By the next morning, I was actually glad that Sid had gone out the night before. He's impossibly grouchy when he gets horny, and he was in a much better mood that morning.

After our run and breakfast, we got dressed for house hunting. But before we left, I called Mama to ask about the deposit on the reception site.

"Oh, I am so glad you asked about that," she said. "I plumb forgot about it."

"Hold on, Mama. My friends Kathy and Jesse just decided to get married, and they got George's and my date at the parish. Do you mind if they take booking for the reception?"

"Not at all, but why don't you give me your friend Kathy's phone number?" She paused. "I managed to get us a bit of a courtesy discount, being in the industry and all. So, we're going to have to play this one real careful like."

I laughed. "How about if I give Kathy your number? I can't give hers without permission."

"Fair enough."

Mama then asked me how I was feeling, and I told her I was fine, which I was. I then called Kathy.

"Mama said to call you," I told her. "She says it's going to be a little tricky since she scored what she called a bit of a discount and what I'm willing to bet was a whopper."

Kathy laughed. "I think between my mother and my own money, we'll be alright. Thanks again, Lisa."

I never did find out what Mama had gotten or what Kathy ended up with. Kathy did book the space, though.

Sid appeared in the door between our offices. "Did I just hear you right? Kathy and Jesse are not only getting married, they got your wedding date at the church?"

"Yeah. Turns out George left Jesse everything he owned, which is quite a lot." I smiled at him.

"That's good." He paused. "And how are you feeling about it?"

"Perfectly fine. I wasn't going to be using that date. They deserve it."

"Okay." Sid nodded, then turned serious. "I just spoke with Henry and the news is not good."

"What's the matter?"

"Powers has been leaving the consulate. He's got someone with him, according to our British friends, but they keep ditching the tails."

"Do they have the dossier?"

"The Brits say no. Powers is still being pressured to produce it. And there's one other development. Angelique told Henry this morning that someone followed her home last night. Henry checked with the Brits and Powers was out of the consulate during that time."

I frowned. "Why follow Angelique? That makes no sense."

"I know." Sid shrugged. "Henry does not want Angelique staying alone tonight and suggested that she call me." He winced. "She said absolutely no thanks. The only thing soothing my wounded ego is that she does not want to go over to Henry's, either."

"Hmm. Would it be risking our cover too much if I volunteered to stay with her?"

Sid thought it over. "I don't see why it would. I'll call Henry."

Angelique must have been more worried than she'd let on because she was happy to call me and ask me to stay.

"I feel a little ridiculous," she said over the phone a few minutes later. "It's not that big a deal."

"Better safe than sorry," I told her. "Plus, it will be fun, and right now, I could use a little fun."

"Terrific. If I call in the order, do you mind picking up some pizza on your way over? Henry's putting a tail on me and has told me to go straight home tonight."

"As long as it's a large one."

We laughed and then hung up. I went ahead and packed for that night, bringing along some cards and a board game in addition to my nightgown, robe, and other stuff.

Sid and I took off for the Inland Empire again.

"Henry gave me a list," he told me as we whipped down Interstate 10 in his Beemer. "We got about five tracts, all in the Chino and Ontario area."

"And one in Diamond Bar," I said, flipping through the newspaper ads that Sid had put on a clipboard.

"Yeah. Henry also said that teams have flown in from all over the country. But we still have a lot of ground to cover."

"I guess we hope that the teams can keep following Powers, then get the dossier when he does."

Sid shook his head. "Not likely. If they want him to lead them somewhere, they can't get too close. And Powers is trained the same way we are. He's going to assume that he's being followed whether or not he is and take evasive maneuvers just on principle."

Sid did a last-second lane change, then sped up, sliding around cars, keeping an eye on his rearview mirror, as if to prove his point. Which was kind of funny, since I don't think he was even aware that he was doing it, the habit was so ingrained.

It was a really rough day, pretending to be happy and excited about buying a new home for our little family while wondering if we were going to miss something crucial and end up exposed and possibly dead. We checked house after house, none of which had even the least bit of errant tape, scratches on doors, or cleaned spots. We checked closet shelves, and when there were cabinets, those, too. We found absolutely nothing.

The tract in Diamond Bar was the last, and it was

getting close to five o'clock when we finished with the final house there. Sid's lead foot got a work out that afternoon. There really wasn't much to talk about, so we talked about what we liked and didn't like about the houses we'd seen. We'd both concluded what we most disliked was how they all looked alike, for the most part.

We got to Culver City, where Angelique's apartment was, in good time, and Sid didn't complain about stopping for the pizza. I also bought a salad. Sid had added a bottle of good chianti to the stuff I'd packed earlier that morning, although he pointed out that Angelique was quite a connoisseur, herself, and had a nice collection. The pizza was warm in my lap as we pulled up in front of Angelique's building.

"Lisa," Sid said as he turned off the ignition. "I've got a thing tonight that I can't really get out of. Made a promise weeks ago. Believe me, I'd much rather be here, keeping an eye on you two."

"We'll be fine, Sid."

"Anyway, here's the number where I'll be." He handed me a card.

That was odd, but I was grateful.

"I don't think anything's going to happen," I said.

"Well, call me if it does." He sighed. "And call me at home when it's time to come get you."

"I can take a bus home."

He shook his head. "I'll come get you. I know you can take care of yourself, but there's no point in asking for trouble."

"Fair enough."

I leaned over to kiss him, but he'd already gotten out of the car. Sighing, I got myself and the pizza box out, then leaned in to get my other belongings. Sid stayed out on the sidewalk as I went up to the building's glass doors and got myself buzzed in.

Angelique was waiting and had her table set and the wine already poured. It was something from the Napa Valley, she said.

"I feel so silly," she said as we sat down to eat.

"Can't hurt to be a little careful," I said. "And besides, it'll be nice to do a sleep-over."

Angelique chuckled as she dished some salad onto her plate.

"How have you been?" I asked.

"Really good," she said and took a sip of wine. "The time off has been really good for me. It's kind of funny. I liked the sex, and I was so proud of owning my own sexual power. But in the end, I was really devaluing myself. I'm probably not going to become a nun or anything. Still, I think I'm going to wait for a really good man before I go to bed again."

"You know, I think Sid would support you in that." I munched on a slice of pizza.

"What do you mean?"

"Sid really does care about you as a person," I said. "I mean, there's the thing with me."

"Aha!" Angelique slapped her hand on the table. "I knew it!"

"Okay. You were right about that. Just don't get too excited. We both have a lot to work out, me as well as him." I shrugged. "But he was worried about you and how you were doing and he does care about you as his friend."

"Huh." Angelique looked thoughtful for a moment, then turned her gaze on me. "And how are you doing? I mean, with losing your fiance and all."

"Oh, it's been pretty awful," I conceded. I blinked, then reached for my glass of wine. "Wow. This is really good."

"Are you avoiding me?"

"No. It's just that Sid said you were a real connoisseur and he was right." I set my glass down. "Anyway, thank God Sid has been around. He's been a real rock for me. I don't know what I would have done without him." I looked at her. "He, uh, asked me to move into his bedroom."

"It's about time." Angelique took a bite of salad,

then looked at me. "Uh, was this before or after George was killed?"

"Before," I said. "I couldn't, for all sorts of reasons, but I also decided that I needed to break up with George. I just didn't get a chance to before..."

"That must have made things rough."

And so dinner went on. Angelique was a great listener and agreed with me that Sid was probably not ready for me to move in any more than I was ready.

"I mean, he probably would give up sleeping around," she pointed out as we landed in her living room, wine glasses in hand. "I don't know if he'd be a hundred percent faithful, but it wouldn't surprise me if he was."

"What do you mean, Angelique?"

"Well, it's something he said to me the last time we were together. He liked making love to me because it was familiar and comfortable." Angelique grabbed a wine bottle off her coffee table and opened it. "Cabernet sauvignon, out of Calistoga. You want some?"

"Maybe in a bit."

"Anyway, he had never said anything like that to me before." Angelique filled her glass. "He's always been very complimentary, don't get me wrong. But it was always about how I looked and what he liked that I did. Surface stuff. And I would never have guessed that he'd like being familiar and comfortable. But now, I almost wonder if he's getting tired of playing around all the time. This is, by the way, in addition to being seriously hung up on you."

"Huh," I said. I sipped some more wine. "It's funny, but you may be right. When he dropped me off here tonight, he said he had to go to this thing, that he'd promised, but that he'd rather be here keeping an eye on us." I shuddered. "Henry really got him spooked, and I thought that was why he'd rather be here. But he didn't sound too excited about the thing, either."

"Really?" Angelique's jaw dropped. "Oh, my lord. I think I know what the thing was." She dove for her purse and her pocket calendar. "I was supposed to be there, myself. Here it is. Sex Olympics at Barb Petrie's place. It's in Brentwood. She made a big deal about it because of the Olympics coming to L.A. She even said she was bringing in some foreign talent."

I was blushing furiously. "Uh, Ange, I really don't need to know about all of this."

"You might want to," Angelique said with a snigger. "One of these days, you will get the benefit of his antics."

"We'll see about that." I shifted, feeling far more aroused than I wanted to.

"That's not the point," Angelique said, flopping onto the couch. "Sid loves the Sex Olympics. Really loves them, even when he can't compete and he's been out of the running since taking Best All-Around for the fourth time in a row three years ago. They had to make him a judge. They couldn't get anyone else to compete. If he didn't want to go tonight, that is amazing."

"Ange, he can't compete. Of course, it wouldn't be as much fun to him."

"Hah!" Angelique sat up. "He hasn't been able to compete for three years and still loves the event. Or did. You have no idea what a sea change this is for him."

"Oh."

Angelique flopped back into the couch. "Who would have thought it! Oh, my lord, this is amazing." She scrambled up and tucked her feet under her. "You do know what this means, darling, don't you?"

"Sid is... What?"

"He's getting ready to settle down."

"Ange, that's ridiculous. Even if he was, he's not capable of it."

She looked at me severely. "What about you?"

"What about me? I'm not the issue here."

"Oh, for crying out loud, Lisa. You love the man. It's written all over you, and I sure as hell know what that looks like better than anybody."

"Okay, so I do. But that doesn't help me right now. He's not ready."

Angelique looked at me with a sweet grin. "Neither are you. Don't you get it?"

"Apparently not, although I think we already came to agreement on the not ready part." I blinked and looked at my glass. "And what about you? You love him, too!"

"Yes! But Sid was my fantasy." Angelique came toward me, shoving her way through the couch cushions on her knees. "I have finally gotten that. What you haven't gotten is that he is your reality. That you two have something that even he doesn't know what to do with. And you don't either!" She laughed loudly.

"This isn't helping."

"Lisa, it's what you told me about deserving more in my relationships."

"So, this is your revenge." I gulped the rest of my wine.

Angelique laughed and poured more wine into my glass.

"No!" She shook her head, clearly trying to find the right words. "You and Sid are trying to figure out what works for you two, as individuals and a couple. It may not be the marriage thing. It may be. I do not know and do not care. The thing is, you two love each other and want each other, but neither of you has figured out what that means or how that's going to happen. And that's okay."

"Huh?"

"It's okay. You and Sid do not have to do anything. You're fine. Whatever will happen, and I believe it will, will happen in its own good time and you, my dear friend, do not have to do anything, not one little thing, to make it happen. You're okay. Sid is okay."

"I never thought otherwise."

"Bull puckey." (Okay, she used the naughtier version.) "You've already told me that you've been freaking out since Sid asked you to move into his bedroom. Lisa, sweet Lisa, what I'm trying to tell you is that it's all going to be fine. Really. You probably know Sid a little bit better than I do, but I also know him and in ways you will never know him. I've known him longer..." She paused. "And I've spent a lot of time in bed with him. The thing is, we both love this man in very different ways. I can see where his heart is in a way that you can't because you're too close to him. I love you and adore you. You are, without question, the best thing that ever happened to that idiot. So do not doubt your feelings. Do not worry about it. You and Sid will be fine. I know that more than I've ever known anything. You and Sid will be fine."

"Okay."

I really wanted to believe her. I probably knew, in my deepest gut, that she was right, but I couldn't make my head understand it. Angelique bundled me into her arms and held me close.

"You guys are going to be fine," she said again. "And if I have to lose Sid, I am so grateful that it was to you." She pulled away a little and looked me in the eyes. "You will take good care of him, won't you?"

"Of course, Ange!" I gasped and looked at her again. "I have to. I love him."

"I know. That's the only reason I don't mind losing him to you too much." She sniffed.

The next thing I knew, we were both crying and holding each other. Later, in my more rational frame of mind, I had to put the incident down to too much wine. But I had only drunk the one glass. Ange had drunk more, but she wasn't slurring or otherwise showing the effects. Nope. The reality was, we were both crazy, head over heels, in love with Sid Hackbirn, and she had just relinquished him to me. And I had no idea what I was going to do about that.

We staggered to bed another hour or three after that. My board game sat forgotten on the coffee table. The second bottle of wine lay on its side, completely empty, and it had been really, really tasty. I went to bed in Angelique's second bedroom with my mind whirling.

She had certainly offered me some perspective that I had not considered. That maybe Sid was getting tired of sleeping around? Okay, that one seemed doubtful and perhaps reflected her own state of mind. And the idea that I was not ready to settle down myself? Probably. I had resisted George's hovering and had found myself chafing at Sid when he'd tried to be there for me. Then there was the idea that I really didn't need to do anything and that everything would work itself out. Hmmm. It was probably true, but I couldn't see it. On the other hand, I didn't necessarily need to see it.

All these thoughts kept chasing themselves around my brain, and as it turned out, it was probably a good thing. I was the first to hear the steps in the front of the apartment that shouldn't have been there. That being said, Angelique was not that far behind me, although I had no idea of that because she was in her bedroom.

I crept toward the bedroom door and oh, so softly, opened it and peeked through. I saw a dark figure in the dining area, opening the drawers in Angelique's breakfront, and tossing the contents out right and left.

"What are you doing?" Angelique screamed, her words sprinkled with cuss words.

The figure turned toward her. I thought I saw a gun. I wasn't sure. I just knew that I was almost in reach, so I screamed and ran at him. He turned toward me and I jumped him. In the struggle, I felt something sting my left arm, but I kept screaming and hitting at him, barely noting the white glint on the outer edge of his left hand. A minute later, a gun went off and the man slipped out of my arms and ran for the front door. The gun went off again. The man was gone.

Angelique yelled something obscene and ran for the front door. I sank onto the couch, feeling more than a little woozy.

"He's gone," Angelique snorted, coming back into the apartment. "Lisa! Are you alright?"

"I think so." I looked down at my left arm, which was burning. "Oh. I think I got cut."

I have to give Angelique an enormous amount of credit. She grabbed a dishtowel and told me to press it against my cut, then called somebody to get help. The paramedics arrived soon after and insisted on taking me to the emergency room. Angelique came with me. I was able to get my purse and produced the card that Sid had given me.

"He asked me to call if there was trouble," I told Angelique in the ambulance.

Some minutes later, I was unloaded and put in a curtained cubicle. Angelique had disappeared, but then returned.

"Sid's on his way," she told me. "So is Henry." She sighed. "I think we're both in trouble."

We weren't, but both Sid and Henry were not happy. Henry insisted on bundling Angelique up and taking her to his place. Angelique wasn't thrilled, but when Henry took her home, she didn't protest that much. Sid remained with me, holding my right hand and keeping me distracted while the cute intern stitched up the cut on my arm.

"You'll need to keep your stitches dry," the intern said as he finished.

"Yes. I will," I said.

The only thing that was left was for me to sign the paperwork and for Sid to agree to pay the hospital for the visit and the ambulance ride.

July 19–21, 1984

The next morning, I awoke a little woozy, but mostly okay. I'd told Sid the night before all about what had happened. After breakfast, Sid called Henry to check in on Angelique and to tell Henry that I'd seen Powers' scar, which meant that he was the one who had attacked us.

"He's pretty angry," Sid told me as he came back into the breakfast room. "The Brits had called him to let him know that Powers was gone again, but he'd missed the call."

"Oh, dear. Did Angelique tell him about her gun?"

"If she did, he seems to have missed that part," Sid said.

"Well, he does have that paternal thing for her," I said. "Could be a blessing. Now that Powers has touched his family, so to speak, Henry will be even more motivated to catch him."

"Possibly."

Shortly after, Sid and I went on our designated way, back to the Inland Empire, not really expecting to find much. We did find signs of squatters at one housing development, but no dossier or anything else left behind.

I had declined to tell Sid about Angelique's observations from the night before. It didn't make sense to. If she was right, everything would fall together at the right time. If she was wrong, it would just make everything even more awkward. I still had plenty of food for thought and was a little distant in the car that day. Sid didn't really notice. He was a little distant, too, for some reason. [Not really. I'd just been bored out of my mind the night before and couldn't figure out why. - SEH]

We looked at house after house, getting more and

more frustrated because we weren't finding anything. We even re-checked a couple, worried that because we hadn't found anything, we hadn't looked as thoroughly as we could have. We didn't get back onto the freeway until almost six.

"We need to re-check that one house we couldn't get into the other day," I said. "The one in Pomona."

"It's been sold, Lisa," Sid grumbled. "They've been working on it. If that dossier was there, it's been found and thrown out, I would imagine."

"Still, we haven't found anything."

"It's an incredible long shot, Lisa." Sid sighed and started for the nearest off-ramp to turn around.

Only our pagers went off. I checked mine and frowned.

"We've got to radio in," I said, getting my keys out of my purse.

I unlocked the glove box and switched on the radio there.

"This is Little Red, Big Red, come in," I said into the mike.

"This is Red Knight." It was Henry. Sid and I glanced at each other. "We have a meeting in Pasadena at nineteen hundred hours, over."

"We copy, Red Knight, but we were going to check one more house, over."

"Leave it 'til tomorrow. We have to find a new plan, over."

Sid and I shrugged, but there wasn't anything we could do. I got the address for the meeting from Henry and after shutting down the radio and re-locking the glove compartment, got out the Thomas Guide map book to find it.

The place was a mansion in the southern part of Pasadena. The exterior was brick and half-timbered and the place was huge. Sid and I were not surprised to see a Rolls Royce limousine in the driveway. Inside was gorgeous. Wooden floors gleamed with fresh polish. Antiques were set here and there, arranged to create the most pleasing effect possible. The dining room table was set for a buffet, with fine china and real silverware. Marian spotted me first, as she came out of one of the rooms in the hallway.

"Oh, there you are. Very good." She nodded at the table in the dining room. "Get yourselves some dinner and bring it into the study, will you? We're eating there tonight. We have a great deal of work to do."

Sid and I got plates and filled them. Grabbing some silverware and napkins, we went into the study to find that Marian had poured us glasses of wine in beautiful cut crystal glasses. Henry was there, as was another man dressed in a black vest, white shirt, and black pants. He had a headset on, with the earpiece only covering one ear, and was facing a radio that had been set up on a typing table in a corner. He finished scribbling something on a note pad.

"Here you, Ma'am," he said, handing the pad to Marian.

"Excellent work, Brixton," she said after reading it over and handed it to Andrew.

He read it over. "Well, that settles it. What are our resources?"

"Three of our chaps," Marian said. "Not including us."

"We've got about eight people from out of town," Henry said. "Plus six more resident here, and two B-1s."

B-1s were safe houses and other liaisons. Every Quickline city had at least one. They handled things like paychecks, weapons, and other administrative issues.

"The problem is our best tracker got made by these guys last month," Henry said.

It hadn't been the tracker's fault, but sloppy work by that idiot on the Blue line.

"So we've about twenty of us." Marian shivered.

"What are we covering?" I asked.

"All ways of getting out of here," Henry said

grimly.

I shivered. Los Angeles is a huge region and there were a lot of directions that could be taken.

"What's going on?" Sid asked.

"The Rumanians have given Powers an ultimatum," Henry said. "He will be moved tomorrow afternoon, whether he likes it or not."

"And this latest bit," said Andrew, holding up the notepad. "Says that Mr. Powers has agreed to let Mr. Mihaili accompany him tomorrow morning to get the dossier."

"Did any of the other teams find anything?" Sid asked.

"Absolutely nothing," Marian said with some disgust. "Well, they did find two other houses that someone had been using, but each team checked them over extremely carefully."

"And I also went over them," Henry said.

"What about that notice about the fake FBI agent?" I asked.

"Hasn't turned up anything." Henry shifted in his chair, then set aside his plate and rubbed his face with his hand.

"We simply must get our hands on that dossier," Marian said, pouring herself a glass of something amber from a decanter. "It will be disastrous if we don't."

"We have checked every potential house in three counties and have found nothing," Henry said. "It's either hidden somewhere here in L.A. Or maybe it doesn't even exist and he's trying to make one up. That would explain why he attacked Angelique last night. He was looking for something, and Angelique said that she'd thought someone had been in her apartment a couple weeks ago. Things not quite where they were supposed to be. She hadn't said anything to me because she thought she was imagining it."

"But why would he think your secretary would have any information?" Andrew asked.

"I haven't the faintest idea," Henry said. "But you saw him last night, Lisa."

"I saw the scar," I said. "It was definitely him."

"Round and round and round we go," Marian complained.

"There was one house we didn't check," I said. "In Pomona. The one Sid had been kept in. We couldn't get in."

"Surely he wouldn't be stupid enough to return to a place that we know about," Marian said.

"But he could be that cocky," said Henry. He sighed. "We're trying to find out who bought it. It's probably a long shot, but that could be the house."

Marian and Andrew agreed that it might be. However, it made more sense to follow Powers and let him lead us to the dossier. Other resources would be used to watch airports, seaports, even the train station. Several of us would be on the freeways, in case Powers and Mihaili tried to leave that way. Henry agreed to meet Sid and me at the house in Pomona on the off chance the dossier was there.

We finished dinner in the dining room, after all. Andrew kept giving me the eye until Marian got disgusted and told him to let me alone. We left fairly early and went home.

"How's your arm?" Sid asked as we came in from the garage.

I shifted it. "Sore, but not too bad."

"Good." There was an awkward pause. "Goodnight, Lisa."

"Goodnight, Sid." I watched as he moved on down the hallway to his bedroom.

I sure hoped Angelique had known what she was talking about. I pushed thoughts of Sid out of my mind as much as possible. In my room, my sleeping bag was out and airing before I would take it to camp on Saturday. If I went. It sure looked like I was going to make it, though. I shuddered and went to bed.

I was surprised that Sid let me sleep in.

"Well, you're injured," he told me as I came in to breakfast.

We were still dressed casually, in jeans and a sport shirt for Sid and a blouse for me. We were also wired with transmitters hidden under our waists and earpieces in our ears. That would make it easier for us to communicate with Henry and the rest of the crew. We took Sid's car. Henry broke in on the radio from time to time to update us.

Powers left the consulate about twenty minutes after we'd left Sid's house, and was headed for Interstate 10. Sid and I were already on that freeway, and not that far from downtown. If Powers was, indeed, going to that house in Pomona, we'd probably have less than twenty minutes to find the dossier.

We were halfway to Pomona when Henry broke in again.

"Home base just radioed me," he said. "Powers bought the house about a week after you were extracted Sid. Used a phony ID and paid cash. Over."

Sid stepped on the accelerator. "We're about halfway there, over."

"I am, too." Henry cussed loudly. "Just got this on another channel. Powers killed Mihaili and dumped him on the Pomona freeway just past the Long Beach Freeway. Our tail got caught in the crash. But he's definitely headed our way. Over."

Sid looked grim as he wove his way around the traffic.

"So, he bought the house," I muttered. "That would explain why he stopped using paid help. He probably sank all of his cash into the house."

"Probably," said Sid.

Some minutes later, we tore up the street to the target house. Sid parked the Beemer in a driveway across from the house. As we ran across the street, Henry's car pulled up and parked next to Sid.

"Looks like it's clear," Sid said as we went in. "Lisa's going upstairs. I'm checking down here."

All the cabinets had been put in. There was terra cotta tile in the entryway and carpeting everywhere else. The smell of fresh paint hung in the air. The only thing missing was the furniture.

I ran straight upstairs. I checked every bathroom, every closet, and found nothing.

"It's gotta be here somewhere," said Sid's voice in my ear.

"I'm not finding it," I said. "Maybe it's under some carpet."

"Nope," said Sid. "Everything is firmly tacked down here."

We heard the car pull into the driveway.

"I'm on it," said Henry.

I was in the bedroom closest to the stairs. Sid came running up and we both hid in the closet there. I pulled the double sliding doors closed. Sid swore.

"What?" I mouthed.

Sid showed me the hidden panel at the bottom corner next to him. Inside was a manila envelope and several bundles of cash.

"Henry? You?" The voice grated in our ears, then we heard the chirp of a silenced pistol.

My heart stopped. Henry had to be down. I tried not to think about it. The presence of the panel meant that Powers was on his way upstairs to the room we were in, the new carpeting muffling his steps.

"Cover me," Sid mouthed and slid out of the closet.

Nodding, I got in position. I tried not to worry about Henry. I tried not to worry about Sid stepping right into gunfire from a heartless killer. I tried not to worry that I had missed that hidden panel when I had first searched the closet. I tried to stay focused on listening for steps, listening for where Sid and Powers might be.

Sid was braced and ready when Powers came into the room, his gun also drawn and ready. I peeked through the crack where the sliding door didn't quite meet the jamb and inched the door open an inch or two more. I still couldn't get a clear shot at Powers. Still covering Powers, I could hear Sid sliding along the bedroom wall toward Powers.

"It's too late," Sid said. "I've got your dossier."

"Big deal," Powers said. A shadow passed the crack as Powers went past the closet door. "I got you dead."

I slid to the other side of the closet and peeked through that door, poking my gun out, as well. Powers was facing into the room, his back to the wall, still aiming at Sid. I thought I saw Powers' finger tighten on the trigger and felt my own finger squeeze, as well. My gun roared.

Powers didn't have a chance to ask about it. Sid was there in a flash, pulling me out of the closet. I looked back into the room. Bright red blood had splattered across the wall. There was a dark crumpled shape below the splatter. My stomach heaved and emptied itself.

Sid whispered something in my ear and gently tugged me out of the room. My brain began to clear.

"I didn't have time to aim," I said as he led me down the stairs.

"I know," he said.

We found Henry sitting up in the dining room, his right hand covering his left sleeve.

"He just winged me," Henry said. "He must have been pretty anxious to get upstairs."

Sid nodded. "We have the dossier."

"Powers?"

Sid shook his head and my stomach heaved again. I turned and vomited all over the hall.

"First kill," Sid told Henry.

"Get her out of here," Henry said. "We've got a whole crew coming."

"Will you be okay?" Sid asked.

"I'm fine. Just a scratch."

Sid pulled me from the house and got me into the Beemer. We pulled out quickly.

"If you've got to heave again, let me know and I'll

stop.”

I took a deep breath. “I think I’m okay now.”

I started crying and kept at it until we were almost home. We got off the freeway, and Sid put his hands on mine.

“In Nam,” he said quietly. “When you killed your first person, they took you off the lines for two weeks. It looks like your camp week is certainly well-timed.”

He almost never spoke about his time in the army in Vietnam, so I was a little surprised, and oddly, comforted. I got my purse off the floor and dug around inside. My pocket bible was there, and I knew exactly which part I wanted, Psalm Fifty-One.

“A clean heart create for me, O God,” I read aloud, then skipped down. “Free me from blood guilt, O God, my saving God, then my tongue shall revel in your justice.”

“That’s nice,” he said.

I sniffed. “I’m glad you like it.”

I continued flipping through the bible, praying for solace or at least guidance.

Sid stayed with me for the rest of the day, helping me pack for the church camp. That night, I woke up, crying. The bright red splatter of blood filled my dreams and I couldn’t shake it away. Sid was there in minutes, holding me and letting me cry. Some minutes later, he looked down at my hands.

“You’re still wearing George’s ring,” he said.

“Yeah. I guess I am.” I slid it off my finger. “I suppose I should return it to his family. What do you do with engagement rings?”

“As I recall, you only return them if you’re breaking up.”

I sniffed. “We need to spare them, that, don’t we? I guess I’ll just put in my drawer.”

Sid took the ring from my hands. “That is a really beautiful diamond. It’s far too nice to be hiding away in a drawer.”

“Do what you want, then,” I said dully.

Sid smiled softly at me, then kissed my hair and said goodnight. He was there another hour later when the dream returned.

The next day, he took me to the church, where kids and grownups were trying to sort out luggage, boat tickets and a host of other things. I managed to catch Father John for a second.

"What's wrong?" he asked. I guess it was pretty obvious that I was a bit of a mess.

"We got George's killer," I said. "And I could really use a chance to talk to you."

John, as always, came with the youth group to camp, saying that he needed it as much as they needed him.

Parents car-pooled, bringing all the campers and our gear to Long Beach to catch the ferry to Catalina Island. I waved at Sid as my ride bore me and the others out of the lot. He looked a little forlorn.

The camp was in a nice, secluded cove on the island. Most of the afternoon was taken up in getting kids and luggage to their correct cabins, plus a meeting to explain the rules and the theme of the camp that year. Most of the kids were there because they wanted to be, but there was the usual small group of scowling faces, there because Mom and Dad had forced them to come.

In the chaos, I finally found a chance to talk with Father John. We went to one of the more private areas of camp, which was right next to the beach, so no one could overhear us.

John looked at me, waiting.

"I killed a man yesterday," I said softly. At least, my stomach didn't heave.

"I see." John closed his eyes and swallowed. "Am I correct that it was George's killer?"

I nodded. "He was ruthless and he would have killed Sid and I didn't have time to aim, and..."

"Yeah." John looked out over the ocean. "Killing in self-defense is not a sin, as I'm sure you know."

"I couldn't sleep last night," I said. "I kept dreaming about it."

"Yeah." John took a deep breath and then swore. "I've done this confession before."

"You have?"

"I've counseled a few cops in my time." John took another deep breath. "Just not when I've been this close to the case."

"Oh, dear. I'm sorry."

"Lisa, there's a reason I am your confessor, just like there's a reason you are doing what you do." He put his hand on my shoulder. "We will ride this out together. We will deal with our feelings in a healthy way and we will be stronger. Now, you do not technically need absolution, but we will pray that prayer and you will have it. And I want you to remember that you have been absolved of this killing. Because you already feel guilty and you're not going to stop feeling guilty for a long time. That's what happens."

I snorted. "Funny. I can be absolved for killing somebody, but I can't justify making love to a man I love with all my heart."

"Sid?"

I nodded. "He asked me to move into his bedroom. I couldn't, though. I... I couldn't justify it."

"Oh, I think you can justify making love to Sid."

"What?" I looked at him in wonder.

"Lisa, you are simply not that rule-bound. It's not the religion thing that's holding you back. It's something else."

"You think so?"

"I do." He smiled at me. "I'll let you figure out what on your own. In the meantime, be thankful for the religion thing. It's probably keeping you safe." He sighed. "Any other sins to absolve while we're here?"

I had to laugh a little. "Not at the moment. If I think of any new ones, I'll let you know."

John smiled and began the prayers of absolution.

I left camp early that year, with a group of kids who were also coming home early. We all had tickets to the opening ceremonies for the Olympics, so we caught a boat right around dawn on Saturday morning. As the sun climbed into the sky over the water, I looked at the letter Sid had sent me while I was away. It had arrived the previous Wednesday.

"Dear Lisa," it read in his cramped handwriting. "Greetings and all that stuff. I hope this finds you well and wearing your sunscreen. I'm doing well, myself, indolently basking in the sun all day. Well, I can't say I'm being completely indolent. I've been doing a lot of thinking. Unfortunately, our impasse has been haunting me. I have come to the conclusion that I must support your religious beliefs. They are too obviously the glue that holds you together. Were I to stand between you and The Church, it would destroy you and I cannot do that. I applaud the strength of your faith, even if, at the same time, I must applaud and support that which is our only barrier to our complete happiness. Take care and please try to avoid the junk food. Yours, as ever, Sid."

I still couldn't figure out what to do about him. He couldn't stop being his randy self any more than I could stop being religious. In some ways, I didn't want him to change who he was, especially if he only gave up sleeping around because of me.

I was not surprised that Sid was at the landing when the boat docked. I was surprised to see Nick there. As it turned out, Nick had gotten kicked out of his camp and Sid had agreed to take him for the rest of the summer. Fortunately, Sid hadn't scalped the ticket to the ceremonies that he'd originally bought for Nick earlier that spring.

We had a wonderful time that night and watched the ceremonies again the next day because Sid had taped them on his VCR. By Monday, life was back to usual.

Except that I was depressed. Some of it was the guilt and Sid was pretty helpful with that part. He'd gone through the exact same thing and knew what I was feeling. Some of it was that I really wanted to be living in his bedroom. Every night he went out, I felt it a little more.

But then, when I'd been home about a week, Nick had gone to Mae's to visit with Darby and I was resting in the rumpus room. Sid popped up in the doorway.

"How does New York sound for dinner?" he asked merrily.

"It's too late, Sid," I said.

"I had a feeling you'd say that." He slid down next to me on the bean bag chair and handed me a long, narrow gift-wrapped box. "Here."

"Sid..."

"No protests. I've heard them all."

"I know, but—"

"Lisa, I just want you to have this. Maybe help us both move on."

"What?" I opened the package.

It was a necklace, with a nice s-chain, and a pendant shaped like a figure eight. The bottom circle featured a large, round cut diamond, surrounded by tiny aquamarines, and the top circle had an aquamarine surrounded by tiny diamonds.

"It's beautiful. But what am I going to do with it?"

"Wear it, silly girl. I told you that diamond was too nice to sit in a drawer."

"Sid, this isn't..."

"The diamond George gave you? It is. I had it reset. I did buy the aquamarines, though. I believe that is your birthstone."

"Yeah." I looked at the flashing pale blue and white gems. "Thank you so much."

"You're very welcome."

I looked at the necklace and thought about what he'd written about my faith being the barrier to our happiness. I felt the same way about his fooling around.

"You know, Sid, I am who I am, and you are who you are. And that seems to get in our way, sometimes."

He looked at me warmly. "I suppose it does."

"But I can't change who you are, and really, I don't even want to. So, like you, I have to applaud and support that which is most in our way." I looked down at the necklace in my hands. "I have no idea how this is all going to fall out, but you were right when you said when we come together rather than if." I looked at him and smiled. "It will happen, sometime, somehow. And I'm willing to wait until does of its own accord. I don't want to push it, any more than you do, I think."

"I definitely don't want to push it." He scooted closer to me and pulled me into his arms. "May I kiss you?"

In answer, I pressed my lips against his. As we held each other, the depression slowly left and I began to be filled with joy. And the song that had been haunting me for the past month and a half drifted away. We had, at last, found what we could tell each other.

Coming Soon...

The next Operation Quickline book is **These Hallowed Halls.** Lisa and Sid take up undercover roles at a university in a small town in Wisconsin to try to find out who is smuggling out a top-secret formula. Lisa's teaching an English composition class and Sid is studying for a degree in music. Their only chance to connect? Sid's in Lisa's class.

Given that their relationship is still at an all-too-awkward impasse, this might not be the best time for them to pretend a romantic relationship. Unfortunately, Sid has picked up a tail and needs to convince the unseen bad guy that his interest in his teacher is more than academic. Lisa can't resist. Then one of the English Department faculty is murdered. Lisa can't let her feelings for Sid get in the way of catching an increasingly desperate killer.

Read the first four Operation Quickline books:

That Old Cloak and Dagger Routine – Unemployed and desperate, Lisa Wycherly accepts a job working for oh, so randy Sid Hackbirn, even though it means living in his house. It turns out that Sid has recruited Lisa as his partner in a thriving undercover espionage agency. But it isn't just her life that got turned upside down when he did.

Stopleak – Sid and Lisa hit the road to lure out who's trying to bring down Operation Quickline, with themselves as the bait.

Deceptive Appearances – Someone is stealing secrets, and Sid and Lisa are sent to Lisa's hometown of South Lake Tahoe. Only the case gets way too close to home for Sid, as well.

Fugue in a Minor Key – There's a ring of bad guys selling secrets from some local defense plants in the area. But setting up the sting will be the easy part when Sid finds out he has a son and Lisa's nephew Darby is in trouble.

Other books by Anne Louise Bannon

I'm so glad you liked this book! Check out my other novels, available in print or ebook at your favorite retailer:

Freddie and Kathy Series:
Fascinating Rhythm
Bring Into Bondage
The Last Witnesses
Blood Red

Old Los Angeles
Death of the Zanjero
Death of the City Marshal

Mrs. Sperling
A Nose for a Niedeman

Brenda Finnegan
Tyger, Tyger

Romantic Fiction
White House Rhapsody, Book One

Fantasy and Science Fiction
A Ring for a Second Chance
But World Enough and Time

And I would be honored if you left a review for this and any of my books on GoodReads or any other retail site. It really helps.

Connect with Anne Louise Bannon

Thank you for sticking it out this long! Please join my newsletter. It's the best way to stay up-to-date on my upcoming projects, blog posts and even games and giveaways.

Sign up here: http://eepurl.com/zH0Ab

Or connect with me on your favorite social media platforms:

Visit my website: http://annelouisebannon.com

Friend me on Facebook: http://facebook.com/RobinGoodfellowEnt

Follow me on Twitter: http://twitter.com/ALBannon

Favorite my Smashwords author page: https://www.smashwords.com/profile/view/MsBriscow

Connect on LinkedIn: http://www.linkedin.com/in/annelouisebannon

Follow me on Pinterest: http://pinterest.com/msbriscow

About Anne Louise Bannon

Anne Louise Bannon is an author and journalist who wrote her first novel at age 15. Her journalistic work has appeared in Ladies' Home Journal, the Los Angeles Times, Wines and Vines, and in newspapers across the country. She was a TV critic for over 10 years, founded the YourFamilyViewer blog, and created the OddBallGrape.com wine education blog with her husband, Michael Holland. She is the co-author of Howdunit: Book of Poisons, with Serita Stevens, as well as author of the Freddie and Kathy mystery series, set in the 1920s, the Old Los Angeles series, set in 1870, and the Operation Quickline series and Tyger, Tyger. She and her husband live in Southern California with an assortment of critters.

www.ingramcontent.com/pod-product-compliance
Lightning Source LLC
Chambersburg PA
CBHW070918190726
48292CB00004B/1015